Texas Bomber

by

Ernest Francis Schanilec

DORRANCE
PUBLISHING CO
EST. 1920
PITTSBURGH, PENNSYLVANIA 15238

Dorrance Publishing Co
585 Alpha Drive
Suite 103
Pittsburgh, PA 15238
Visit our website at *www.dorrancebookstore.com*

ISBN: 978-1-4809-4955-3
eISBN: 978-1-4809-4932-4

Also By Ernest Francis Schanilec

Blue Darkness

The Towers

Danger in the Keys

Purgatory Curve

Gray Riders

Sleep Six

Night Out in Fargo

Gray Riders II

Ice Lord

Rio Grande Identity

War & Beyond

Revenge

ACKNOWLEDGMENTS

I thank Suzanna, my family partner. She has been very patient with me while I have been writing *Texas Bomber*. Thank you to Tony Held for editing and proofing the manuscript.

I thank the following for using their names in this novel. They are: Jesse, at the gate in Victoria Palms; Judy, the manager of the Inns & Suites at Victoria Palms; Tim with Winter Texan Home Sales, Inc.; Doug, my neighbor at Victoria Palms; Steve Bruhn, the author's former farming friend; Margie Schwandt, former neighbor, and Steve's mother-in-law; Greg Barta, a locksmith in Grand Forks; Irma, a resident of Victoria Palms and B.G., a waiter at Chili's Restaurant in Weslaco.

DEDICATIONS

I dedicate my thirteenth novel to the Police, Sheriff's officers, Constables, FBI agents, Border Patrol agents, and any other law enforcement officials of Hidalgo County in Texas. They keep us safe.

I also dedicate my novel to all the Winter Texans in the Rio Grande Valley and to my former farming neighbor near Vergas, Minnesota, Steve Bruhn.

Texas Bomber

Chapter 1

THE THREE PARTNERS OF SUN ENERGY CORPORATION sat around a table in their meeting room at Sun Energy's headquarters in Bloomington, Minnesota. They glumly listened to their financial consultant, Leslie. He lightly thumped his fist on the table and said, "It's all over boys—under the current circumstances there's no way Sun can survive!" He moved both arms upward, making them look like a wall. "Bankruptcy is the next logical step!"

Mick Brown, one of the partners, stood. "I realize that we've run out of money, but cripes, I was hoping we could hang on longer—our sales could change." His dark hair was combed straight back. He stroked his short, dark beard which extended down from a narrow mustache circling part of his round face.

"What type of bankruptcy are you talking about, Leslie?" another partner, Norm Blaine, asked.

The consultant narrowed his eyes. "It looks like chapter seven. The good news is that your personal properties are protected and there's just enough money left in your account to take care of my company's fees."

The room went silent as Nick Giggs, the third Sun Energy partner, lowered his head and looked at the top of the conference table. Norm got up and walked over to the window, his dark-skinned forehead furrowing as he looked out.

Leslie stood and grabbed his satchel. "Good day to you, gentlemen. If you need me further, give me a call. Meanwhile, I'll get the papers prepared and should have them ready by this time tomorrow. Is 10:00 a.m. okay?"

Mick nodded. "We'll be here."

The consultant cleared his throat and left the room.

NICK GIGGS RETURNED TO HIS APARTMENT. I don't like what's going on in my life, he thought. I don't have a girlfriend, and I'm starting to lose money. Cripes sakes, bankruptcy is going to only temporarily save me.

He sat down in front of his computer. His blue eyes focused on the screen and after entering his password, he accessed his TD Ameritrade account. I have enough assets and cash to hold me over for several years, he thought. A chapter seven corporate bankruptcy can't get into my account...I think I'm safe.

Nick then spent a little over an hour at an Applebee's drinking beer and enjoying ribs for dinner. Tomorrow, I have no choice but to sign the papers, he thought. At least my debts will disappear.

He went home and stretched out on his bed. Nick closed his eyes, trying to get the recent meeting out of his mind. After tossing and turning for over an hour, he finally fell asleep.

NORM BLAINE USED HIS KEY to unlock Sun Energy's front door the next morning. My God, he thought, we are no longer open for business.

He entered the meeting room and saw Mick standing and looking out the window. "Hey, Mick, what's happened to Alana?"

Mick turned around. "We are no longer in business, so why would we need a receptionist?"

Boy, this is moving along a lot faster than I expected, he thought. I think I better share this situation with my wife today. She's going to be shocked...worse than that, we could lose our house...not enough income.

Norm heard the door open and he saw his other partner, Nick, walk into the room. "Hi Nick, are you ready for a big day?"

Nick's expression is scary, he thought. Maybe I should be scared, too. I wish I was somewhere else. He closed his eyes for a moment. He hit the side of his head with his right palm. Wake up buddy...reality is here.

THE THREE PARTNERS SAT DOWN AT THE TABLE. Their mood was glum as Mick, Norm, and Nick thumbed through the paperwork Leslie had slapped down in front of them.

"If you need more time, let me know, otherwise I'll call my notary. She can be here in a few minutes," Leslie said.

Mick nodded and said, "We're ready. Cripes, let's get it out of the way."

Nick partially opened his mouth. "Hey, Mick, don't you think it would be smart to have our lawyers go over this?"

Mick sneered. "What the hell good would that do? This is a standard chapter seven. No lawyer can change that."

Norm set his fingers down on the paperwork. "Okay, hell, let's get it over with."

"Atta-boy Norm," Mick said. He looked at Nick.

Nick threw up his hands. "Alright, doesn't look like I have much choice," he said.

Minutes later, the notary public arrived. The three partners gathered close to her and signed the papers.

"Thanks Mary," Mick said.

Mary picked up her briefcase and left the room.

"That's it for now, boys. I want us to get back together here in a few days," Mick said.

THE THREE MEN MET IN THEIR OFFICE AGAIN IN FIVE DAYS. "Hey, don't look so glum guys, I have some new and exciting news," Mick said.

Mick sat down and his eyes sparkled as he looked at Nick and then Norm. His eyes narrowed and his mouth tightened into a forced smile. "I talked to a gentleman yesterday who is going to bail us out of this mess."

Nick's chin elevated. His blue eyes opened wider than usual and he ran a finger through his gray-blond hair. "What the heck do you mean by that, Mick?"

"You guys are aware that D.C. has legalized marijuana, aren't you?"

"Yup, I heard that on the news the other day," Norm said, rubbing his thumb under his thin chin.

Mick tightened his lips together for a moment, then he opened them slightly and said, "The man I talked to is going to provide us with eight oil tanker transport trucks. Each one of them has three special rounded tanks—they each have a narrow, twelve inch compartment surrounding each tank, leaving the inside of the tank open for storage. The base of the tank is lined with lead. An electronic control is used to swing each tank open."

Nick raised his hand. "What the devil would we use those trucks for anyway?"

Mick's eyes widened. "Marijuana! Pot! Each truck will have the hidden spaces filled with pot and because each truck has two drivers, they can drive to Bloomington from Mexico in two days. We're going to clean out both of our big warehouses and fill one with the loot and store the trucks in the other."

Norm chuckled. "Come on, Mick, how the heck are the trucks going to get through the border checkpoints?"

"I knew you were going to ask that," Mick replied. "The oil compartments block some of the odor, but we also use a special spray to totally fool the dogs at the stations. The trucks have already been tested. All the dog can sniff is oil—no pot.

"So the trucks will fool the border agents into thinking they have oil in them. This will work both ways, when the trucks come out of Mexico and when they return. This has all moved along so quickly that we've already hired sixteen Mexican drivers from Texas.

"The company we are doing this for has pre-arranged the excise tax going both ways—into the US from Mexico and into Mexico from the US. That means the trucks should be able to pass through customs in both countries very rapidly."

Mick laughed loudly and placed both hands on top of his head. "Tell you what boys, we'll meet again day after tomorrow at 9:00 a.m. I'll have more information on the trucks and the pot, but I'll give you something more to think about.

"We've been offered to manage the oil pot trucks at a price of a hundred and fifty thousand bucks for each delivery—that means fifty thou each. If we go along with the offer, that means we each have to invest a hundred thousand dollars up front."

"Whoa," Norm said. "That's a lot of bucks."

Mick pointed his finger at him. "Yes it is, but when the first load from Mexico shows up in Bloomington, we get half our original investment back. Then with each subsequent load, we each get another fifty thousand. So to put things in perspective, each year, if we bring in twenty-four loads, two per month, we each make over a million. Think about that, boys, and I'll see you here at the same time tomorrow."

NICK GOT UP AND WALKED TOWARD THE DOOR. He stepped outside and walked toward his vehicle. Mick's wild idea about getting involved with marijuana sounds extremely risky, he thought. But then, there's a national trend to make pot legal. It's possible that Minnesota could become a pot legal state in the near future, too.

One hundred thousand bucks is a lot of money, but I'm sure I can come up with that amount in a flash, he thought next. Heck, we'd have our money back in two weeks...and we already have a market in Oregon, Colorado, and D.C.

Nick's thoughts continued as he unlocked his car. If we succeed, and we will, the three of us are going to get very rich. He made a fist and raised it into the air. We're going to do it!

Chapter 2

THE TWO SUN ENERGY WAREHOUSES in Bloomington had been cleaned out of all materials and vehicles. Mick, Norm, and Nick sat around a table in the small corner office of one building, anxiously staring out the window.

"They're going to arrive any minute," Mick said after sliding his phone back into its holster.

Minutes later, Norm yelled, "They're here!"

The three men left the office and entered the huge warehouse. Mick pressed a button and a huge folding door opened. He pressed another button and a second door opened.

"Man, it looks like a parade of oil tanker trucks," Nick said. He felt excitement building in his stomach as the first oil truck passed through the closest doorway. I can't believe this is happening, he thought. They came all the way from Progreso, Mexico.

Nick watched the first truck come to a stop near the back wall. The driver was guided by Mick, who was waving an orange wand. The truck had an icon on the door which contained a section of the Mexican flag and a title that read *Sardoza Oil*. Four of the trucks formed two columns, two in each one, with lots of space in between. The fifth truck entered through the second door and two more columns were formed.

The trucks' engines shut down and their drivers disembarked.

Hey, where are they going? Nick thought, watching the drivers board an old small school bus. I bet they're heading for a motel.

After the drivers left, Mick pressed the buttons to close both overhead doors. Then he walked back to the first truck. Mick stepped up the driver's door and entered the truck. He emerged a second later carrying a key fob.

What's he doing? Nick thought.

Mick reached up to a small lockbox just below the first tank. He inserted one of keys into a slot and turned it. Then he opened the top of the case. He reached over with a finger and pressed something inside.

A section of the tank rotated and opened, exposing two huge bales covered with plastic. They look like farm hay bales, Nick thought.

Mick pressed a second button and another section rotated. Then he pressed another button and a third section opened.

The truck contains a total of six bales, Nick said to himself.

Two mini loaders pulled up. Nick watched the first one slip its bucket under the first bale. The loader lifted the bale up and toward the far wall, away from the truck.

It looks like they're going to set that bale down on the plastic-lined floor, Nick thought.

Two hours later, the last bale was lifted from the eighth truck. Both of the mini loaders parked next to the bales. The two drivers got out and each of them walked to one of the rear trucks, got in, waited for Mick to open the overhead door, and backed them out.

The drivers parked the trucks in the adjoining building and walked back to move the next two trucks. Within ten minutes all the trucks had been moved. Now the big room contained only forty-eight bales and the two loaders.

This unloading process is totally amazing, Nick thought.

Norm and Mick headed for the office.

I best join them, Nick thought.

Mick, Norm, and Nick each took a seat around the small table. "The three semis will be here within the hour," Mick said. "Our two mini loaders should get them loaded up within a couple of hours. Pretty slick, huh guys?"

Nick nodded. "Yeah, quite the procedure, and the trucks didn't leak a drop of oil."

Norm said, "I can't even guess where you came up with this technology to mask pot."

Mick laughed. "You really don't have to know, Norm. And it's probably best each one of you know as little as possible. Your jobs will be to oversee the loading and unloading of the pot in the trucks—and the management of the drivers.

"Each truck will have two drivers when it leaves Mexico—it's very important that each driver doesn't know a thing about what he is hauling. Mick, I heard that the agents at the border checkpoints are guided by people's expressions—guilty-looking or normal."

Norm said, "So that's why the drivers all left when the trucks arrived."

"You're catching on, Norm," Mick said, smiling widely.

.

NICK WATCHED AS THE MINI LOADERS EACH MADE TWENTY FOUR-TRIPS moving the pot bales off the floor and into the semis. Wow, it's been close to three hours since they started, he thought. This unloading-loading procedure can easily be done in one day.

The first semi is headed for Oregon, Nick mused. It'll get there in a couple of days. The second semi is driving to D.C. That'll also take a couple of days. The last one being loaded will leave for Colorado as soon as it is full.

It's amazing how Mick has planned all this, Nick thought. Norm and I didn't have a clue. Tomorrow the oil trucks will head back to Mexico. When they return there, I'll have my investment paid for...then after that, I'll make fifty thousand each tip. Mick is amazing person. He's taken us out of a deep hole and led us up a mountain.

MICK TAPPED HIS PEN ON A THIN STACK OF PAPERS on the desk. “Norm, I’m putting you in charge of managing the eight oil trucks when they arrive from Mexico. This includes keeping an eye on unloading them, and then loading of the semi-trucks. It’s going to happen every two weeks.

“Nick, you’re a lucky guy. You are going to be in control of marijuana loading in the Progreso, Mexico area. I have information for you about a popular RV Resort in southern Texas. I want you to rent a suite immediately. The name of the place is Texas Palms.”

“What!” Nick exclaimed. “I’m moving to Texas?”

Mick said, “When winter comes, you’ll thank me. They don’t have snow storms in southern Texas.”

“Do you want to trade places, Nick?” Norm asked with a laugh.

Mick handed Nick a piece of paper. “The phone number and any other information about the resort in Texas is all there. If I were you, I would call them today.”

Chapter 3

Tom and Samantha Hastings PARKED CLOSE to the office of the Texas Palms Inns & Suites. He grasped the ignition key and shut the car off. Tom looked at his wife and said, "Sammy, we're here."

She smiled and reached into her purse. "I have our reservation right here. Let's get it done."

Tom opened the door and followed Sammy inside. She walked up to the counter and announced their arrival. "Okay, we'll have a seat," Sammy said to the receptionist. She turned to Tom. "The lady will be with us soon. Let's sit down by the window."

After they sat down, Sammy said to her husband, "Look at that woman behind the counter. Her hair is spiked."

Tom chuckled. "Yeah, I've noticed, but she really looks good, and did you know that she's from Minnesota?"

They both returned to the counter and signed some papers. The woman with the spiked hair said, "My name is Judy. Good to meet the two of you. Follow my golf cart. I'll lead you to your unit. "

Minutes later they parked in front of suite 4907. Judy unlocked the front door and waved for them to follow.

"This looks good, Tom," Sammy said. "It's got an efficient kitchen and table; a big flat screen TV and a nice sectional; and a bedroom-bathroom with a second TV."

Tom looked at the woman. "It's a go—thanks a lot, Judy."

"Have a pleasant stay folks. I'll talk to you later," Judy said and walked out the door.

"I need a hug," Sammy said, extending her arms.

"You got it," Tom said.

He gave her a firm embrace.

NICK GIGGS LOOKED OUT THE AIRPLANE WINDOW and saw patches of roof tops as his flight approached the airport in Harlingen, Texas. I'm almost home, he thought…new second home. Nick laughed. It's going to be quite exciting driving across the Rio Grande into Mexico twice a month.

Minutes later, he felt a nudge as the wheels touched the landing strip. Nick grabbed his carry-on bag from the overhead storage and headed for the door. He and the other first-class seat-holders led the passengers through the slightly sloped ramp and into the airport terminal.

He quickly found the luggage carousel and stood next to a tall, dark-haired, skirted woman. "Good afternoon, ma'am, how are you today?" Nick asked.

Wow, he thought. This is one attractive woman. She has unbelievable long, purple finger nails.

"Good, thank you," the dark-haired lady replied and turned her head slightly to look at Nick.

"Are you from Minneapolis?" Nick asked.

She nodded. "Yes, and now I plan on becoming a Texan."

"Then we have something in common," Nick said. He gave her a tap on the shoulder.

"There're my bags," the woman said, reaching out for them.

"Here, let me help you with them. Are those both yours?" Nick asked.

"Yes, they are."

Nick grabbed one in each hand and set them down in front of her. "Can I ask you where you're staying here in Texas?"

She hesitated. "I'm Pam, she finally replied, "and I have rented a suite at Texas Palms in Donna."

Nick shook her hand. "I'm Nick, and by coincidence that's where I'm staying, too. Whoops, there are my bags," he said, stooping to pick them up off the carousel. "Hey, I plan on renting a car right now. If you wish, you can join me—we're both going to the same place."

Pam smiled and said, "Sorry, but I have some other stops to make, so I need to rent my own vehicle—thanks anyhow."

NICK AND PAM SAT SIDE-BY-SIDE in the Avis shuttle as it headed to the Avis office. "It's a beautiful day out there," Pam said.

"Not bad for November. The Twin City area has snow falling as we speak. We're fortunate to be here," Nick said.

The shuttle stopped and all the passengers disembarked and entered the reception area. Half an hour later, Pam got into her maroon Ford Focus. She rolled her window down so she could shake hands with Nick before she left.

"See you at Texas Palms," Nick said.

She nodded and handed him her card, which had her phone number.

A few minutes later, Nick got into his rental, a brown Honda and drove westward toward Highway-77. I'll be meeting new people and will start a whole new life, he thought as he sped onto Highway-83 west of Harlingen. One of the first things I have to do is to pick out a new bank.

This Pam girl looks like a Hollywood star. I'll have to look her up after settling down at Texas Palms.

Nick felt excitement building in his brain when he saw the large "Texas Palms" sign to his left. He exited Highway-83 onto the ramp which accessed Texas Road. Minutes later he parked in the Inn & Suites lot. Nick used a credit card to pay for a one-month stay. He looked at his door access card. It read *4910*.

Two things I have to do tomorrow, he thought. I need to turn in the Honda and change vehicles and then I need to open a bank account.

PAM COLLITON ENTERED THE Texas Palms Inn & Suites office and edged over to the counter. Her dark brown eyes narrowed as she used her right hand to sweep away locks of dark hair from her left eye.

She signed some papers and in minutes reached out her hand and accepted a keycard. I have suite 4705, she said to herself. I bet that Nick guy has a suite in the same area as I do. My boss in Minneapolis sure hit it right, getting me on the same plane. Master Buddy, Mick always seems to be ahead of the game since I started working for him.

I wonder how long it will take before this Nick guy calls me, she thought... probably this evening...maybe even sooner.

Chapter 4

SAMANTHA LIFTED A GLASS OF GIN AND TONIC to her lips while sitting on the couch. Tom came out of the bedroom and stared. "Wow, that's an awesome skirt you have on, Sammy."

Samantha smiled. "Thank you, Tom. I got it at TJ Maxx just last week."

"Whenever you're ready, let's head out. I'm anxious to see the restaurant," Tom said.

"I just need to get my shoes on and I'll be ready to go."

Tom grasped Sammy's hand as they walked on the sidewalk toward the huge activity building. They crossed Kingston Road and entered the parking lot. "Lots of vehicles out here," Tom said.

He opened the restaurant's front door for Sammy and followed her inside.

"My Gosh, Tom, this place is full," Sammy said.

She felt a tug on her arm.

"Why don't you join us?" a dark-haired woman asked her.

"Hey, Tom, we've got a place to sit," Sammy said.

"My name is Pam, and this is Nick," the woman said.

"I'm Samantha, and this is my husband, Tom. We really appreciate this.

They all shook hands and sat down. "So, how long have you two been here?" Nick asked.

"Just got here today," Tom said. "How about you two?"

"Three days ago. We each have a suite. Pam and I are just friends. We met at the airport," Nick said.

Sammy's eyes gleamed as she smiled and took another sip. "Everything has to start somehow."

Pam grimaced and said, "Is it time to eat? That buffet looks real good—a lot of choices."

Nick stood. "I read you, let's go." He led the way, and minutes later, they all returned to the table with full plates.

An hour later, they left the restaurant and walked toward the rows of suites.

"I've got to leave you guys," Pam said. "I live in the next concourse of suites." She pointed.

"Nice meeting you, Pam," Tom said and shook her hand.

Sammy waved.

Tom, Sammy, and Nick walked down the sidewalk. "I live over there in suite 4910," Nick said.

"That's right across the parking lot from us," Sammy said. "We're in 4907."

"Neighbors," Nick said. "Great meeting you guys."

"Same with us, Nick. I'm sure we'll see you and Pam again," Tom said.

NICK GIGGS SLIPPED HIS CELL PHONE back into the holster attached to his belt. I'm off to Mexico today, he said to himself. All eight trucks are back and a huge load of marijuana is arriving tomorrow. It's my job to make sure the pot gets loaded properly and the sixteen drivers from Texas are contacted so they are available to drive the eight trucks to Minnesota.

I am going to enjoy my ride today, he thought. My updated rental Lincoln Navigator looks great. My big choice at Boggus Ford in

Harlingen yesterday was color: black or white. I chose the black because it's not as noticeable...right now, I need to remain as anonymous as possible. It was great of the dealer to return the Honda to Avis.

Nick's thoughts flowed on. The Lone Star National Bank on International Boulevard in Weslaco had just received my money transfer from my bank in Bloomington and they were more than gracious in telling me they would finance an automobile if I decided to make a purchase, Nick said to himself. My account will be getting another boost after the eight oil tanker trucks make another delivery to the warehouse in Bloomington.

He checked his passport and dropped it into his shirt pocket. Nick stepped outside and looked at his new rental car. It's a beauty, he thought. He glanced across the street and saw a man sitting on a bench. It looks like that Hastings guy, he thought. He appears to be of above-normal intelligence. Maybe I can make use of him as this pot thing moves along. I'll definitely need some help in moving the drivers around.

Nick got into his Lincoln and drove out of the RV Park onto Highway-83, heading toward International Boulevard. Minutes later, he crossed the Rio Grande River and stopped at the Mexican border station. He handed the uniformed border agent his passport. Nick drove down Benito Juárez, the main street in Progreso, and continued until reaching the outskirts. He made a right turn at the Veracruz sign and followed a blacktop road for about four miles.

Nick slowed his car. There's a gravel road, he thought, but it appears to lead to about four houses. This can't be where the warehouse is.

He sped up and kept looking to his right.

A-hah, there it is, that big building over there. And that gravel road will lead right to it.

He turned onto the gravel road. Minutes later, he stopped in front of a large building. It has a light gray metal exterior, Nick thought. It's got two huge overhead doors, obviously for the trucks to get in and out of. At the north end of the building is a small door and a window. The window is protected with bars and the door looks like it is made of steel.

Nick entered the building and saw a man sitting behind a desk.

"Yes, sir, can I help you?" the man asked.

"I'm Nick Giggs from the U.S.," Nick replied. I've been assigned to manage the Sardoza oil-tanker trucks which you have inside. They are inside, aren't they?"

The man nodded and stood. "I've been expecting you. I'm Marcos."

Nick saw a fairly tall, pudgy guy with a heavy head of hair and a mustache, both pepper-colored. His voice is sure squeaky, Nick thought. According to Mick, the guy is totally trustable.

MARCOS GARZA'S MARITAL PROBLEMS had accelerated to the point that he had to move out of his house. This came only days after he lost his job with a computer technology firm in Progreso.

I've got two choices, he said to himself. Either I cross the border illegally and look for work in the US or I join the drug gang. Pedro has offered me a position where I would connect with an American smuggling company out of Minnesota. About twice per month, they would send us eight trucks and my job would be to make enough marijuana available to load all eight of them.

I think it's really clever how they disguise the trucks to make them appear to be hauling oil. This guy Nick, who is living in Donna, Texas, right now hires eight Mexican drivers to simply drive the trucks to a gas station in Progreso. Then the drivers are replaced by sixteen guys from Texas who move the trucks through customs and the border agents. They keep the wheels rolling all the way to Minnesota non-stop except for changing drivers and refueling.

That whole trucking process is none of my business, he thought. I'm being paid to speak to no one about it except the Nick guy. He's in charge of all the drivers. I'm glad that I don't have that job. Fooling the border agents with the phony oil tanks is one thing, but the installation of a base made of lead, adding to the weight and masking the pot's scent, is another. When the trucks stop at a weigh station, the agent who manages the scales is totally fooled.

Marcos ran his fingers through his pepper-colored hair. Now that I have met Nick, I feel more comfortable with this job, he thought. I will get paid when we transport the loaded trucks to the Tesoro in Progreso. Actually, I am doing nothing illegal here in Mexico.

Chapter 5

SAMANTHA HASTINGS WALKED TOWARD THE RV PARK'S activity area. Today, I'm going to have a swim and lay in the sun, she thought. This is such a great place. Maybe I can talk Tom into buying a Mobile Home. Then we would have more space and not bump into each other so much.

She passed through a gate and into the pool area. I see they have two spas, she thought. I know Tom will enjoy those. She set down her bag and took off her robe. Sammy stretched out on a lounge chair and adjusted it so she could see the people in and around the pool.

"Good morning, Samantha," she heard someone say.

Sammy turned her head and felt excited. Her new acquaintance, Pam, sat in the lounger next to hers. "Well, how surprising to see you Pam. Good morning to you, too."

"This is really the life," Pam said. "Instead of going to work, I go to the pool on a warm morning in November."

"What kind of work did you do, Pam?" Sammy asked.

Pam's face slightly contorted. "I work for my father. He has an investment business in Minneapolis," she replied.

Sammy puckered her lips and said, "I worked for an aircraft company until I met Tom. Now, I'm retired."

"How long have you two been married?" Pam asked.

"Less than a year—we actually got married here in Texas before we left for home earlier this year," Sammy replied with a wide smile.

"How nice," Pam said. "Actually, I've never been married. I've come close a couple of times, but so far the right person hasn't come around. Have you ever been married before you met Tom?"

"Yup, a couple of times—neither one lasted very long," Sammy said, her brow slightly furrowing.

Pam puckered her lips. "Do you have any children?"

Sammy sat up. "It's time for a swim. Are you going in, too?"

"No, not right now, but you go right ahead," Pam said.

NICK SET DOWN HIS PHONE. Mick has lined up a van for me to transport the sixteen Texan drivers from Texas to Progreso, he said to himself. The only catch is that I have to drive to a place called Valley Transit in Harlingen to pick up the van this afternoon so it's ready to go in the morning. Mick said that the Texan drivers will check in this afternoon, and he's given me the phone number of the head guy, Menzo. They are going to stay in eight of the ten rooms across from the main office...rooms 4001 to 4008.

He removed two pieces of toast from the toaster and set them on a plate. Nick buttered the toast and placed the plate on the table located in front of the kitchen window. He opened the microwave, reached inside, and brought out two sausage patties. Nick took them to the table, put them on his plate, and sat down.

He picked up his cup of coffee and looked out the window. There's that Hastings guy, he said to himself. He's having coffee outside. He could be just what I'm looking for. Marcos has his hands full and obviously needs help now and then. I can't be in two places at the same time.

I've met Hastings only one time, and by just talking to him, I know that he would do a good job moving the drivers back and forth between here and Progreso, Nick thought. It's obvious to me that I'll need someone to do that for me. He wouldn't have any trouble at the border on either side.

TOM HASTINGS SIPPED COFFEE WHILE SITTING ON A CHAIR, watching the sky, looking for birds. I see a bunch of birds over there…they look like vultures, he thought. Those huge birds sure hang around this area a lot. Tom reached up over his cap and grabbed his sunglasses. He put them on and continued to watch the large birds.

He noticed someone coming out of a door across the wide driveway. Hey, it looks like that new guy we met at the restaurant yesterday, Tom thought. He watched the man for a few moments, and then felt his body tighten. Looks like he's headed this way.

Tom raised his arm as the man stepped onto the sidewalk. They shook hands and the man said, "Remember me, Mr. Hastings? We had dinner together last night. I'm Nick."

"Tell you what, I'll get you a chair and we can visit."

Nick nodded. "Sure."

Tom stood and pulled open the door to the suite. Moments later, he returned with a chair. "There you are, Nick. Have a seat."

"Thanks."

"So are you a Winter Texan like Samantha and I are?"

Nick shook his head. "No, I'm not. I'm here on business. Actually, I come from Bloomington, Minnesota. Do you know where that is?"

Tom nodded. "Yup, it's a suburb of Minneapolis. I've been through there many times—and that's where the North Stars and Twins used to play. I went to a lot of their games."

"I work for a company from that area. We ship crude oil from Mexico to the Twin Cities area."

Tom raised his chin. "Hmm, that's unusual—considering that Texas is the number one crude oil producing state."

"Yes, it is unusual, but we buy the oil at a reduced price and don't have to pay a tariff when we cross the border. Later this afternoon, I have sixteen drivers coming by and I will deliver them to the trucking site in Progreso."

Tom nodded. "Interesting."

"Are you retired, Mr. Hastings?" Nick asked.

"You can call me Tom. Yes, I am retired."

"The reason I ask is because I'm looking for a part-time assistant to help me with the truck drivers. It's not very complicated. Right now, I have to make sure they show up and have rooms to stay in. They all park their vehicles in the parking lot outside the fence, right by the frontage road. After staying here overnight, I bus them to Progreso in a van. They take over the trucks and drive them to Bloomington.

"They return to Progreso with the trucks in about five days. At that time, I drive to Progreso to pick them up and return them to their vehicles. In about a week the drivers return on a Sunday, and I bus them to Progreso again. There is a round trip made every two weeks.

"I need someone to drive them to Progreso on a Monday morning after they stay at the Inn on Sunday. Then in five days, that someone's job would be to pick them up in Progreso. I hope you accept this position, and if you do, there will be no scheduling and reservations at the Inn for you to make."

Tom smiled. "I'll have to think about it. Actually, it sounds real exciting to me, but I'm sure Samantha will have something to say."

"I understand. In summary, every two weeks you would deliver the drivers to Progreso and pick them up again. That's about three hours of work. If you decide to take this on, you would get three hundred bucks for each trip—that means six hundred dollars every two weeks."

Tom's eyes widened. He gasped. "Are you going to be here tomorrow? I'll have made my decision by then."

Nick stood. "It's a deal—I'll check with you then."

He shook Tom's hand and walked back across the street.

THE VULTURES HAVE DISAPPEARED, Tom said to himself as he scanned the sky. Nick's proposal sounds real exciting to me, but I wonder what Sammy is going to say when I tell her. She is usually very suspicious of someone offering a high price or wage.

He opened the suite's door and entered. Sammy was sitting in an easy chair, reading. She looked up. "Who were you talking to out there?"

Tom cleared his throat. "It was that Nick guy we met yesterday. He walked over for a chat."

Sammy tightened her lips and slightly raised her chin. "Oh yeah—and what did the Nick have to say?"

"He's offered me a part-time job."

Sammy planted the tip of her forefinger on her chin. "What! You just met him yesterday. What kind of a job?"

"Nick works for an oil company and he needs help moving the drivers back and forth between here and Progreso."

She shook her head. "Sounds weird. How much do you get paid?"

"Three hundred bucks for each trip, and there will likely be four trips each month."

Samantha sighed. "Well, you do what you want, but it sounds rather fishy to me."

Chapter 6

NICK GIGGS HAD BREAKFAST AT A NEARBY IHOP and then headed for Boggus Ford in Harlingen. I need to get rid of this rental and buy myself a permanent vehicle, he said to himself. Nick continued southward on Expressway-83 after passing through the city limits. I see it...the sign...it says *Boggus Ford*.

He spent the next hour with a salesman named Sanchez looking at vehicles. Nick's morale lifted while driving a black Ford Mustang Eco boost Coupe. This is exactly what I'm looking for, he thought. I like the white color. An hour later, he signed the purchase agreement and financing contract. I'll have this paid off in a couple of weeks...and they're going to return my rental to Avis.

Nick arrived at Texas Palms in the late afternoon. He parked close to the Inn & Suites office. Looks like Menzo and his boys are here, he said to himself after noticing several vehicles parked in the visiting area. He walked across the roadway and knocked on room 4001's door.

Moments later, he shook hands with Menzo, the leader of the drivers and one of the few who spoke English. They talked for a few minutes, and Nick said, "I'll be here at eight a.m. with the transit van."

NICK DROVE BACK TO HIS SUITE in his new Ford Mustang. He got out of the car and walked a few steps toward his room. He paused to turn around and admire his new car. This is a classic vehicle, he thought. Then he looked across the street. I've got to connect with Hastings today, he thought.

He unlocked his front door and entered the suite. Pushing away the curtain from his front window, he stared across the street. I've got to connect...and right now, he thought.

Nick walked across the street and knocked on the door. It opened moments later and he stood face to face with Samantha. "Hi there, Miss Samantha—hope your day is going well."

"Thank you, Mr. Nick. I assume you're here to talk to Tom."

Nick nodded.

"He'll be out momentarily."

"Great, I can wait outside."

"Sure, have a seat. Tom will join you soon."

Nick sat down on one of the two chairs in front of the suite. I don't think this woman is for her Tom working for me, he thought. But, her feelings don't matter to me. I have a job to do.

One minute later, Tom came out of the suite and walked over to Nick. "Hi, Mr. Nick—good to see you again." They shook hands and Tom sat down.

"Tom Hastings, I repeat that I would like you to work for me by transporting the sixteen truck drivers. Tomorrow morning, I am picking up those drivers here at Texas Palms. I will use a transit van, which I will pick up in Harlingen today. I invite you to join me tomorrow morning and get a view of what your job will be."

"Nick, this is a little unusual for me, but I'm going to go along for your delivery tomorrow. How do I get started?"

"Hey, thanks, Tom. I'm picking up the transit van today and it will be parked in front of my unit. I'll be leaving about seven fifty-five to pick up the drivers in the motel area."

"Okay, I'll come over."

"Great!" Nick stood and shook Tom's hand. "I'll see you tomorrow morning—oh, by the way, if you decide to go along, bring your passport or at least some kind of picture ID."

Tom nodded. "I've got a passport."

Nick walked toward his suite. I've got the guy sold, he thought.

TOM AND SAMANTHA GOT UP AT 7:00 A.M. He made coffee while she took her daily bath. I better share my plan with Sammy as soon as she gets out of the tub, he said to himself. She won't be too happy, but that's the way life is...people don't always agree.

A few minutes later, he delivered a second cup to Sammy in the bathroom. She'll be out pretty soon, he thought. Tom pushed aside the drapes on their front window. There's the van...it's the same color as my SUV. I've got about an hour before I head over there.

Samantha came out of the bedroom all dressed and holding an empty cup. She filled her cup and sat down. "What's up today, Tom?"

"I was hoping you would ask," he said. Tom cleared his throat. "Remember yesterday when I sat outside and talked to Nick?"

"Yes, I certainly do, and I would sure like to know what you two were talking about."

"I hope this doesn't shock you, but I have agreed to ride with Nick to Progreso today—we're leaving about eight."

Samantha leaned forward. "What! You're going to Progreso?"

"You know that I like challenges, Sammy. This is certainly one. It will help me make a decision on whether I want to go to work for him."

"How long will you be gone today?"

Tom shook his head. "I really don't know, but Progreso is less than an hour away, probably closer to half an hour."

“So, you should be back this afternoon then?” Sammy asked.

Tom nodded. “I would think so. Nick’s job is to assign the drivers to eight trucks—that means two guys in each truck. Once the truck takes off, his job is done.”

“Well, okay Tom. I have to go along with it. Actually, it sounds very exciting. Maybe I could go along.”

Tom laughed. “The transit van has sixteen seats for the passengers, and two seats in the front—one for the driver and one for me. Sorry, no room for Sammy.”

Chapter 7

TOM AND SAMMY HUGGED EACH OTHER TIGHT shortly before 8:00 a.m. He kissed her on the lips, released his grip, and opened the door. "See you later, sweetie."

He headed across the street and stopped next to the van. The suite's door opened and Nick stepped out. "Hey, Tom—glad you're here."

Tom pointed at the sky. "It's a great morning. We should have a good day."

Nick smiled. "Hop in and we'll get underway."

Two short turns later, the van stopped in front of a long row of motel rooms. Nick pressed a button above his head and the two back panel doors opened. Tom watched as the motel doors begin to open and several men approached the van. Each of the drivers received a belt packet to hold their identifications. Minutes later, Nick pressed a button and the doors closed.

Nick turned slightly in his seat and looked back at a man seated behind him. "Menzo, this is Tom," he said, tapping Tom on the shoulder. "He's my assistant today."

Tom turned and extended his hand. "Good to meet you, Menzo."

"Si amigo."

TOM WATCHED THE TRAFFIC AFTER NICK DROVE onto Expressway-83 and headed east. Tom saw the highway exit sign that read: International Boulevard. We'll be getting off here, he thought. I've never been to Progreso but I remember looking at a map, and seeing a street that looks like an extension of International Boulevard.

Tom patted the packet strapped to his belt. He had his passport and driver's license with him.

Within minutes the transit van lined up behind other vehicles at the Mexican border. When they approached the gate, Tom unsnapped his belt packet and brought out his credentials. Moments later a border agent approached his door. Tom opened the window.

"Hello, sir, can I see your ID?" the agent asked.

Tom handed him his driver's license and passport.

"Thank you, sir," the agent said, returning Tom's papers.

Tom turned his head and watched the other passengers go through a similar process.

The sliding doors closed. Nick drove the van forward in response to an arm wave by one of the border agents.

The first few blocks moved by very slowly. Sure are a lot of little girls begging out there, Tom thought as he gazed at the waifs on the sidewalk while Nick waited for a red light.

Minutes later, Nick drove the transit van into the lot of a Tesoro Truck Stop. Tom gasped with amazement when he saw eight Sanchez oil trucks parked at a fueling station in various formations. Nick parked the van in front of the food service building. Nick turned his head to face the passengers in the rear seats. "All of you remain right here until the trucks are ready." He turned to Tom and said, "Follow me."

They exited the van.

"That man standing over there by the other van is Marcos Garza," Nick said. "He's our head guy here at Progreso, and right now his job is to have all the trucks driven to this station from the warehouse. The drivers each fill their trucks with diesel and leave their keys in the cab. Then they will all get into the other van you see. Marcos will drive them back to the warehouse where they have their cars parked."

Tom nodded.

"Come on and join me at the other van," Nick said. "I want you to meet Garza."

Tom followed Nick. There's a lot of Mexican chatter around those eight trucks, Tom thought as they arrived at the other van. Tom shook Garza's hand after Nick introduced him. Minutes later Garza opened the two side-panel doors of his van. Tom watched the eight drivers approach and get into the van. Nick waved as Garza backed up the vehicle a little and made a turn. "The warehouse is only about five, ten minutes away," Nick said to Tom.

Tom nodded.

"Okay, Tom, let's get back to our transit van," Nick said.

Nick opened a side panel door and said, "Okay, *amigos*, I want you all to come out in pairs and take over a truck. All trucks are full of fuel and ready to go. One at a time you will leave the station. I will lead you through Progreso and the American customs."

Tom stared at the group of drivers as they meandered into the truck parking lot and boarded their vehicles, two men per cab.

Nick and Tom returned to the transit van. I marvel at the sound of those eight engines starting up, Tom said to himself.

Tom got in and Nick drove toward the main street. Tom looked back and saw a truck following. Wow, he thought. All eight of them are following us.

NICK DROVE THE VAN AWAY FROM THE TESORO STATION and glanced at Tom as he drove up Progreso's main street. Minutes later, he stopped at the border station, and got the go ahead to continue northward. When he arrived at Expressway-83, he turned the van toward Harlingen. "I'm going to show you where I pick up this van. It's a place called *Valley Transit*."

Sammy is going to ask me a lot of questions, Tom thought. Heck, I'll take her out to dinner and cool her off. I think she'll go along with the deal.

"Well, what do you think, Tom?" Nick asked.

Tom shrugged. "It looks pretty straightforward to me. I imagine that after a time or two, going through customs will be routine."

"I think you have that right. Anyhow, you don't have to decide right now, but sometime this week, I'll give you a call. I could sure use your help. The guy who supervises loading the trucks has his hands full with other tasks, and that's why I need you. I need to be at the loading site."

Half an hour later, Nick drove the van into the parking lot of Valley Transit. Minutes later, Nick and Tom got into the white Mustang. They got back on the Expressway and headed west toward the city of Donna. Minutes later, Nick exited and drove onto the Texas Road. He stopped at the Texas Palms gate and the gate attendant waved him on through. Nick parked his vehicle in front of his suite. Tom got out and walked around to the driver's side. "Thanks for the tour, Nick. I think I can handle the job. Hopefully, I can swing it by Samantha. You know how women are."

Nick chuckled. "The trucks will return from Bloomington in about five days and will be ready for another haul about a week after that. When the time comes, I'll let you know, and you can come with me to pick up the van for the next run."

"Sure," Tom said. "See you later."

TOM WALKED ACROSS THE STREET. He looked back and saw Nick enter his suite. He paused and frowned. I hope I know what I'm doing, he said to himself. Well, here goes nothin'.

Tom opened the door. "Hey, sweetie, I'm back. How was your day?"

"My day was no big deal. I'm anxious to hear what happened to you," Samantha said.

"Tell you what, Sammy, I'm going to get cleaned up and then I'll take you out to Arturo's for dinner. How does that sound?"

Sammy stepped over and Tom hugged her tight for close to half a minute.

TOM OPENED THE DOOR OF ARTURO'S RESTAURANT. He tapped Samantha's shoulder as she passed by him.

"A Gin and tonic for the young lady and a glass of Chardonnay for me," Tom said to the young waiter.

"Okay, let's have it," Samantha said after the waiter left. "I need to know what happened."

Tom pinched his nose and smiled. "It's been an exciting day. I witnessed the drivers and their trucks being managed. This Nick guy has a lot on the ball. The job he is offering me doesn't seem very difficult and it allows me to connect with people."

"How often do you make the trip to Progreso?" Sammy asked.

"Twice a month, I use the van to deliver the drivers and then pick them up," Tom replied. "That means four trips, but—but, I get paid twelve hundred bucks. That's pretty good change for a retired guy like me."

Samantha took a sip of her drink. "Well, okay. I suppose, if you need something like that, it will work. I'll be okay."

Chapter 8

JON CORLONE TOOK A SEAT AT A SMALL TABLE in the far corner of Milano's Restaurant in Weslaco. He ordered a whiskey and water and looked around the room. Tony should be here anytime, he thought. I've got some news which is going to invade his brain big time.

He watched a couple get seated at a table in another section. Somehow that guy looks familiar, he thought. Suddenly his friend Tony Fabzonni appeared, quickly walking around a short room divider. The guy is built like a brick, Jon thought. Tony has almost no neck and a round face which smiles almost all the time. The hair on top of his head looks like a spike of brown grass jutting out from a flat field.

Jon was slim and tall. He had a dark-skinned, narrow face with a narrow black mustache. His dark hair was combed straight back.

Jon pointed at a chair next to him as his friend approached. Using his low, husky voice, he said, "Have a seat Tony. Good to see you again."

Tony let out a loud laugh and said in his high-pitched voice, "We meet again."

Jon waved at the waitress. "This gentleman needs a drink."

The two men exchanged small talk until Tony's drink arrived.

"Tony, I heard a rumor the other day that someone is making a fortune in this area by shipping marijuana from Mexico to somewhere north in central Minnesota."

"That doesn't surprise me. With pot getting more legalized, smuggling is expected to pick up," Tony said. "The cost of pot coming from Mexico will be a lot less expensive than growing it here in our country."

"Okay, you're absolutely right. Now get this. I got word that lately, a transit van unloaded a bunch of guys at Texas Palms. Why? Not sure, but it has something to do with pot being smuggled from Mexico."

"So, what's your plan, Jon?"

"To keep Texas Palms RV Resort under surveillance and wait and watch for a van to show up."

"How are you going to do that?"

Jon looked Tony straight in the eye, his face contorting. "I want you to rent a motel room at that resort right away. The van may never return, but my instinct tells me that it will. You can rent a golf cart and easily keep the place under surveillance."

"Hell almighty, what's in it for me?" Tony asked.

"The motel room will be paid for and you'll get fifty bucks a day—plus I'll take care of the golf cart rental. If you spot the van and follow it, you will get a big bonus."

"Hell almighty, it's a deal," Tony said.

TOM PARKED THEIR VEHICLE NEXT TO MILANO'S. "I'll get the door for you," he said and raced around to the other side. Taking Sammy out for dinner wins me a lot of points, he said to himself. I just took her out to dinner a couple of days ago, and here we are again...all dressed up and doing it again.

He reached inside and grasped Samantha's hand, gently assisting her out of the vehicle. "You look great, Sammy. That long dark blue skirt really looks nice."

Tom closed the door and pressed his key lock button. He held Sammy's hand as they entered the restaurant.

They stopped next to a counter area in the foyer and were greeted by a hostess with dark sparkling eyes.

"Table for two," Tom said.

"Right this way," the hostess said.

They followed the woman into an area with six tables. Two of them were occupied and they were led to a table with four chairs at the far wall. Tom pulled a chair out for Samantha and he seated himself across from her.

"Richard will be your waiter. He'll be with you soon."

Within a minute, the waiter arrived. "I'm Richard and I will be your waiter. Do you wish for anything to drink?"

"Yes," Tom said. "The lady will have a Gin and tonic and I'll have a glass of Chardonnay."

"So, Tom," Sammy said after the waiter left. "You're taking on a responsibility with Nick's company. Do you know anything about it?"

Tom shook his head. "No, but it apparently involves hauling crude oil from Mexico to Minnesota."

Samantha raised a finger. "My question is: Why do the drivers stay here at Texas Palms? Why don't they stay in Progreso where the oil comes from?"

Tom chuckled. "Sweetie, the business world is very complicated. One plus one is not always two."

"Time will tell," Sammy said. "At least you don't have to stay anywhere overnight."

Tom smiled. "No, I don't. Actually my job will not take that much time. I'll always be around."

Samantha took a sip of her Gin and tonic. "Here's to you—I'll be there for you no matter what happens."

They clicked glasses.

Tom glanced at two men leaving from the larger seating area. "Wow, Sammy, look at those two guys over there." Tom pointed.

"One of the guys really looks odd. He's got narrow spike of hair on top, and a body built like a tank. The other guy looks normal."

"The guy does look very odd," Sammy agreed.

They watched the two men leave. Then they took another sip of their drinks.

Half an hour later, Sammy said, "I'm all done. How about you?"

"Great meal—I'm all finished, too," Tom said. "I think it's just great to have this quality a restaurant located so close to where we stay."

TONY FABZONNI ENTERED THE TEXAS PALMS INNS & SUITES OFFICE. He introduced himself and explained he was here representing Jon Corlone, who had made the reservation and was responsible for the payment. The woman brought out a document and nodded. "I'm Judy. Do you wish a room in the Inn or a suite?"

Tony hesitated and cleared his throat. "A suite—a suite!"

"Okay, we'll take the golf cart out and you can look at some," Judy said.

They walked outside and got into a four passenger cart. Moments later they parked in front of suite 4401. Tony followed Judy around for about a minute and said, "I'll take it." This costs a lot more than a single room, but Hell almighty, Jon said he would be paying for it, Tony said to himself.

After returning to the office, Judy handed him a key. "Hey, thanks Judy," Tony said. He grabbed the key and walked outside. He glanced at the sign that read *Kingston Way,* identifying the short roadway separating the parking lot from the Inn's rooms. He got into his dark blue Toyota Corolla and drove to suite 4401. Tony went into the suite, dropped off his luggage, and then left for the

H.E.B. grocery store to supply his kitchen. The weekend is coming up and I'll need food and drink, he said to himself.

Chapter 9

NICK WALKED OUT OF SUITE 4910 and got into his white Ford Mustang on a Thursday morning. He headed for the Texas Palms exit and took a right onto the frontage road. Minutes later, he drove onto Expressway-83, headed toward the International Boulevard exit while on his way to Progreso. The trucks are returning tomorrow and I need to make sure that Marcos is ready, he thought. Then when I get back, I'll meet with Hastings and we'll go over the plan to get the van in Harlingen and pick up the drivers at Tesoro.

He smiled while handing his passport to the border agent. Should be no problem, he thought. They're getting to know me.

Half an hour later, he parked in front of the door of the huge light-gray warehouse. Nick glanced at the bars which protected the lone window. It would be almost impossible to break into this building, he thought.

He entered and sat down next to Marcos's desk. "Hello, Marcos. Do you have the eight guys lined up to pick up the trucks at the Tesoro in Progreso?"

Marcos nodded. *"Si, amigo."*

"Can I see your list?" Nick asked.

"List, I don't have a list—it's all up here," Marcos said and pointed at this forehead.

"I prefer that you make a list of all the drivers. We need their addresses." Marcos frowned and nodded his head. *"Si,* I can do that."

Nick scratched the top of his head. "One more thing, Marcos. Do you know anybody who lives in one of those houses over there?" he asked, pointing.

Marcos nodded. "Yes, I know Emile. He lives in the one that's white."

"Good, here's what I want you to do. Talk to Emile and offer to pay him to keep an eye out on our warehouse. We're not here that much and we need to know if someone shows up to spy on our building."

Marcos nodded. "How much should I offer him?"

"A hundred bucks a month, and if he spots someone and reports it to us, he will get an extra fifty dollars."

"Yes, *amigo,* I will talk to Emile soon."

An hour later, as Nick was driving back to Texas Palms, he thought about Marcos. I need to watch that guy like a hawk, he said to himself.

Tony Fabzonni sat next to a table and looked out his suite's window. The golf cart people should be here any minute, he thought. I hope Jon doesn't get upset with me for moving into a suite rather than a regular Inn room.

Suddenly he saw a pickup truck pulling a small trailer. It's the golf cart company, Weslaco Wheels, he said to himself. That's it! Hell almighty, the golf cart is here. That'll help me tremendously in watching the rooms where the drivers are apparently supposed to spend some time.

Tony stood and opened the door. He stepped out and waved to the pickup driver. Then he motioned for him to stop. Heck, he can unload the cart right here, he thought.

Tony walked over to the pickup and saw two golf carts. The driver rolled down his window and asked, "Are you Tony?"

Tony raised his arm. "Yes, I am. You can drop the golf cart off right here."

"You are assigned the green one. The brown cart goes to someone else."

The driver walked to the rear of the trailer. He flipped down a metal ramp and ran his fists over the top to verify its security. Then he stepped onto the trailer and removed a series of chains which anchored the cart to the trailer bed. He sat down behind the steering wheel and inserted a key. Slowly he backed the cart onto the parking lot.

The man got off the cart and walked back to the pickup. Opening the door, he brought out a clipboard with a form attached and took it over to Tony. "Sign right here, Tony, and the cart is yours."

Tony signed his name in the signature box.

"The electric charger is in that box in the back part," the man said. "Turn it on and give it a try."

Tony sat down, turned the key, and pressed his foot down on the pedal. The cart took off. He circled the lot and parked the golf cart next to his Toyota. "It works fine. Thanks."

Tony watched the man get back into the pickup truck and drive off. The truck took a left turn. Looks like someone else in the Texas Palms area is getting a cart, too, he thought.

PAM COLLITON STOOD OUTSIDE THE DOOR OF SUITE 4705. She saw the pickup truck turn into her lot. "Weslaco Wheels has brought my cart," she muttered.

The truck stopped in front of her and the driver's side window opened. She walked over and said, "I see you've brought my golf cart. It looks nice—neat brown color."

The driver looked at a piece of paper. "Are you Pam Colliton?"

She nodded. "Yes I am."

The man got out and proceeded to unload the cart. After it was on the pavement, he sat down and placed a key in the ignition. He started the golf cart and did a short circle in the parking lot. He stopped in front of Pam and said, “It’s all yours.”

She watched the deliveryman leave before she sat down on the cart. This is super, she thought. I won’t have to do any more of that walking while spying on Nick. So far, he seems to be on the right track for what Mick is expecting. The guy I actually have to watch now is Tom Hastings. He has been hired by Nick to transport the drivers from the resort to Progreso. Then he picks them up in five days after they return from Bloomington.

Pam parked the cart next to her rental vehicle, a maroon Ford Focus. Master buddy, this should help me a lot in keeping an eye out on what’s going on here, she thought.

Chapter 10

TOM HASTINGS KISSED SAMANTHA GOODBYE in the doorway of their suite. "I'll be back before you know it," he said.

He got into his vehicle and drove toward the gate. Minutes later, he drove onto Expressway-83 and headed east toward Harlingen. This is going to be my first trip with the van, he said to himself, feeling a pang of excitement.

I looked up Monroe Avenue on my smart phone, so I shouldn't have any trouble finding Valley Transit, and the rental has already been setup by Nick, he thought.

He passed through Mercedes and La Feria before arriving at Harlingen's outskirts. He made a few turns and ended up on Monroe Avenue. Minutes later he pulled into the parking lot he was looking for. He entered the main building and approached a desk. The woman on duty looked up at him and said, "What can I do for you?"

"I'm her to pick up a transit van. The rental has been set up by Mr. Nick Giggs."

"Yes, the van is waiting for you outside. Here are the keys. There's a parking place for your vehicle over that way," she said, pointing.

Tom opened the door to the van and stepped up onto the rung. He got inside and inserted the key into the ignition. The vehicle started and he placed the gear into reverse. Driving slowly, he got onto a service road and then entered the Expressway. Tom stayed in the right lane and kept his speed down to sixty.

Close to half an hour later, he exited at International Boulevard. Progreso isn't too far from here, he thought. Fortunately my ride with Nick the other day tells me exactly where to go on this run.

The border agent waved him on after Tom showed his identity. He stopped at a few stoplights before turning left and entering the huge parking lot at Tesoro Truck Stop.

He parked in front of the main building and watched as sixteen men walked toward his van. Tom recognized the man who led the group. That's Menzo. I've met him before, he said to himself.

"Hi Menzo. Good to see you again," Tom said.

The man opened the sliding passenger door and continued waving until the last of the drivers had entered and sat down. Menzo closed the sliding door, opened the front passenger door, and sat down next to Tom. "We are ready," he said.

Tom drove the van back onto the main road and headed north. "So how was your trip to Minnesota?" he asked.

Menzo nodded. "It's a long ride, but it went well. Each of the trucks has a sleeping cot. That really helps."

"How many nights does it take?" Tom asked.

"Only one. We sleep in a motel in Bloomington for two to three nights after that."

Tom felt uplifted after seeing the Texas Road sign. He exited the Expressway and worked his way to the Inn & Suites gate. He parked the van and watched as Menzo opened the side panel door.

The passengers disembarked and headed for their parked vehicles.

Menzo returned to the van and reached up to shake Tom's hand.

"Thank you for the ride, sir."

"You're welcome," Tom said.

Tom remained parked and watched the vehicles leave Texas Palms and enter the frontage road leading to the Expressway. He backed up the van and drove to his suite.

"Hi Sammy," he said after opening the door. He hugged her feverishly. Tom kissed her on the forehead and relaxed his arms. "I've got to take the van back to Harlingen right now, and I should be back in about an hour and a half."

"Have a safe trip, sweetie," she said, placing her hands on his shoulders.

"Thanks. See you soon," Tom said.

TONY FABZONNI SAT ON A CHAIR PLACED NEXT TO HIS SUITE'S DOORWAY. His blocky body tightened and he sat up straight when he saw a van drive by. It's heading in, likely coming from the office area, he said to himself. Jon's been telling me to be on the lookout for a large silver-colored van. It's likely the one that I see right now.

He rushed to his golf cart and drove toward the main roadway. Tony took a left and drove to the farthest row of suites. He took a left and slowly drove up the middle, watching the area where the van was parked.

Tony continued to the end and made a slow turn. He stopped when saw a man come out of a suite and enter the van. I need to know who is driving it, he said to himself. After the van exited the area, he stopped the golf cart close to the door the man had left minutes earlier. It's number 4907 and doesn't have a vehicle parked out front. Hell almighty, that means he is returning the van and will come back in his own vehicle.

Tony increased his golf cart's speed and drove toward the main office area. He turned the final corner and saw the van exit the park through a gate and take a right on the frontage road which led to the Expressway.

TONY FABZONNI HAD FINISHED HIS BREAKFAST and sat sipping coffee on the couch. I expect the phone to ring any moment, he thought. I called Jon last night and told him about the new van driver. I don't know his name yet, but I do know where he lives: *Suite 4907*.

He heard a buzz at his waist. He pulled out his cell phone and flipped it open. "Hello Jon."

He nodded several times, and about two minutes later, he snapped the phone shut and placed it back into his cell phone holster. Hell almighty, I need a beer, he thought. He got up and headed for the refrigerator. After removing the cap, he returned to the couch.

Jon wants me to find out the name of the new van driver, he said to himself. He also wants more information on the guy, such as where he's from and who is with him here in Texas. I'm not sure how I can do that. It's doubtful the Inn & Suites people would pass that type of info on to me. My biggest problem is to remain as anonymous as possible.

He looked up at the calendar he had taped to the wall, which separated the sitting area from the bedroom. It's Saturday today and Jon suspects the sixteen drivers will show up sometime this weekend, probably tomorrow on Sunday, he thought. That means the van will return and haul them away on Monday morning.

Tony stepped outside and got into his golf cart. He drove it onto Kingston Drive and headed for the office. After parking, he stayed in the cart and watched the traffic coming and going to and from the Expressway.

Minutes later, he walked up the office counter. "Can I help you?" a woman asked.

"Yes, I'm staying in suite 4401 and would like to know who is in 4907. I know that I could go knock on the door, but I'd like to be sure who lives there first." Tony extended his hand, which had two twenty dollar bills clutched between his thumb and forefinger.

The woman stared at him and hesitated for a few moments. Then she opened a file cabinet drawer. After thumbing through a series of files, she grasped one and pulled it out. "I shouldn't do this, but since you are a current customer, I will give you the names. Suite 4907 is currently occupied by Tom and Samantha Hastings."

Tony smiled. "Thank you, ma'am. I appreciate it." He gave the woman the money, turned, and left the office. Hell almighty, I got the guy's name. Then he saw a woman in a brown golf cart parked in one of the parking lots. I wonder who that is, he thought. She looks like a movie star with that long dark hair. He waved as he passed by. She didn't wave back. I should stop and meet her, but I best not, right now.

PAM COLLITON SLIPPED HER PHONE INTO THE CHARGER. Well, I told Mick exactly what appears to be going on, she said to herself. I'm doing my job. He sounded confused when I told him about Nick hiring Hastings to help with the truck drivers. But Mick did understand Nick's claim that he has to spend time at the warehouse to monitor the truck loading and their drivers. There are eight of them, and they do only the driving from the warehouse to the Tesoro station.

I think Mick is a little distrustful of hiring a stranger to be a part of the driver transportation services, she thought. However, I totally don't agree with him, and I totally trust the Hastings guy. What I'm more concerned about is the recent emergence of a green golf cart. There's a strange looking heavyset guy driving it. He could be a spy because he cruises around this area every single day.

When I saw Hastings driving the van yesterday, heading out of the park, the green golf cart driver was following him, she thought. Master Buddy, I'm not sure if I should report this to Mick or not.

Chapter 11

NICK GIGGS CLICKED "LOGOUT" ON HIS LAPTOP. TD Ameritrade is doing well for me, he said to himself. My first payment from Mick has already grown by 2%.

It's Sunday morning and I'll head for Progreso right after breakfast, he thought. The bales of pot are arriving today and Marcos needs to be watched regarding loading them properly into the oil trucks. Sealing all of the tanks in all the trucks has to be done right. A mistake could be fatal. The dog at the border station would sniff us out of business.

But now there's a new problem, he thought. According to Mick, someone is spying on our drivers and Hastings, His information suggests a heavyset guy in a golf cart. That would mean the guy is living here. Mick has someone else looking into it...not sure if it's Hastings or someone else.

He locked his suite's door and clicked his key fob to unlock his Ford Mustang. He drove onto Kingston Drive and headed for the Expressway.

The Mexican agent at the border waved him on through. Driving into and out of Progreso is not much different than driving to Minneapolis from Bloomington, he thought. They know me and my vehicle real well.

Minutes later, Nick arrived at the warehouse west of Progreso. He walked into the office and greeted Marcos who was waiting for him. "Okay, *amigo* Marcos, let's load the trucks."

Nick stepped up to the driver's door of the first truck and got in. He pulled out the ignition key, which was attached to a fob with three others, and got out of the cab. One of these keys is used to open the lockbox, Nick thought, studying the keys.

He selected the seventh key and slipped it into the lockbox's slot. This must be the one, he thought. It fits. He turned the key and the top of the box flipped open. Nick pressed one of the buttons and the top of the first tank slowly flipped open.

Wow, this is something.

He pressed the other two buttons and opened the tops of the other three tankers.

This is tedious, he thought, but I have to do this with every truck. "Hey, Marcos, do you know how to open these tanks?"

Marcos nodded.

"Great, then do the four trucks over there," Nick said.

Half an hour later, all the tanks were open. Nick and Marcos walked over to the two loaders. "Let's get the loading under way," Nick said to Marcos.

They loaded six bales into each truck. An hour later, Nick muttered, "Looks like we got them all."

He walked back into the office. "Okay, Marcos, I'm headed for home. I'll be here about seven in the morning to help you with the Tesoro drivers. Oh, by the way, did you get your friend Emile lined up to watch this place?"

"Yes sir, he is watching it every day."

"Good. Here's a hundred dollar bill to pay him for the first month."

TOM HASTINGS EXITED THE EXPRESSWAY. HE WAS BEHIND THE WHEEL OF THE VAN, which he had just picked up in Harlingen on Sunday afternoon. I'm really looking forward to seeing Samantha, even though I've been gone only about an hour and a half, he said to himself. I know that she is really concerned about me joining Nick and helping him transport those truckers from here to Mexico.

The trucks these men drive are only hauling oil. That shouldn't be a problem.

He slowed the van and followed the frontage road to the Inn & Suites gate. The oil truck drivers will be here early tomorrow morning, he thought. My trip to Progreso will be a lot easier on the next run…it will be my second one, but my first one alone…I'm pleasantly surprised how easy it is to pass through the border stations, especially the U.S. one.

He drove down Kingston Drive and parked in front of suite 4906. Tom quickly unlocked the front door and entered. "Hi Sammy," he said, extending his arms. He hugged Sammy around her waist and tightened his grip until he heard her gasp.

"I'm real glad that you're home safe, Tom. I worry when you make these mysterious trips," she said. "I understand that you're making a lot of money by assisting an oil company, but the whole thing sounds shaky to me."

"Well, hauling guys back and forth across the border certainly shouldn't be a crime. All the drivers appear to be legitimate citizens. Nobody is hiding anything."

"So you left our SUV at the transit place, huh?" Sammy asked. She looked dubious at the thought of their vehicle not being safely parked at Texas Palms.

"Yup, it will spend the night there, but they have fenced and gated security. Should be no problem."

"When are the truck drivers supposed to arrive here?" Sammy asked.

"Sometime this afternoon, actually, or they could already be here. They all get to enjoy an evening at Texas Palms," Tom replied.

"So, how early do you have to pick them up tomorrow?" Sammy asked.

"I'll be there about seven. That means I have to get up about six, but you can certainly sleep in," Tom replied.

"I plan on doing exactly that," Sammy said.

Chapter 12

PAM WATCHED THE GREEN GOLF CART GO BY. Something is wrong here, she thought. The heavyset man in the green cart is spying on the drivers. I know that I cannot mention this to Nick, but I'll pass it on to Mick soon as I get back to my room.

She pushed her cart's accelerator and followed the heavyset guy. I best stay a good distance behind, she thought. Uh-oh, he's making a left turn into the first concourse...and he's parking in front of the first door. Whoever this guy is, I now know where he lives.

She continued her drive and parked in front of her suite.

Pam entered and sat on the couch. She flipped open her cell phone and called Mick.

"Hi Mick, things appear to be going well. This Hastings guy looks like a good choice, and he's getting the job done."

Pam listened, nodding a few times. Then she said, "There's one more thing. There is a guy hanging around in a golf cart. He appears to be interested in the drivers and the van."

She listened for another minute and then shut down her cell phone. Uh-oh, Master Buddy, I've got a new job...watching the guy in the green cart and finding out who he is, she thought. This may not be easy. I've got to think on this one. I'll see what happens when the van picks up the drivers tomorrow.

THE SKY WAS THICK WITH CLOUDS AND PRODUCED an occasional drizzle on Sunday afternoon. Tony drove his golf cart onto Kingston Drive and soon took a right onto Kingston Way.

He took another quick left and parked in a small lot close to the Inn & Suite's office. I'll just have to keep doing this until the drivers show up, he thought. This is my sixth run today. Jon insisted that they will arrive sometime on Sunday afternoon.

He looked at his watch. It's close to four, he thought.

He looked up and saw a vehicle exit the frontage road and take a left into the first parking lot. It parked in the far corner.

Hell almighty, I think that's one of 'em, Tony thought. There should be more coming shortly.

Two more vehicles entered and they both parked next to the first. About ten minutes later an eighth vehicle entered and parked.

Tony watched as sixteen men got out of the vehicles and walked toward the main office. That's them. They're checking in and soon will access their rooms.

He started the golf cart, crossed Kingston Way, and drove into the parking lot in front of the ten rooms. He parked close to Room 4001.

Hell almighty, there's that dark-haired woman again, he thought as he saw a brown golf cart turn off Kingston Drive and slowly head his way.

She took a left and parked where I was a few minutes ago, he thought. It looks like she's spying on me.

Tony turned his attention to the office when he saw several men exit and walk toward the Inn's rooms. Within minutes two men had entered each room.

One of the men walked out of room 4001 and walked his way.

The man stopped next to the golf cart. "Can I help you, sir?"

Tony pulled the brim of his cap slightly down and said, "No, thank you, I'm just killing time."

The dark-skinned man gave Tony a slight nod. He shrugged and returned to his room.

Tony turned the switch and pushed the pedal. He headed for Kingston Drive and waved at the woman in the brown golf cart. She didn't wave back.

SAMANTHA HASTINGS ELEVATED HER CHIN. "Tom, are you going right now?"

"Yup, actually, it's much better for both of us if I pick up the van right now on Sunday, rather than early in the morning—I should be back in about an hour and a half. Do you want to come along?"

She slowly shook her head. "No thank you, I'd much rather stay home and wait for your return."

Tom walked over to the couch. He reached down and pulled her up onto her feet. He hugged her tightly.

"Have a safe trip, Tom," Sammy said.

Tom walked out the door and clicked his fob to unlock his vehicle. He stood next to his black SUV and looked across the street. Nick has been gone all day, he thought. He's sure a busy guy.

Tom drove onto Kingston Drive and headed for the gate. Uh-oh, there's that green golf cart again, he said to himself. It's parked in the Kingston Way parking lot, and there's that same oddball looking creature sitting in it. Tom drove slowly through the gate. There they are...about eight vehicles...the drivers must all be here. He turned onto the frontage road and headed for Harlingen.

An hour and a half later, he drove back into Texas Palms, slowly made his way down Kington Drive, and turned left to park the van in front of his suite.

Opening the door, he said, "I'm home, Sammy."

Chapter 13

TOM HELD SAMANTHA TIGHT AND KISSED HER ON THE LIPS. "Wish me luck, sweetie. I need to go."

"I totally understand, and I know you will be back before we know it."

Sammy followed Tom outside and she watched him get into the silver van. She saw him wave as the van rolled toward Kingston Drive. Sammy continued to watch until the vehicle disappeared from view.

Tom turned the van right onto Kingston Way. There's no one around except for that blue vehicle parked in the Way's lot, he thought.

He stopped close to the last unit, number 4001, and stepped out. "Hey, Menzo, are your drivers ready to go?"

"Yes, sir. I'll knock on their doors and let them know that you are here."

Tom watched with amazement as the drivers, one by one, stepped into the van.

"Hey, Menzo, you can sit up front if you wish," Tom said.

"Thank you, Mr. Hastings. I'll do that." He looked at this watch. "We are on time, sir. It's not quite eight. We'll be at our destination within half an hour."

Tom got back in the van and put on his seatbelt. He drove through the gate and onto the frontage road. Looking into his side view mirror, he saw a vehicle following. That looks like the same one that was in the Way's parking lot, he thought.

My ears are full of verbal chatter coming from the rear, he thought. He smiled. It's part of my job.

He activated his left turn signal and slipped into the right lane of the Expressway. That pickup truck that just passed me must have been going a hundred miles an hour.

Minutes later he saw the sign that read *International Boulevard*. Tom slipped into the next right lane and headed for the stoplight. We'll be at the Mexican border station in about six minutes, he thought, looking at his watch. I hope Sammy is okay.

There's the Tesoro station, he thought. I'm almost done with my delivery. He took a left into the large parking lot. Wow, those eight trucks look awesome. Tom parked the van in front of the main building. He turned his head and looked at Menzo. "Everyone waits here in the van until the trucks are ready."

Tom stepped out and looked across the lot. The other van is still here, so the original eight drivers are still in the trucks, he thought. He saw Nick emerge from behind a truck. Looks like he's leading the original eight drivers to the van, he thought. He apparently drives them back to where their vehicles are parked

Tom watched as all eight drivers got into the van. There comes Nick, he said to himself, watching his boss walk across the lot.

"Good morning, Mr. Hastings. Good job, you got all the drivers here on time."

"Hi Nick, they're a bunch of good guys."

Nick smiled. "Great. It'll be about five days before they get back. I'll give you a call when they do return. So thanks again, and you can take off. Menzo and I will get the drivers into the trucks."

Tom nodded. He got back into the vehicle and watched the drivers leave and follow Nick toward the trucks.

Tom closed the window. He drove onto the main street *Benito Juárez* and headed north. "I'm on my way home, Sammy," he muttered.

TONY FABZONNI SAT AT HIS EATING TABLE IN HIS SUITE. He munched a piece of toast and sipped coffee as he stared out his window. I now know who the van driver is, he said to himself. He is obviously going to pick up all those guys staying at the Inn. I don't know when, so I will need to get out there early. My plan is to follow that silver van...find out where it is going.

Jon will be very upset with me if I don't succeed, he thought. Suddenly his body muscles tightened. Hell almighty, the van is going by. I better get out there. Tony grabbed his vehicle keys and suite key off the kitchen counter and headed for the door. He turned the latch button and quickly walked to his dark blue Toyota Corolla.

He backed out of his spot and drove towards the Inn's office area, next to the rooms where the van passengers were staying. Tony turned the corner and saw some of the men entering the van. He backed his vehicle into the Kingston Way parking area. They're still coming out of their rooms, he thought. Hell almighty, there sure is a bunch 'em.

Suddenly he detected movement to his right. It's the Hollywood dame again...the brown golf cart, he thought. He watched as it wheeled to the right and parked a distance behind the van. I've got the driver Hastings identified, but now I need to know who the dame is and what she is doing here. Jon will want to know.

Tony saw the last passenger get into the van and he slowly moved his golf cart ahead as he watched the long silver van roll forward. Tony drove out of the parking lot and caught up with the van as it approached the frontage road. He looked in his rear view mirror. The dame's golf cart hasn't moved, but she sure as heck is watching me, he said to himself.

Tony Fabzonni had remained a few vehicles behind the van as it drove onto the Expressway and headed east. A few minutes later, he saw the van's right turn signal blink. Tony moved into the far right lane and came within two vehicles of the van as it stopped at a red light on International Boulevard.

The van took a right. It's headed for Progreso as sure as I'm sitting here, Tony thought.

Minutes later the van stopped at the Mexican border station. Tony was right behind it. He fished out his driver's license and passport and readied for the agent.

He watched the van move up Benito Juárez, the main street in Progreso. The agent returned his two identity items and waved him on. Tony sped ahead to catch up with the van. This is going to be very interesting and informative on where the van stops, he thought.

We're almost out of town, Tony said to himself. Then, he saw the van pull into a Tesoro Truck Stop. "Hell almighty," he muttered. There are eight big oil trucks parked next to the pumps. They all have the same marking on the doors: *Sardoza Oil*. The van has stopped next to the main building. Uh-oh, there's the other guy from Texas Palms, Nick is his name, Tony thought. He's leading all the drivers towards the trucks.

According to Jon, there is marijuana in each of those trucks and they are hauling it to Minnesota, Tony said to himself. I imagine they will resell it to people and businesses which live in the three states where pot is legal. The people running this trucking expedition must be filled with technical genius to get the stuff by those dogs at the border station.

Tony watched as the drivers disappeared. I can hear doors slamming, he thought. They should be leaving soon. There goes Hastings with the van. He must deliver the vehicle back to some place in Texas near Texas Palms.

Tony left the station just as the eight trucks begin their movement up Benito Juárez. He got through American customs and continued going north on International Boulevard. His mind focused on the man at the truck stop who drove the white Ford Mustang. The Inn & Suite's office people gave me Hastings's name, he said to himself. I need to find out which unit the Nick guy stays in. The white Mustang should tell me that.

Tony drove onto the Expressway and in minutes he took an exit and drove onto Texas Palms Road.

Chapter 14

PAM COLLITON WATCHED THE VAN LEAVE THE RESORT. There's a blue vehicle following them, she said to herself. I bet it's that heavyset guy who's been cruising around in the green golf cart. I need to get on the phone with Mick. He's not going to like this.

She returned to her suite and sat down on the couch. She flipped open her cell phone. Mick Brown answered on the third ring. "Hello."

"Hi Mick, this is Pam."

"Well, hi Pam, how are things going? Good, I hope."

"Transporting the drivers across the border and the general delivery flow is going excellent. Hastings is doing a great job."

"So why did you call?" Mick asked.

"There's a guy hanging around. He's staying in a suite not far from here. He appears to be spying on Hastings and the drivers. He drives both a blue Toyota and a green golf cart. He hangs around the Inn's gate with the cart a lot. When Hastings left on today's delivery run, this guy followed the van in his car. That's all I know for now."

"Pam, listen carefully. You need to get the name of the man and as much information as you can. Then get right back to me."

"I shall do," Pam said. "Master Buddy, what do I do now?" she muttered after the call ended.

She closed her phone. I know where the guy lives, she said to herself. I wonder if the cleaning people have been there yet. I better check this out.

PAM FELT HER STOMACH TENSE. She stepped outside and got into her golf cart. She headed for Kingston Drive. After turning right, she slowed at the 4400 concourse. There's the guy's golf cart, she said to herself.

Pam drove very slow and backed into the parking area across the street.

Half an hour later, a cart carrying two cleaning ladies turned into the concourse. Hopefully, they will start at the first unit, Pam thought.

"Master Buddy, it's my lucky day," she whispered.

Both of the cleaning women got out of the cart. One of them entered suite 4401. The second one opened the door of suite 4403. After the women disappeared inside, Pam thought, this is my chance.

She drove across the concourse and parked next to the cleaning ladies' golf cart.

Pam entered the suite. The cleaning woman inside looked up. "Pardon me, but I need to find something. It will only take a moment," Pam said. She felt pleasantly surprised when the woman nodded.

Pam spotted a desk next to the couch. She opened a narrow drawer and saw a small stack of envelopes. She picked up the first one and saw the name: *Tony Fabzonni*.

"Thank you very much, I found what I needed," Pam said to the cleaning woman.

She closed the drawer, rushed outside, and got into her golf cart. Within minutes she parked in front of her unit and entered. "Master Buddy, I've got the name of the guy," she muttered.

Pam set the envelope down on her small desk. She flipped her cell phone open. She pressed her finger on the dials three times and waited. When Mick answered, she said, "Mick, I've got the intruder's name."

TOM CRANKED THE CORK OUT OF A BOTTLE OF CHARDONNAY and filled his glass. He took a seat on the couch next to Sammy, who was watching television. "What are you watching?"

"Look at that house. Those two people are going through it and if I was them, I would buy it."

Tom smiled. She's watching her Home channel again, he thought. That's one of her favorites. Sammy likes to look at different types and styles of homes.

Sammy turned her head. "Tom, I talked to the local realtor when you were gone and he said there were four mobiles homes for sale on Kingston Drive. If it's okay with you, he'll pick us up after lunch tomorrow and we can look at them."

Tom nodded and laughed. "Yup, I remember. We talked about the possibility of buying a place here."

He watched Samantha's face light up as he took a deep sip of wine from his glass.

"Then it's a deal. I'll give Tim a call back," Sammy said.

"Who's Tim?" Tom asked.

"He owns and runs the local real estate company which has a headquarters in this park."

Tom took another sip. This could be a good distraction for me after being involved with Nick's drivers, he thought. Maybe Sammy is right and we should buy a home here in Texas Palms.

Chapter 15

MICK SAT BEHIND HIS DESK IN THE BLOOMINGTON WAREHOUSE'S OFFICE. He looked at Norm Blaine, who stood in front of the window, his hands on his hips. Norm is watching for the trucks, which should be here anytime, Mick thought. This is the third load and all three of us get to pocket another fifty thou. That will put us in the clear.

"Hey Norm, see anything yet?"

"No, Mick, but they should be less than an hour away."

"Yup, I talked to Menzo about half an hour ago. They had passed Owatonna some time ago. They're making good time on Interstate-35."

He thought about Pam and how she had found out the name of the man who was apparently spying on the drivers and the van. I'm going to have to do something about that guy.

I made a good decision in hiring Pam to watch over the action at Texas Palms...it's certainly paid off to this point, he thought. He looked at a document which he had lying on his lap. The man who is spying on us in Texas is a guy with the name of Tony Fabzonni. He has a long record, most of which is criminal or related. The question in my mind is how am I going get rid of him. Should I have Nick take care of the guy or should I rely on Pam?

Mick picked up the report and brought it up to his eyes. Cripes, this guy has spent seven years in prison, he said to himself. He's been convicted of four crimes, all related to stealing money or property from people. I'm certain that he's working for someone. A guy like that doesn't have enough brains to plan and execute a formal crime. Before I get rid of him, though, I need to know who he's working for.

Pam can't do that for me. I need to hire a professional, and I know one who can do the job. Stuart lives here in Minneapolis. He can likely gather all the information we need.

Mick walked over to his desk and sat down in front of his computer. Four clicks later, he had Stuart's phone number on the screen. I'll call him right now, he thought.

Mick punched in the number and waited. Moments later, he heard Stuart's hello.

"Hi, old buddy, this is Mick Brown."

Mick listened and chuckled for a few moments. "So I suppose you want to know why I'm calling you." Mick chuckled some more. "Okay, here's the deal. I need to know who a man is working for. His name is Tony Fabzonni and right now he's living in Donna, Texas. He's got quite the criminal record. You will get well rewarded if you get this information for me."

Mick listened for part of a minute. "Okay, Stuart. You can call me anytime you wish. Thanks old partner. It's good to hear your voice again."

Mick pressed Pam's number in his contact list. "Hey, Pam, you're doing a great job in Texas. Within a day or two, I'll have more information on this Tony guy. Then I'll decide on how to handle it, so just keep up your surveillance and you'll be hearing from me again soon."

She's a beautiful girl, Mick thought as he put his phone away. I should be spending time with her instead of messing with marijuana.

"They're here!" Norm exclaimed.

Mick left his desk and joined Norm at the window. "Let's get the doors open," he said and headed out the door.

TONY SAT DOWN IN HIS GOLF CART and took a right onto Kingston. There are two other concourses other than mine, he thought. One of them is going to have a white Mustang. His eyes scanned the concourse next to his. Nothing there resembles what I am looking for. Then he drove by the third concourse.

"Uh oh, there it is," he muttered.

He took a right and drove up the middle. It's a Mustang, and parked right in front of number 4901, he said to himself. Tony drove by slowly. Who's living in 4901? He definitely has got something to do with those eight trucks.

Tony drove to the office. He parked and went inside. "Can I help you" the young lady on duty behind the counter asked.

"Yes, I need to know the name of the person who is staying in suite 4901. I owe him some money and need to drop it off in the mail. Could you help me out?"

The woman smiled and turned a few pages in a large booklet which lay on the counter. She scanned the final page. "It's a man by the name of Nick Giggs."

"Is Giggs spelled like this?" Tony asked, handing the woman his notepad.

She nodded.

I'll call Jon soon as I get back to my room, Tony thought. Hell almighty, I've done my job. It's pretty obvious that this gang from Bloomington is illegally shipping marijuana from Mexico to their home base. And! And, I have the name of the guy who seems to be running the show here.

A few minutes later, Tony called his boss. "Jon, I've got the name of the guy who appears to be in charge of the trucks here in Texas."

"Let's have it," Jon said.

"It's Nick Giggs, and he's staying in suite 4901 here at Texas Palms. He drives a white Ford Mustang."

"Good job, Tony. Now, I want you to follow that vehicle when it heads to Progreso. We need to know where he goes. Likely it's where the trucks get loaded."

"I shall do so."

Chapter 16

TOM SMILED AT SAMANTHA AS THEY ATE BREAKFAST while looking out the window. "I see Nick's car is gone. He's probably already in Progreso organizing the trucks."

"Is today the day you do a transport of the oil truck drivers?" Sammy asked.

Tom nodded. "Yup, today is the day—another three hundred bucks in our pockets."

"It sure helps pay the rent for this place," Sammy said.

"This will likely go on all winter long, but when April comes and we head back to Minnesota, Nick will have to find himself a new driver. Oh, by the way, I would like to delay our meeting with the realtor for a week or so. Okay?"

"I suppose that would be alright. Is there any special reason for your request?"

"Yup, I've just got too much going right now. Later, it will be better."

Two hours later, Tom held Samantha tight while they stood close to the door. He kissed her on the lips. "I'll be back before you know it."

"Have a safe trip. See you in a couple of hours," she said.

Tom got into their SUV and headed for the Expressway. He looked into his side view mirror when he drove onto the Frontage Road. I don't see the blue Toyota behind me that followed me the last trip, he thought. Oh what the heck...whoever drives it does not involve me...it's probably no big deal.

Half an hour later, he arrived at Valley Transit to pick up the van. Minutes later he signed a paper, picked up the keys, and headed out to the silver van. He backed out of the parking spot and headed for Progreso. About half an hour later, he pulled up at the

Tesoro station and muttered, "There they are—all eight trucks." Tom chuckled. Looks like all the drivers have already gotten out and are hanging around the station store, he thought. They've all got food either in their hands or their mouths.

Uh-oh, Tom thought. There's Nick's white Mustang and a black van coming over with new drivers to pick up the trucks.

"Okay, Menzo, do you have everyone in here?" Tom asked.

"*Si, senòr*—all set to go."

Hmm, Tom thought. There's that blue vehicle again. It's not going to follow me. Instead it's filling up with gas.

He pressed the gas pedal and headed out of the station and onto the main street in Progreso. I'll have the driver's back to Texas Palms within an hour.

TONY FABZONNI HAD ANXIOUSLY WAITED FOR THE VAN TO PASS BY. Finally the guy has showed up, he thought. It'll take him close to an hour to get to the truck stop in Progreso. I think I'll head out in about a half an hour and get there before he does.

Sometime later he looked at his watch. It's time hit the road, he thought.

Tony got into his blue Corolla and headed for Progreso. When he arrived at the station, he parked in a customer parking space. Minutes later, he said to himself, Oh my God, there come the trucks. He felt excited as he watched them approach from the north.

Tony opened his window. It sounds like a race track, he thought.

The first truck pulled into the station and parked next to the farthest pump at the far end of the station. He watched with anxiety as three more trucks stopped next to a pump. The other four trucks lined up behind the others to fill their tanks. Tony again noted the name on the trucks: *Sardoza Oil*.

Looks like the fuel tanks are all filled, Tony thought as he watched the drivers leave the trucks and meander toward the convenience store.

Tony looked across the station lot and saw the white Mustang. He watched Nick return from the trucks area. The man waved at the black van parked behind the Mustang. Eight guys exited and headed toward the trucks. Each of them walked up to a truck cab and got inside.

Tony kept an eye on the convenience store's door.

The truck drivers emerged minutes later. A van drove up to them. This is confusing, he thought. I have seen both Giggs and Hastings driving that van. Apparently Giggs has hired Hastings to deliver the drivers from Texas Palms to Progreso, and then pick them up later.

The first truck is leaving, Tony said to himself as he watched it drive away from the pump and slowly make its way to a road heading west. Soon, three more trucks followed. Should I go now or wait until the last truck leaves? Heck, I'll follow the first four and assume the others will follow.

Tony drove away from the station and got onto the highway the first four trucks had taken. He followed at some distance behind. In his side view mirror, he could see the other four trucks coming his way. Then he saw the lead truck in front of him take a right and drive onto a gravel road. He lifted his foot from the gas pedal to slow down and watch. After the fourth truck turned off, Tony kept driving west. He stopped after half a mile and turned onto an approach. He reversed directions and stopped as the second line of four trucks turned onto the gravel road.

That looks like a very large building about a half a mile away, Tony thought. That's where the trucks are heading. I bet Hastings is back at Texas Palms by now, with his load of drivers from the north.

I'm going to have some big news for Jon when I get back, he said to himself.

PAM HAD DRIVEN HER GOLF CART TO THE KINGSTON WAY parking area. She saw Hastings's vehicle go by, heading for the Expressway. Within half an hour she saw Tony's blue Toyota head in the same direction. The spy is going to end up in Progreso, she thought. I best call Mick and let him know.

Now that both Hastings and Tony are gone, there isn't anything for me to do, she thought. I'll head home and make the call.

Instead of driving into the concourse where her suite was located, she drove into the one next to hers. Nick's white vehicle is gone, so he's in Progreso managing the trucks, she thought. That's exactly where Hastings and Tony have headed. I'm glad that I'm here, safe and sound.

After sitting down on the couch in her suite, she called Mick. "What's up Miss Pam?" he asked.

"Our spy Tony has followed Hastings again, and they're likely both in Progreso where the trucks are arriving. I can't be absolutely sure, but I'm sure Nick is there in the middle of it all. His vehicle is gone, too."

"Thanks Pam. I'll give Nick a call. Talk to you later," Mick said.

Chapter 17

NICK HAD DRIVEN AWAY FROM THE WAREHOUSE BUILDING. Marcos's Progreso drivers are following me, he said to himself, seeing the black van in his rear view mirror. Minutes later he parked at the far side of the parking area at the Tesoro station. According to the call I got from Mick, the eight trucks from Bloomington should arrive in minutes.

Nick continued to stare out the window, watching the traffic on Benito Juárez. He gasped. They're here! He thought.

Nick watched the first truck enter the lot and park next to a fuel pump. Three other trucks followed. Then he saw the next four trucks arrive and park in back of the others.

Nick stepped out and walked over to the black van behind him. The driver's side window opened. "The trucks are getting fueled by the drivers who got them here. Stay put until all sixteen of the drivers leave the trucks."

He went back to his Mustang and sat down. His phone vibrated. It's Mick, he thought. Snapping it open, he said, "Hi, Mick." His face furrowed as he listened. Then he said, "Ah-ha. Ah-ha."

A minute later, he put his phone back in its holster. He saw the fourth truck leave and head west. There it is, he said to himself, a blue vehicle's following them. That's apparently Tony the spy, who is currently living at Texas Palms. Surely, he's not dumb enough to follow the trucks to the warehouse.

The trucks and the spy disappeared from view as the other four trucks headed west. He looked at the convenience store and saw the Minnesota drivers getting into Hastings's van. My neighbor is doing his job well, Nick thought.

Nick started his Mustang and led the black van to their warehouse.

Nick kept looking around for the blue vehicle as he turned onto the gravel road. All eight trucks have already arrived at their destination. The blue vehicle has disappeared, but I sure know who the hell it is, he thought.

MICK BROWN SAT BEHIND HIS DESK. He held his phone up to his lips. "So, Nick, you couldn't track down who's behind the spy at Texas Palms?"

Mick nodded and set the phone down on his desk. This is a serious problem, he thought. Tony followed the trucks from the Tesoro to the warehouse, and he likely knows that they load the pot there. He's obviously not a cop, and we don't know who he works for. My old friend Stuart, who rarely fails my requests, couldn't track down this guy. I'm a hundred percent certain that the spy has a leader.

We do know where Tony lives, however and what kind of vehicle he drives, and we know his full name, Mick thought. This investigation will not stop.

Mick clasped his hands to the sides of his head. I have a tough decision ahead of me, he said to himself. I know that it's all up to me what to do with the spy. I can't rely on either Nick or Norm to be part of how I deal with this problem. It's time to go home and take a break.

Maybe I should call Angela, he thought. She could settle down my mind. But then I don't know what her situation is. We've been divorced for over a year now. Mick decided to give his ex-wife a call. They talked for close to an hour. After putting the phone away, he opened a beer and returned to the couch. Cripes, I think we could get back together, he thought.

Mick finished the first beer and opened a second one. After finishing that and a snack, he fell asleep on the couch.

Tom's thoughts focused on Samantha as he drove the van from Progreso to Texas Palms. She's handling this adventure of mine real well, he thought. The intense chatter in back of me is something I've never experienced before, but I'm getting used to it. He smiled. I'll deliver the drivers to their vehicles within half an hour.

I wonder why the company needs another set of drivers after the trucks get to Progreso, he thought. I guess it's none of my business, so I'm certainly not going to ask Nick.

The chatter has stopped, Tom thought as he pulled into the parking lot next to the Inn. He smiled as his passengers said goodbye to him.

After the last person got out of the van, Tom called Sammy. "Hi, I've just dropped off the drivers. I'm heading for Harlingen and should be back home in about an hour."

Chapter 18

PAM COLLITON PLACED HER PHONE BACK IN ITS HOLSTER. This is the first time that I've ever talked to Mick when he felt insecure about the problem...the spy, she said to herself. He did push the idea that we need to get rid of this Tony guy.

It's now been a few days since Hastings and the van returned from Progreso with the drivers who do the Bloomington run, she thought. He's fortunate that he's not involved with the spy, and there's no reason he logically should. This Tony guy has been driving me nuts. I'm glad that I don't have a gun. Otherwise I might blow him away.

Actually, what Mick's guys are doing is somewhat legal, she thought. Three states in the US have legalized the stuff. They have to be supplied from somewhere. There's no way they could grow enough pot in the US to satisfy the local needs.

Pam walked outside and sat down in her golf cart. I'll take a spin around and see what's going on, she thought. Tony hasn't been around much lately. But then, he probably has all the information he needs.

She drove toward the office area and slowed. "There's the spy again," Pam muttered. The bastard will not go away. He's parked in his usual spot, she said to herself.

Pam turned her cart into the main parking lot close to the Events Center and the Park Restaurant. She stopped in a parking spot from where she could see the spy. Hastings hasn't gone by yet, she thought. He usually leaves the park about noon to get the van sometime during the afternoon.

TONY FABZONNI SIPPED A BEER AND STOOD IN FRONT OF THE WINDOW. Jon sounded like he was very satisfied with my last trip to Progreso, he thought. Yet, he wants to know more about the warehouse where the trucks all went after being at the Tesoro. I think that he wants to know exactly where the pot comes from. Jon has to realize that I cannot hang around that warehouse building. I would get caught.

Jon has made it clear that he wants me to continue my surveillance of the van and the truck drivers, he thought. Today, it's Sunday, and I expect Hastings to pick up the van in Harlingen today, and then deliver the drivers to Progreso tomorrow morning. If he does that, I'm not going to follow him this time. I already know where they're going to go.

Tony stepped outside and got into his golf cart. He backed up and drove it onto Kingston, heading toward the office area. He spun around in the Kingston Way parking area and parked so he could continue his surveillance.

There's the movie star, he said to himself. She's on her way over here. She's likely coming here to check on me.

Tony laughed loudly.

His golf cart exploded in a ball of fire, sending a large plume of smoke into the air.

A woman with spiky hair came dashing out of the office building. Her jaw dropped when she saw the fiery spectacle in the parking lot. At that moment, she also saw another golf cart, a brown one, driving at top speed away from the area, toward the suites.

She dashed back inside and called 911.

Chapter 19

"Hey, Sammy, how about if I take you out for lunch?" Tom asked, holding his wife by the shoulders on Sunday.

"I would love it," Sammy said, snuggling up tight to Tom.

At close to 12:30, Tom parked their SUV in front of the park restaurant. He exited his vehicle and opened the side door, bringing out a cooler.

"What you got in there? Do I dare ask?" Sammy said.

Tom laughed. "Milk and water."

"Just what I am looking for," Sammy said, laughing and heading for the door.

Tom pushed it open ahead of her and they entered.

"How's this table?" Sammy asked.

"Looks great."

They were greeted by a waiter and then headed for the buffet.

Tom returned to their table first and sat down. Sammy followed soon after, sitting down across from him.

Suddenly, they heard a very loud explosion.

"What the heck was that?" Sammy asked.

"Sounded like a bomb over towards the Inn's office. I'm going to have a look."

Tom quickly walked to the far door and stepped outside. Sammy followed him. They walked into the parking lot. "Oh my God, Sammy, look over there. It looks like a golf cart's burning," Tom said.

"There comes a fire truck," Sammy said as they both walked toward the far side of the lot.

"And there's another siren. This time it's an ambulance," Tom said.

They watched as the firefighters sprayed the golf cart and put out the fire. Moments later, two ambulance men dashed over. One of them shook his head. He went back to the ambulance and returned with a body bag. The two of them carefully moved the human remains into the bag.

Sammy placed a hand over her face.

A police car arrived. Tom watched two officers get out of the car and hurry over to the golf cart. He saw them talking to the ambulance crew. One of the men nodded, and the ambulance crew carried the body bag away. A couple of minutes later, the ambulance exited the park.

"The exit area should be open by the time I head for Harlingen to get the van," Tom said.

CAPTAIN JESSE TREVINO CLEARED HIS THROAT as he hustled over to the destroyed golf cart. He shook the hand of one of the ambulance men. "How many bodies in the cart?"

"Only one, sir."

The captain nodded. "Not much left is there?"

The white-clad medic shook his head. "Nothing. We will deliver the remains to the forensics department. They will prepare a report and it will be available to your office within a day or two."

"Thanks boys," the captain said. "You may leave. There's nothing else for you to do here."

He looked at Sergeant Maria. "Will you give the technical department a call? We need help and right away. Meanwhile, Jesse will be here any moment. Get him to help you tape off the perimeter of the explosion. Looks like that concrete fence in back of the lot absorbed the explosion and protected the building in back of it. But there's a lot of debris on the street. We need to get it cleaned up."

Sergeant Maria walked back to the car. She talked on her phone for a short time and then opened the trunk. She brought out some metal stakes and a roll of bright yellow tape. She waved at an officer getting out of the police car that had just arrived. "Help me with this, Jesse. Looks like about a thirty foot distance from the cart we need to mark, except the fence, of course. It doesn't look like any shrapnel penetrated. It sure created a lot of marks and slivers, though."

Captain Trevino assisted his two sergeants in marking the periphery of the explosion. He occasionally glanced at the four technicians who sifted through the remains. I'm sure glad the state patrol sent over two troopers to help us secure the area, he thought. They are handling all the traffic.

"SAMMY, I'VE GOT TO GO. IT'S TIME FOR ME TO PICK UP THE VAN. The investigation will likely continue on for some time."

"Okay, let's go home—oh my God, we need to finish our meal."

"I'm sure it's been collected by the staff by now, but I need to pay our bill. Let's go back inside."

They walked back into the restaurant. "Looks like our food is gone," Sammy said.

Tom walked over to the hostess's station. He wrote out a check and looked back at Sammy. "Let's head home. You know what I have to do."

Tom held Sammy's hand as they walked back to their suite. "I'm not sure what to think about what has happened. I have to assume it has nothing to do with Nick and what I'm doing for him."

Chapter 20

CAPTAIN TREVINO SAT BEHIND HIS DESK IN HIS OFFICE at the Donna police department. He tapped his knuckles on the desk top and looked at Sergeants Maria and Jesse. "I've been here for twenty years, but never, never have I ever been exposed to a scene like we had at Texas Palms.

"The victim has been identified as Tony Fabzonni. He had been staying at suite 4401. He had a vehicle. It is a blue Toyota Corolla and is still parked in front of his rental unit.

"A background investigation has been conducted and there is absolutely no information on the victim. He has been living totally anonymously. The rent has been paid with cash. The vehicle was paid with cash. We don't know why he was here—and that's where you two come in."

He pointed at Maria. "You will lead the local investigation and Jesse will be your assistant. Judy, the head person at the Inns & Suites office is the first person to talk to. By now, she has communicated with the cleaning people. Judy has mentioned that she has seen Tony in his golf cart, either driving around, or parked in the Way's lot, where the his cart blew up. One of Judy's assistants has mentioned that Tony did ask who lived in suite 4907. I do know it is a couple by the name of Tom and Samantha Hastings.

"So that's all we have so far—any questions?"

Jesse nodded. "What caused the explosion?"

"So far the technical investigative team from McAllen has said it was a pipe bomb of some kind. I don't know any of the details, but if this is important, we can find out."

"Anything else?"

Sergeant Maria asked, "When do we start?"

"Right now," Captain Trevino replied. "First you stop to see Judy at the office. Ask her anything you want. She is going to give you a key to suite 4401. You will be the first persons to investigate it—and also the blue Toyota.

SERGEANT JESSE DROVE. Sergeant Maria sat on the passenger seat. He parked the squad car next to the Inn & Suites office. "Judy is her name," he said. "She is expecting us."

The two officers entered the building. "Can I help you?" the young lady behind the desk asked.

"Yes you can," Maria replied. "We have an appointment with Miss Judy."

The young lady walked over to a door and gave it a gentle tap. She opened the door slightly and said, "Two police officers are here to see you, Judy."

The receptionist nodded to the officers. "You may both go in."

Maria led the way and shook hands with Judy. Jesse followed and did the same. They both sat down.

"I know why you are here and I will do my best to answer any questions you have," Judy said.

Maria leaned forward. "We will need a key for suite 4401. That's apparently where the victim stayed."

Judy nodded and slid the key across the desk. "Thank you," Maria said. "So far all we have is the name of the victim. Is there anything unusual that you noticed during the past week?"

Judy touched her fingers to her mouth. "Yes, there are some things that I and my staff have remembered this past day. First, the victim, Tony, he came in the office one day and asked Sarah, who was on duty at the time, about who was staying in suite

4907. I'm not sure what reason Mr. Fabzonni gave her, but Sarah did honor his request and told the man that Tom and Samantha Hastings are in that suite." Jesse busily took notes.

"Then, when we were interviewing the cleaning women, one of them told us a strange story. She told me that when she was cleaning the Fabzonni suite one day, a woman came in and looked around. I'm not a hundred percent sure, but I think it was the same woman who I saw driving a golf cart away from the explosion. She has long dark hair, and I've seen her hanging around a lot, just like the Fabzonni guy."

Maria asked, "Do you have her suite number?"

"Yes, it's 4705."

"Thanks Judy, anything else?" Maria asked.

"No, that about does it."

"Thanks so much, Judy, you've been a big help," Jesse said.

The two police officers returned to their vehicle

JESSE AND MARIA PARKED IN FRONT OF SUITE 4401. Jesse exited their vehicle and unlocked the door. He entered and Maria followed right behind him.

Maria said, "Here are the victim's car keys. Why don't you check out the vehicle and I'll get started in here?"

"Sure, I'm on my way."

Maria opened the refrigerator. Lots of food in here, she thought. She left the kitchen and opened the drawer of a small stand by the couch. Uh-oh, we got some stuff in there.

She reached in and brought out four envelopes. Maria sat on the couch. One of these is a letter from his daughter, she thought. She lives in Waco. It's a major connection. The woman needs to be contacted right away.

She heard the door open. "Find anything useful in the Toyota?" she asked Jesse.

"Nope, nothing," Jesse replied.

"I've only got the bedroom left," Maria said. "So far nothing except a letter from his daughter."

"So there is a family connection," Jesse said.

"Yup, that's going to be very important for us and Texas Palms."

She entered the bedroom and opened the closet door. "Not very many clothes."

Then she opened the four drawers in the dresser. Nothing here, she thought. She spotted the small nightstand by the bed. It had a drawer and a small door. She opened both and shook her head. Maria returned to the main room. "Find anything, Jesse?"

He shook his head.

"Okay, let's head over to suite 4705. The woman's name is Pam Colliton, and I need two explanations from her," Maria said.

Chapter 21

JESSE DROVE THE POLICE CAR INTO THE MIDDLE CONCOURSE. He parked in front of suite 4705, next to a brown golf cart and a maroon Ford Focus. "Here it is, Maria. This is going to be a little sticky."

"I've got two questions written down here," Maria said, pointing at her notebook. I think you know what they are."

He nodded.

Maria knocked on the door. It opened a few moments later. A tall young woman stood in the doorway. She frowned and said, "Can I help you?"

"Yes, I'm Sergeant Maria Salinas and this is Sergeant Jesse Herarra. We're with the Donna Police Department and are investigating the killing of a resident, Tony Fabzonni."

"I am aware that a golf cart blew up," Pam said.

"Can we come inside?" Maria asked.

"Sure," Pam replied. She walked back into her suite. "Have a seat on the couch," she said.

Jesse cleared his throat after he sat down. Speaking in his low tone, almost a whisper, he said, "Sergeant Maria has some questions for you."

Pam nodded, looking concerned.

Maria looked down at her notebook. "Miss Colliton, we have received information from someone who saw you leaving the scene of the explosion. This person said that you were in your golf cart and sped away. Can you explain to us what happened?"

"Yes—yes," Pam stuttered. "It was terrible what I saw! I immediately reacted to my fear, and got the heck out of there."

"Did you see the explosion?" Maria asked.

"No, I was in my golf cart, driving around slowly in the main parking lot, when I heard the boom—it sounded terrible." Pam placed both hands over her mouth.

The two officers remained silent for a few seconds. "Yes, it was terrible," Maria said. "My second question is, did you ever meet Tony Fabzonni?"

"No, I didn't," Pam quickly replied.

"One of the cleaning ladies at this resort reported that she saw you in Mr. Fabzonni's suite. Is this lady telling the truth?"

Pam looked up at the ceiling. "I went into the suite to talk to the cleaning lady, but when I got in there, I realized that she wasn't the one who does my suite—so I left."

"Can I ask you if you are employed or part of a business?" Maria asked.

"I'm actually semi-retired, but I do some consulting regarding public relations. I have about two dozen businesses up north who call me now and then for input on how to handle employees. In spite of all that, you can view me as a typical Winter Texan."

Maria closed her notebook. "Thank you very much, Miss Colliton. If you ever hear anything from anyone here in the park about Fabzonni, please give us a call."

She stood and handed Pam a card.

The two officers left and got back into their vehicle.

Jesse said. "The woman lied in her answer about why she was in the Fabzonni suite."

Maria nodded. "I agree. Now we have to find out why."

Samantha Hastings placed a hand on Tom's shoulder. He sat in the recliner, having just told her that the police had called and were coming over. "Why Tom? What reason do the police have to question you?"

Tom sucked in his cheeks. "Don't know, Sammy, I really do not know."

I wonder if the guy who was blown up had a blue vehicle, Tom asked himself. I remember seeing it following me when I headed for Progreso...and I remember seeing it at the Tesoro station. Then, there has been this guy hanging around in a golf cart. I suppose it's possible that he was the one blown up...and...he and the guy in the blue vehicle was one and the same.

He edged forward when he heard a knock. Tom got up and opened the door.

"Mr. Hastings, I'm Sergeant Maria and my partner is Sergeant Jesse. We are investigating the explosion. Could we ask you some questions?"

"Sure, come on in."

Tom shook hands with the two officers and they both sat down on the couch.

Sammy entered the room. "Ah, this is my wife, Samantha. She likely would like to know what's going on," Tom said.

"No problem, it's okay for her to be here," Maria said.

Tom brought in two chairs from the kitchen and both he and Sammy sat down.

Maria brought out her notebook. "Mr. Hastings, the only reason we are here is to ask you why the deceased—Tony Fabzonni—would stop at the Inn & Suites office and inquire about who is staying in suite 4907."

Tom's brow furrowed. "Geez, I really don't know." He looked at Sammy. "Is there something you could add to that?"

"No there is not, Tom. I have no idea why that guy would ask that question."

"Have you ever met Tony Fabzonni?" Jesse asked.

Tom shook his head. "Heck no. I don't think I've ever actually ever talked to the guy."

Sergeant Maria smiled. "Mr. Hastings, have you ever noticed someone hanging around a lot—someone unusual?"

"Now I have a question: did this Tony guy drive a blue vehicle?" Tom asked.

Maria nodded. "He certainly did—a blue Toyota. Why did you ask this question?"

"During my recent travels, I noticed a blue vehicle—sort of following me."

"What kind of travels? Can you explain?"

Tom cleared his throat. "About every week, I pick up a van and haul sixteen truck drivers to and from their trucks in Progreso."

Jesse said, "Sixteen drivers! Can you tell us who you do this for?"

"Yeah, it's for an oil company—I don't know the name of it—but I am actually doing this to help out a neighbor here at Texas Palms."

Maria leaned forward. "Who? Who is the neighbor?"

"It's a guy by the name of Nick Giggs. He is staying here at the resort."

Maria picked up her notebook. "Is Giggs spelled G, I, G, G, S?"

Tom nodded.

"Do you know his suite number?" Maria asked.

"Yes, it's 4910."

"These trucks you mentioned, where do they go to after leaving Progreso?"

Tom shook his head. "Sorry, but I really don't know. My job is to transport the drivers to and from the trucks."

Jesse said, "Mr. Hastings, how much time goes by between your trips to Progreso?"

"I make two trips there every two weeks, one to deliver the drivers and another to pick them up in about five days."

Maria closed her notebook. "Thank you so much, Mr. Hastings. Hopefully we will get to the bottom of this tragedy. We appreciate all the help we can get," she said.

The two officers left.

CAPTAIN TREVINO TURNED HIS CHAIR and stretched out his legs parallel to his desk as he waited for his two sergeants to come in. I wonder if I should contact the FBI, he thought. This is a very unusual case. I'll wait and see what Maria and Jesse come up with.

One minute later, the two sergeants entered the office and sat down. Trevino straightened out his chair and placed his hands on the desk. "I'm anxious to hear your results," he said.

Maria opened her notebook. "Our first visit was with Miss Pam Colliton. She is semi-retired, but does some work as a consultant in public relations—or so she says. She was near the explosion when it happened, but claims that she dashed away because of fear. She did admit that she earlier had entered the suite where Fabzonni stayed. She claimed that she went there to talk to a cleaning lady."

The captain looked at Jesse. "What do you think of Miss Colliton's answers, sergeant?"

Jesse took a deep breath. "I don't think Pam Colliton was telling us the truth, especially regarding the visit to Fabzonni's suite."

"What do you think, Maria?"

"I agree. This woman is likely connected to the victim somehow. We need to find out the truth."

"Okay, we'll drop that for now. What did you learn from Mr. Hastings?"

Jesse's quiet words came out slowly. "He appears to be honest, but he did say some interesting things—such as he helps out a local guy who works for an oil company from Progreso. He transports truck drivers between here and Progreso."

The captain's eyes widened. "Did he give you the name of the local guy he helps out?"

Jesse nodded. "Yes, a Nick Giggs, who currently lives in a suite at the same RV Park."

"How about the oil company? Do you have a name?" the captain asked.

Jesse shook his head. "No we don't. But, I think we can find that out from that Giggs guy."

NICK GIGGS SIPPED COFFEE EARLY IN THE MORNING. Hastings did a good job to get all the drivers to the Tesoro on time, he thought. He's going to be a huge help. Next Monday we'll do our fourth run. This will mean another money order from Mick for another fifty thousand.

He heard the sound of a vehicle pulling up. I'm going to get a visitor, he thought...and I bet it will be the cops. Then he heard a car door slamming shut. Nick took a deep breath and waited for the knock.

I may as well get this over with, he thought as he approached the door and opened it. He saw two uniformed police officers standing in the walkway, a man and a woman. Both of them were looking at him.

"Are you Nick Giggs?" the male officer asked.

"Yes, I certainly am. What can I do for you?"

The female officer said, "As you are probably aware, this area had a golf cart blow up, killing the guy who was driving it. We are investigating the case."

"So what do I have to do with it?"

Maria looked up at the sky. "The guy who was killed by the bomb had shown some interest in one of Texas Palm's residents—a guy by the name of Tom Hastings. We have interviewed him and he said that he works for you."

"Alright, I'll give you two the situation. I'm a consultant for a Mexican oil company—it's called Sardoza Oil. They ship raw crude oil generated in Mexico to Minnesota at a very low price. I do a lot of monitoring of the shipments and I hired Hastings to help me out once in a while—no big deal."

Maria put a finger to her lips. "Have you ever met or known a man by the name of *Tony Fabzonni*?"

Nick smiled. "No, I have not. Who are you talking about?"

Jesse's expression hardened. "Fabzonni was the name of the man blown up in the golf cart."

Nick shook his head. "I know nothing about what happened. In this park, I mind my own business and enjoy the weather, and do only what I need to do for Sardoza."

Maria lifted her chin. "Do you drive to Mexico to do your consulting for Sardoza?"

"Yes I do, but only on occasion. I'm semi-retired, and I need a few extra bucks once in a while."

"Al right, Mr. Giggs, we appreciate visiting with you," Maria said. "And if you ever receive any information which may lead to the bombing being solved, please give us a call."

Maria handed Nick a card.

"I certainly will," Nick said.

The two officers left the suite.

Nick opened the refrigerator and plucked out a beer bottle. He removed the cap and sat on the couch. I'm pretty sure that Mick had the spy removed, but that's a possibility I cannot dwell on. The spy is gone, he said to himself.

Chapter 22

NICK GIGGS SAT IN FRONT OF HIS LAPTOP on Sunday morning. This past week was one of the worst I've ever experienced in the stock market, he thought. He clicked on the TD Ameritrade icon and accessed his account. He shook his head. I lost a lot last week, but I should be able to put a lot more cash in there after this next week. I'll be getting another fifth thou after the trucks reach Bloomington.

Soon as daylight comes, I'll be off to Progreso, he thought. Marcos needs to be supervised every time the bales come in. He's got some connections which are negative to our operations. I think Mick should get rid of him and find someone else. He took a sip of coffee and opened his front window blinds.

On the other hand, Nick thought, Marcos has this Emile guy lined up to keep an eye out on the warehouse when we're gone. Mick knows about that, so I best not try to get rid of Marcos.

He looked outside. Tom and Samantha are home, he thought, seeing the black SUV. My biggest concern is whether he mentioned me to the cops yesterday. They were there for at least an hour. Maybe I should move. But then they don't have the authority to investigate a Mexican oil company.

My best news lately has been that the spy is gone...gone for good, he said to himself. I will not see his vehicle in Progreso today...nor any other time. I suppose I should call Mick and find out what he knows about the explosion.

Nick finished his coffee and headed outside. He got into his Mustang and drove out of the park.

TOM SAID GOODBYE TO SAMANTHA and left their concourse. That's where the bomb victim lived, he thought as he looked at the number *4401* on the door while turning left. Moments later he entered Kingston Way. Wow, look at that fence, Tom thought as he noticed for the first time the splattered surface of the concrete fence. The smears on the fence are all sorts of colors, including some reds. At least the bomb didn't blow down the wall and blast into the RV's behind it.

Half an hour later, he started the van in Harlingen. "I'll be home before you know, Sammy," he said to her via his cell phone.

Tom drove the van very slowly as he turned into the resort. Hey, the drivers are all here, he said to himself, while glancing at the parking lot to his left. He parked the van next to his suite and rushed inside. Sammy came dashing across the room and they hugged very tightly.

CAPTAIN TREVINO SAT BEHIND HIS DESK. He lowered his glasses and reviewed a sheet of paper lying in front of him. He looked at his two sergeants. "So we have a murder and have a couple of suspects, but nothing close enough for an arrest."

"I have a theory. Would you like to hear it?" Sergeant Maria asked.

Captain Trevino nodded. "Let's have it."

"I think that Fabzonni was killed because he was spying on an organization which is doing something grossly illegal," Maria said.

Trevino placed a hand over his mouth. "Alright. Do you have any more?"

Sergeant Maria cleared her throat. "I think that the oil company which has been mentioned is smuggling in drugs from Mexico."

The captain sat back in his chair. "Do you have some evidence or is that all speculation?"

"It's some of both, captain. If the trucks are totally legitimate, why would there be a spy? According to what Hastings said, he did notice a blue vehicle following him and hanging around in Progreso. If Fabzonni was in that vehicle, he was spying on the trucks."

Captain Trevino brought out a document from his desk drawer. He looked at it for a few seconds, then said, "I have a choice between contacting the Drug Enforcement Agency or the Federal Bureau of Investigation. If the activities at Texas Palms had suggested straight up drug trafficking, I would have called the DEA. But Fabzonni's suspicious actions suggested an organized crime angle, and so I called the Bureau. If drugs were indeed involved, the DEA would have been brought in as well."

Maria asked, "So what are you going to do?"

"Sometime later today, I am going to consult with the FBI. We have no authority to investigate beyond our town," Trevino replied.

Chapter 23

JON CORLONE PACKED HIS BELONGINGS into his black GMC pickup truck. He stopped at the apartment office to pay his bill and drop off the key. He then drove out of Brownsville and headed for Donna.

An hour later, he parked in front of the RV Office at Texas Palms. Within minutes, he put a wad of bills down on the counter and filled out a rental agreement. After signing on a line at the bottom, he gave the agreement to the woman behind the counter. In return, she handed him a key.

Jon drove down the one-way street and turned onto York Drive. There it is, he said to himself...park model 3435. He turned into the small driveway and parked his vehicle. Jon walked up three steps onto a small porch. He used his key to unlock the front door and entered.

Hey, this is a real neat place, he thought.

Jon returned to his pickup truck four times, returning with a box of bottles on his last trip. He placed them in the fridge and opened a kitchen cabinet door. He closed it and opened another door, bringing out a tall glass. Jon partially filled it with whiskey. I've got a lot of planning to do, he said to himself. One of the things I need to do is to find a large storage building near here on Highway-77.

Jon sat on the couch. He gulped down a mouthful of whiskey and set the glass down on a stand next to the couch. According to Tony, this outfit out of Minnesota is smuggling pot from Mexico, changing drivers at a Tesoro Truck Stop in Progreso while on their way north.

I could blackmail that Giggs guy, he thought. They cannot afford to have the Fed's take apart the tanks. The game would be over and the operators would go to jail. I could probably pop half a million, but then, that method would make me vulnerable.

He refilled his glass and took a deep breath. What if I stole one of their trucks? He asked himself. That would shake them up pretty good, and I could make a lot of money selling the drugs.

Jon quietly sat on the couch for an hour. I'm going to call my son Michael, he thought. He knows how to drive a truck, and he is very good at controlling people.

JON CORLONE PARKED IN FRONT OF A REALTY OFFICE IN HARLINGEN. HE went inside and was greeted by a man sitting behind a desk. "Can I help you, sir?"

"Yes, I am looking for a warehouse in this area with very large doors, preferably north of here. It doesn't have to be fancy, just as long as has at least one very large door."

The man behind the desk nodded. He looked confident as he said, "Yes, there is a building north of here, probably just what you're looking for. We can show it to you within the hour."

"I prefer to rent. Do you have any idea what the place rents for, or is it even for rent?"

"I'm Dave, and you're—?"

"Jon—I'm Jon Corlone."

"Okay, Mr. Corlone. Would you like to have a look at it? I can get someone to show it to you, almost immediately."

Jon smiled. "I would like that. Let's get the job done."

"Tell you what, I'll show it to you myself. We'll take my pickup," Dave said.

Jon waited for a minute while Dave made a phone call. Then he followed the realtor outside. Dave pointed at a blue pickup truck. Jon got in and sat down on the passenger seat.

They got on Highway-77 and headed north. Dave got into the exit lane at Primera Road. He followed the Frontage Road and within five minutes, he turned onto a gravel road. "There it is," Dave said, pointing.

Jon's eyes fixed on a green building. It's located in the middle of nowhere and it's huge, he thought.

Dave parked the pickup in front of the building. He opened the warehouse's office door.

Jon followed him into a small office. Dave opened another door and they accessed the largest room in the huge building. He pressed a button and one of the big doors rattled as it opened.

"How much is the rent for this building?" Jon asked.

"Four hundred and fifty bucks for the first month—then five hundred bucks per month after that."

"I'll take it," Jon said.

"Great," Dave said. "Let's go back to my office and we'll draw up an agreement."

Twenty minutes later, Jon signed a paper and wrote out a check.

Chapter 24

JON SNAPPED HIS PHONE SHUT. Michael is on his way and should be here soon, he thought. I know my son. He is a very reliable person and no matter the challenge, he knows how to get the job done.

Five minutes later Jon heard a vehicle stop next to his unit. He opened the front door and saw his smooth-looking, dark-haired son standing next to his light-blue convertible with a black top.

“Good morning, my son.”

Jon opened his arms and the two men hugged.

“Good morning to you, too, father. What can I do for you today?”

“Come on in and I’ll get you a cup of coffee.” They hugged a second time on the small porch next to the door. “How’s Sonny?”

“He’s a junior in high school this year and doing great.”

Jon smiled and nodded. “Glad to hear that. Does he go to school in Mercedes?”

Michael nodded. “Yes, he does.” Michael sat down by the small table and his father extracted a cup from one of the cabinets. He filled it and set it down in front of his son.

Jon sat down and took a sip. “Michael, I need you to travel to Progreso with me this morning. I have a plan to hijack an oil truck—well, it’s not actually an oil truck. Instead it hauls marijuana from Mexico to the Twin Cities in Minnesota.”

“Wow-wee!” Michael exclaimed. “That sounds exciting. What can I do to help?”

“There are eight trucks in all. They get loaded in a warehouse just west of Progreso. Then they get driven to the Tesoro Truck Stop in south Progreso. The eight drivers are replaced there at the station by sixteen new drivers, who drive the eight trucks all the way to the Twin Cities, non-stop.”

"Wow-wee!" Michael exclaimed again.

"My plan is to have you take over one of the trucks while it's at the Tesoro station, just after the drivers change. You will offer two of the Minnesota drivers a thousand dollars each to cooperate. You will tell them that we need to service the truck. You will direct the two drivers to get into my pickup truck. I will take them with me and lead your truck to a warehouse building which I just rented. I will get off the highway at the Primera Road exit just north of Harlingen and you will follow me. Do you know where that is?"

"Yes father, I've been in that area many, many times."

"When we get to the warehouse, I will pay off the drivers while you take the truck into the building. Do you understand?"

Michael nodded his head.

"Good, then we better get going."

TOM HASTINGS GAVE HIS WIFE A BIG HUG. He squeezed her so hard, she gasped. "I best get going. The drivers are ready to go, I'm sure."

"Be careful, Tom," Samantha said.

"No problem, it's a pretty routine situation."

Tom got into the van, headed out of the concourse, and got onto Kingston Drive. He took a right and parked in front of room 4001. He got out of the silver van and opened the sliding panel door on the passenger side. Tom waved at the first man who came out. Menzo is ready to go, he thought.

Minutes later, Tom had all sixteen drivers seated. He took off for the Expressway and International Boulevard. There's a black pickup truck following me, he thought. Oh well, probably no big deal.

I still can't believe what happened at the Inn's parking lot, Tom said to himself. A man was killed in that explosion. I haven't heard that anyone has been arrested yet.

Tom reached into his breast pocket and brought out his passport as he approached the Mexican border station. He turned his head and said to Menzo, "Have everyone get their ID out. The border agents are going to want to see them."

"*Si*," Menzo said. He turned his head and said something in Spanish to the drivers.

Tom pulled up at the border station. Two agents came out and one of them addressed Tom through his open window. The other talked to the passengers through the open panel door. Within five minutes, they were cleared to cross.

Tom followed Benito Juárez for several blocks. There's the Tesoro station, he said to himself, and flicked on his left turn signal. He drove into the huge parking lot and parked in front of the food store. Looks like all eight trucks are here. "Al right, Mr. Menzo, you guys all stay in this van until the trucks are ready."

Tom exited his silver van. He looked across the lot and saw a black van. That must be the one Nick came in, he thought. There he is, leading the original drivers to the black van. Soon as Nick gets those drivers inside, he'll head over here.

Tom walked over to the passenger door and opened it. "Alright, Menzo, our boss is approaching, so you and the drivers can get out."

When the last passenger door closed, Tom got in the van and slowly backed away from the building. I'm headed home to Samantha, he said to himself as he drove onto the main street.

JON AND MICHAEL CORLONE SAT IN THE BLACK PICKUP TRUCK, which Jon had parked on the east side of the Tesoro's food station. He had backed the truck into the parking spot so he could watch the trucks as they were fueled at the diesel pumps.

There go the drivers, Jon said to himself. "Come on, Michael, let's go visit truck number eight." Jon led the way and he stopped at the driver's side of the truck. "Okay, my son, give the driver your spiel."

Michael walked up onto the rung and knocked on the window. In his best agent's tone, Michael claimed to the driver that his truck needed servicing north of the border. Hey, he did it, Jon said to himself upon seeing his son step down.

The truck door opened and both drivers disembarked. Michael pointed at his father and said to them, "You go with him, and he'll drive you to the service building."

Michael stepped up into the cab and closed the door.

Jon led the two drivers to his pickup. After he got them seated, he backed out of the parking spot and drove forward slowly. Jon kept looking into his side view mirror, watching Michael's truck as it followed.

Jon drove onto the main street and headed north. He didn't have any conversations with the two drivers. Half an hour later, he turned off Highway-77 at the Primera Road exit. Minutes later, he turned onto a gravel road and parked next to the warehouse he had rented. "You two can come into the office and wait while the truck gets serviced."

Jon got out and opened the office doors. The two drivers meekly followed him inside. After the drivers were seated, Jon walked through a second door into the warehouse. He pressed a button and the overhead door rattled open. He saw the truck coming down the gravel road. Jon waved at his son, pointing to where he wanted the truck to be parked.

After the truck stopped, Jon stepped up to the cab. "Michael, hand me the key fob." After getting the keys, Jon stepped back down. One of these is for that lockbox compartment near the bottom of the first tank, he thought. He tried one of the keys but it didn't fit. Then he tried a second one and it slipped right in. Jon turned the key and the top of the metal box flipped open.

I got it, he thought, and pressed one of the buttons in the lockbox. He watched with delight as the top of the first tank slowly opened. Look at those bales, he thought. They will soon be mine. Jon pressed the other two buttons and the second and third tanks flipped open.

Michael stood next to his father and stared with amazement, watching the tanks open, exposing bales of pot.

Jon placed the fob and keys into the small metal box and looked at Michael. "Okay, my son, see that loader over there? Get it started and use the lift to move the bales from the tanks to the far corner."

Jon watched as Michael made his sixth trip to the truck and removed the last bale. He pressed the three buttons in the metal box and watched the panels close. Jon handed the keys to his son and said, "Okay, Michael, back the truck out."

Jon returned to the office. "Gentlemen, the truck is ready to go. You need to drive it back up the gravel road and turn right on the Frontage Road. That will lead you back onto Highway-77. Thank you both." He handed each of the drivers an envelope. The thousand dollar bills should make both of them happy, he thought.

Chapter 25

NORM AND MICK SAT ON CHAIRS in the small office of the Bloomington warehouse.

"They should be here any minute," Mick said.

Norm remained sitting, twiddling his thumbs. Suddenly, he looked up. "I hear something—bet it's the trucks." He got up off his chair and walked to the window. "Yup, it's them."

Mick stood and walked through the doorway leading to the warehouse, to open the overhead doors.

As the trucks arrived, Mick waved his hand and pointed at one of four orange markers, which were positioned near the far wall. Within minutes, the first four trucks had parked.

Mick directed truck number five towards a fifth orange marker. Norm had entered the area by now and he guided the last three trucks into place. "Looks good, Mick. We've got plenty of room for our loaders," Norm said.

Norm walked to the end wall. He got into the old mini-school bus. He drove it outside and stopped next to one of the garage doors. Norm got out and waved at the drivers who had gathered next to the office door. He got them seated and then drove the bus to a motel ten blocks away. Close to half an hour later, he emerged from the motel office holding eight mini-envelopes which contained room keycards. He handed them out to the drivers and then turned to Menzo. "I'll pick you all up on Friday and take you back to the trucks."

Menzo nodded. "*Si, amigo*."

NORM DROVE THE BUS BACK TO THE WAREHOUSE. He drove it inside and parked next to the far wall. Sure looks like Mick has stacked a whole bunch of the bales in the far corner, he thought. Norm walked back towards the office and saw Mick slide the mini loader's bucket underneath a bale in truck seven. Norm watched him scoot over to the far corner and set the bale down on top of another one. He'll be done pretty soon. The semi-trucks will show up tomorrow or the next day, he thought.

Norm walked into the office and brought out a chair to sit on. There's nothing, I can do to help Mick, he said to himself. The loader does all the work.

Mick let out a loud yell. Norm stood.

"Hey, Norm, come look!" Mick shouted.

Norm rushed into the warehouse. "What the hell is going on?"

"The eighth truck is empty!" Mick exclaimed as Norm walked up.

"This is impossible," Norm said. "All six bales missing—that's crazy."

MICK GOT OUT OF THE LOADER. He waved a fist in the air. "Cripes, some son-of-a-bitch has goofed up!"

Norm banged his knuckles on top of his head. "Did somebody steal them, or did Marcos and Nick screw up the loading?"

"Let's go inside. I've got to call Nick right away," Mick said, his brow furrowing. He swept a palm over his hair and his eyes tightened into narrow slits.

Norm sat down in the office and watched Mick open his cell phone and press two buttons.

"Hey, Nick, guess what's happened?" Mick asked, his face contorting.

Norm anxiously waited for Mick's next words.

"So, you say that all eight trucks got loaded. If so, then how the hell did one of them arrive here empty?"

Mick shook his head. "Alright, Nick, but this means less money coming in and less in your pocket."

Mick snapped his cell phone shut. He opened the desk drawer and brought out a calculator. Mick punched in a bunch of numbers. "Norm, this means close to an eighteen thousand dollar loss for us."

Norm took a deep breath. "Do you plan on splitting the loss amongst the three of us?"

"Hell no. What we know right now is that it's all coming off Nick's share. That could change. We need to find out what happened to the pot bales in truck eight."

Chapter 26

FBI AGENTS SAM PERKINS AND BILL MALONE were ushered into Captain Jesse Trevino's office. Agent Perkins walked over to the desk and extended his hand. "I'm Agent Perkins, and this is Agent Malone. You must be Captain Jesse Trevino."

They all shook hands. "Have a seat, gentlemen. I'm really glad you came. This case obviously involves more than just my jurisdiction." Trevino smiled, his large brown eyes dancing back and forth in his rectangular face. He ran his fingers through his pepper-colored hair.

Agent Perkins, dressed in a dark blue sport coat with a blue tie, also had brown eyes, but they weren't as big. His dark hair was combed back, and he blinked as he said, "We'll do all we can to bring this case to a close."

Agent Malone also had dark brown hair and wore a sport coat and tie, but he was a little shorter and pudgy. He had a bald spot on the back of his head. He licked his lips and said, "We understand that you have three suspects. Could you tell us who they are?"

Trevino cleared his throat. "Yes. First there is a woman by the name of Pam Colliton. She currently stays at Texas Palms in suite 4705. She is a tall, attractive, dark-haired woman and drives a brown golf cart and a maroon Ford Focus. One of the reasons she is a suspect is because she was seen speeding away from the scene of the bombing. When we questioned her, she said that the explosion had frightened her badly and that she reacted on impulse.

"The other reason is because we have evidence that she spied on the suite where the victim lived."

Agent Perkins asked, "Have you come up with any conclusions as to her testimony?"

"I don't think she told the entire truth. We suspect that she lied about the reason for visiting Fabzonni's suite. She may have had a connection to the guy, and that's why she left the scene like she did."

Agent Perkins looked down at his notepad. "What about Tom Hastings?"

Trevino cleared his throat. "The victim, Tony Fabzonni, had previously consulted with someone at the Inn's office. He wanted to know who is staying in suite 4907. The occupants of that room are a couple from Minnesota, Tom and Samantha Hastings."

Agent Malone asked. "Why do you think Fabzonni was inquiring about Hastings?"

Trevino rubbed his nose. "I really don't know, except the fact that Hastings works for a guy who works for this oil company out of Mexico. The victim may have been doing a private investigation. It makes me feel drugs are involved, and that's why I contacted the FBI."

"Do you suspect that the victim may have been involved in organized crime?" Agent Perkins asked.

Trevino nodded. "That's a possibility."

Agent Malone said, "What makes you think drugs are involved, captain?"

Trevino cleared his throat. He brushed the palm of his right hand through his hair. "It's only a gut feeling. I feel it's rather strange that so many people at Texas Palms are involved—and that all the drivers gather there to spend the night and get transported to the trucks."

Agent Malone lifted his chin. "Then there is Mr. Nick Giggs. What's his connection?"

Trevino cleared his throat. "Tom Hastings works for Mr. Giggs. Giggs told us he is a consultant for a Mexican oil company. Its official name is Sardoza Oil. It has a station near Progreso. He claims Hastings helps deliver truckers from Texas to Mexico who then drive the oil trucks to Bloomington, Minnesota."

"Anything else to add, captain?" Agent Perkins asked.

"No. I wish I had more."

The two agents stood. They shook hands with Trevino. Agent Malone said, "Thank you, captain. We may contact you again in the future.

PAM COLLITON HEARD A KNOCK ON THE DOOR. She looked out the window and saw two men dressed in sport coats and ties. Oh-oh, she thought. It must be more cops.

She opened the door. "Hello gentlemen. Can I help you?"

"Are you Pam Colliton?" Agent Perkins asked.

"Yes, I am. Who are you?"

The two men produced their credentials.

FBI, that's not good, Pam thought.

"I'm Agent Perkins, and this is my partner, Agent Malone," Agent Perkins said.

"What can I do for you?"

Agent Perkins blinked his eyes. "We are here to investigate a man who was killed when his golf cart was blown up. Are you aware that this happened?"

"I certainly am. I was in the area when the bomb went off. I got really scared and drove my cart back to my suite—real fast."

Agent Malone nodded. "I understand that, but what I don't understand is why you visited the victim's suite a short time before the explosion occurred."

Pam placed a hand on her forehead. "I explained this to the local police a few days ago. I was looking for the woman who cleans my unit. I saw the cart in front of the suite and hoped that my cleaning woman was in there." She took a deep breath and exhaled.

Malone said. "Is it possible there was another reason why you visited the suite?"

Pam slowly shook her head. "No."

"Alright, thank you Miss Colliton. We appreciate the visit," Agent Perkins said. He tapped his partner on the shoulder and they left.

Pam opened her refrigerator door and brought out a bottle of wine. She filled up a glass and sat on the couch. I hope the Feds are satisfied, she thought. They really can't prove anything regarding my actions in this park. But now, I've got a new challenge. Mick called, and he wants me to help Nick with monitoring the truck loading. I need to be there very early on Monday morning. The trucks get loaded before eight a.m. I will have to leave here at about six-thirty. Nick knows that I will be there, but we will drive separately

-----

SAMANTHA FILLED HER GLASS WITH WINE and sat on the couch. "Hey, Tom, let's go out to eat. I don't feel like making anything this evening."

"Sounds good to me," Tom replied with a bright smile.

His cell phone buzzed. "Hello. Sure, right now would be fine," Tom said and snapped the phone shut. "Sammy, FBI agents want to come over and interview me. It has to do with the golf cart bombing. Apparently, they are taking over the case."

"When are they coming?" Sammy asked.

"In minutes. They're already in the park."

Tom heard a tap on the door. He walked over and opened it. "Hello, you must be the FBI agents."

"Yes, we are," one of the men said. "I'm Sam Perkins and this is Bill Malone."

Both men displayed their credentials and then shook hands with Tom.

"Come on in," Tom said. "This is my wife, Samantha."

"Hello, ma'am. This won't take very long."

Tom pointed at the couch and they both sat down.

Agent Perkins slipped out a notepad from his sport coat pocket. "According to the information you gave Captain Trevino, the only connection between you and the victim, Fabzonni, is his inquiry at the Inn's office wanting to know who you were. Is that correct?"

"That is true. I've never met the guy or even talked to him," Tom replied.

Agent Malone said, "So, you have a part-time job transporting truck drivers from Texas to Mexico. Is that true?"

Tom nodded. "Yes, I work for Nick Giggs. He's a consultant for a Mexican oil company."

Agent Perkins said, "During your trips between here and Mexico, have you ever noticed a certain vehicle following you? Such as a blue Toyota Corolla?"

Tom swallowed. "I have to admit that I did notice such a vehicle, but I really didn't pay any attention to it. I was never threatened."

Perkins asked, "Where did you notice it? Here at this RV Park, on the highway, or in Progreso?"

Tom opened his mouth slightly and rubbed his tongue across his upper lip. "You know, my memory isn't the greatest, but I do remember seeing the vehicle on the frontage road, between here and International Boulevard—and also at the Tesoro station in Progreso," Tom replied.

"Is that where you deliver the drivers to?" Agent Malone asked.

Tom nodded.

"How many trucks are the drivers involved in?" Perkins asked.

Tom shook his head slightly. "I'm not certain, but I think it is eight."

"Do you know where the trucks do their delivery?" Perkins asked.

"Not specifically, no. I never really didn't talk to Nick Giggs about that. All he said is that they go to some warehouse in Bloomington, Minnesota."

The two agents stood up. "Thank you very much, Mr. Hastings. We'll stay in touch," Agent Perkins said.

The two agents left.

"Come on Sammy, let's get something to eat," Tom said.

Chapter 27

NICK GIGGS SLIPPED HIS PHONE BACK INTO ITS HOLSTER. I can't believe this, he thought...one of the trucks was empty. How the hell could that have happened?

Anyhow, it sounds like I'm going to get to know Pam Colliton a lot better, he said to himself. Mick informed me that he is assigning her to witness the truck loading and the driver change. I've felt all along that she works for Mick, so this doesn't surprise me.

I suppose it's possible that Marcos and I slipped up and missed loading one of the trucks, he thought. But then, there would have been bales left on the floor. Or perhaps...perhaps, only forty-two bales got delivered. Mick is going to have to consider that possibility.

Nick walked outside and got into his white Mustang. I've got to check this out with Marcos, he thought.

He headed for Mexico. An hour later, he turned off Veracruz Street west of Progreso and headed for the light gray warehouse. Nick parked in front of the office and opened the steel door. "Hello Marcos, are you staying out of trouble?" he asked as he opened the door.

Marcos laughed. "*Si.* I no like trouble."

Nick said, "There's something I'd like to talk to you about."

"*Si*, what would that be?"

"Marcos, when the trucks got to their destination on the last trip, one of them was empty."

"*Amigo*! Empty!" Marcos exclaimed.

Nick nodded. "Yup, empty. How do you think that happened?"

Marcos frowned deeply. "We filled all the trucks. I know we did. You were here. You did about half of 'em."

"Is it possible that we only had forty-two bales to begin with?" Nick asked.

Marcos shook his head. "I doubt that. We would have noticed."

"Anyhow, it happened, and on this next trip, a woman by the name of Pam is going to watch and count our loading. She works for my boss."

"Si," Marcos said.

NICK TURNED ONTO THE EXPRESSWAY AND FELT HIS PHONE VIBRATE. He answered it and listened. He nodded and said, "Okay, how about in an hour?" He looked at his watch and put the phone back.

FBI this time, he thought. Well, my answers will be the same as with the local cops.

An hour later, he stood in his suite's doorway as Agents Perkins and Malone displayed their credentials.

Nick invited the agents inside. Perkins and Malone chose to sit on the couch. Agent Malone consulted his notepad said, "It says here that you work for a Mexican company, Sardoza Oil. Is this correct?"

Nick nodded, "Yes, I work for them as a consultant part-time."

Malone looked up at Nick. "What do you mean by 'consultant'?"

"I help the company organize their drivers. They have twenty four of them. Some live in Mexico and some live near here in Texas."

"So, this Sardoza Oil delivers oil to Minnesota?" Perkins asked.

Nick tightened his lips. "I don't have any details of what the company actually does. I have nothing to do with that. I'm strictly involved with the drivers."

Agent Malone said, "Did you know the man who was killed here?"

Nick shook his head. “No, I didn’t, absolutely not.”

Malone asked, “Did you know that he was apparently spying on the company you work for?”

Nick took a deep breath. “If he was spying, I didn’t know,” he replied. “Also, if he was spying, I don’t have a clue as to why.”

Agent Malone made some notes and looked up. “Mr. Giggs, does Tom Hastings work for you?”

“Yes, he does, part-time,” Nick replied.

“Can I ask you what he does?”

“Yes, he transports truck drivers between here and Progreso.”

The three men became quiet for a few moments.

“Alright Mr. Giggs, thank you for talking to us,” Agent Perkins said.

The agents left. Nick watched them drive away.

A couple of hours later, Nick got his mail. He almost passed out after he opened the envelope containing his latest check. “Hey!” he exclaimed when he saw the amount: *$33,125*.

I’m mad as hell, he thought. Mick assumed the empty truck was my fault. That’s totally bull!

JON CORLONE SAT IN A CHAIR NEXT TO HIS ROOM’S TABLE. A wide grin formed on his face when he thought about the successful hijack he had just pulled off. I’ve got to give my son credit for taking the truck from its drivers without rousing suspicion.

It cost me a couple of thousand, but that’s a drop in the bucket compared to what I will sell the pot for, he thought. When the boys in Bloomington find out they’re missing six bales, they’re going to have a fit. This Mick guy will really get mad. He'll call the Giggs guy here at the resort and all hell will break loose,

Jon laughed and muttered, "I know for sure they won't call the cops."

I bet this Mick guy will order the trucks be monitored more closely when they're loaded, he thought. But, it's not going to make much difference for them. The drivers of the eight trucks need the bucks. A couple grand for each of them can easily swing the deal.

For the next hijack, I will use a little different strategy, he thought. I'll have Michael give the guys a message at the station and have them drive the truck to my warehouse north of Harlingen. Michael can go with me, and then we will unload the tanks.

Jon laughed. If this Mick guy was mad this time, I wonder how much madder he will be after next time.

He thought about Hastings for a moment. I don't think the Hastings guy is involved in the smuggling. He's got nothing to do with loading the pot, and his only connection is with the drivers. He's not a meaningful person in this game.

Jon heard a knock on his door. Aha, he thought, the Weslaco Wheels guys are here. They've brought me my new golf cart.

He opened the door. "Hello guys, did you bring my golf cart?"

"We sure did," one of the men replied, pointing. "It's right over there and ready to go."

Jon walked over to his new golf cart. It was parked next to his pickup truck. "I see the key is in it."
"Yes sir. Any questions?"

"No. I'll take it for a spin later. It sure looks good. That's a nice gray color."

Jon walked back inside and poured himself a cup of coffee. He reached up into a cabinet and brought out a bottle. He smiled as he poured a small amount of whiskey into the cup.

Jon sat down on his small couch. Michael does not know this yet, but I've changed the title on my pickup truck, he said to himself. It now belongs to him, and the legal form is in the cubbyhole. I have an extra set of keys in the small drawer in my bedroom. Soon, I shall inform him of the change.

AGENT PERKINS BLINKED HIS EYES as he looked across his desk at Agent Malone. "This case is likely to have hit a dead end. The oil trucks have already gone through the border station more than once, and they are apparently clean."

"I agree," Agent Malone said. "The murder of the guy in the golf cart could be connected to the trucks, but on the other hand—" he licked his lips "—on the other hand, it may all be a coincidence."

Perkins nodded. "We'll stay in touch with Trevino. If he picks up some more evidence regarding the bombing, we can return to the case, and if he uncovers drugs, we'll alert the DEA; otherwise, it looks like we have no further to go."

Chapter 28

TOM HASTINGS RELAXED WITH A GLASS OF WINE. Monday will be my fourth trip to Progreso, he thought. Well, actually it will be the third time I am doing the run alone. I wonder how many more times this is going to happen. The FBI will certainly make a difference. I've got the feeling they are connecting the trucks to the golf cart bombing.

"Hey Sammy, how about if I take you out for dinner this evening?"

"Sure, Tom. I would love that," she replied.

I suspect the agents are really after that Pam woman, he thought. She's deeply involved in the trucking operation, just about as much as Nick. I wonder who blew up the guy in the golf cart. Nick's boss, Mick, was probably behind it. But then, I guess we'll really never know.

Two hours later, Tom held Sammy's hand as they walked up the concourse toward the restaurant. Under his free arm, he carried a bag containing two bottles of wine and a bag of ice. "What are you having for dinner Sammy?" he asked as they entered the restaurant.

"A good salad and some beef is what I'd prefer," Sammy replied. "How about you?"

"I'll have the pulled-pork if they have it."

A few minutes later, they sat down at a table and Tom filled their wine glasses. He had Chardonnay and Sammy had Cabernet Sauvignon. He raised his glass. "Here's to us."

They clicked glasses.

Sammy gave him a big smile. "I would like to ask you a favor."

"Sure, what is it?" Tom asked.

"When you drive to pick up the van on Sunday, I would like to ride with you and bring our SUV back. When you drive the van to Progreso on Monday, I would like to go shopping—and you know where."

Tom laughed. "It wouldn't be TJ Maxx, would it?"

Sammy smiled. "You've got that all figured out."

"No problem, sweetie. I can call you while on my way back to Harlingen, and you can pick me up."

PAM COLLITON SIPPED COFFEE IN HER SUITE AT DAYBREAK on Monday morning. I better get going, she thought. I just saw Nick's car go by. At least he knows that I am going to be there.

Minutes later, she got into her Ford Focus and took off for the Expressway. She shuddered as she drove by the site of the explosion. The more I think about it, the better I feel it wasn't me who got blown up, she said to herself.

Pam stared at the eastern horizon. The sun is coming up, she thought. How much more beautiful could it get than that? I haven't seen a sunrise in years.

She used her passport to get through the border station. Okay, I'm on Benito Juárez, she thought. Veracruz Street is supposed to be on south edge of town, about where the Tesoro station is.

Minutes later, she muttered, "There it is." Now, if I go west for about four miles, I should see the warehouse, she thought.

Within minutes, Pam turned onto the gravel road. I see the building, she said to herself. There are four houses over to my right not far away. The other gravel road I passed by must lead to those.

She pulled up in front of the office and parked next to Nicks's white Mustang.

PAM ENTERED THE WAREHOUSE OFFICE. She saw Nick and Marcos sitting at the table. "Good morning gentlemen."

Nick smiled and stood. "Good to have you with us, Pam. We all know why you're here. Let's go get the job done."

Pam followed Nick and Marcos into the warehouse. "Well, it's up to you how you handle this, Pam," Nick said, "but Marcos and I will be hauling the bales and dropping them into the tanks of those trucks. We're going to open up all the tanks right now."

Pam was amazed when she saw the tanks revolve upward, exposing the storage area within. She got out her notepad and made a list that went: *Truck one, Truck two,* etc. After each truck was loaded, she placed a mark next to the truck number. An hour later, she had all eight marked down. That should do it, she thought. They are all full and there are forty-eight bales in all the trucks.

She closed her notepad and placed it in her pocket.

She saw Nick walk over to the big doors and press a button for each one. The overhead doors opened and she watched Marcos walk over to a black van, which was parked next to the far wall. He got in and drove the van outside. Just then some vehicles arrived and eight Mexican men walked into the building. She saw Nick direct one man to each truck. Pam placed a hand over an ear when the engines roared to life. It's amazing, she thought as the trucks backed out of the building one at a time. It looks like a parade.

"Where do I follow?" she asked Nick.

"You follow the van. I'll be driving it. Then you can park anywhere you want at the Tesoro station. Each driver will fill their truck with fuel and then leave the truck and get into the black van. You will see Hastings's silver van parked next to the food store. He will have brought the sixteen drivers who will take over the trucks."

"Master Buddy, this is totally awesome," Pam said.

Chapter 29

SAMANTHA KISSED TOM AND HELD HIM TIGHT after he gave her the keys to the SUV.

"Hey, Tom, I hope you have another successful day. I'll wait for your phone call and come pick you up at Valley Transit."

"Yeah, thanks. And you have a good day shopping. TJ Maxx has been your favorite shopping place since I've known you. Just be sure to take your phone."

"Actually, I already have my phone in my purse, and I have some other stops, so I'm going to take off right away."

Sammy walked out the door and got into the SUV. She waved at Tom as she drove off. This is a heck of a challenge, she thought, but I need to know what is going on in Progreso, she said to herself.

She showed her passport to the border agent and drove into Progreso, looking for a Tesoro station. Ah-ha, there it is, she said to herself. It's a huge station. There are a bunch of gas pumps here. Looks like about ten for my SUV, and about fifteen or so for the trucks.

She drove by the food shop and parked on the east side of the building. I can keep an eye on things from here, she thought. Tom will probably arrive in an hour.

JON CORLONE LOOKED OUT THE WINDOW, hoping to see his son's vehicle. He should be here any minute, he thought. Jon looked at his watch. Hastings doesn't leave for another twenty minutes, but come on Michael, let's stay ahead of the game.

Two minutes later, Jon smiled when he saw his son pull up in his snazzy convertible. He walked outside and opened the driver's side door of his pickup truck. Don stood and waited for Michael to come out of his car. "You made it on time, Michael. Get in and we'll go and wait for the van."

"Father, is that your golf cart?"

"Yes, just got it. It's brand new and runs like a clock."

"Wow-wee, that should be real handy here in the park."

Jon nodded. "That's why I got it. Hey, we better get going."

Jon drove through the gate at Kingston Drive and drove by the first row of Inn rooms. Hastings hasn't picked up his guys yet, he thought. He sped onto the frontage road, getting honked at by a vehicle behind him. Up your butt, buddy, I've got places to go, Jon thought.

He drove at eighty miles per hour on the Expressway and sixty miles per hour on International Boulevard. Jon continued to speed as he drove down Progreso's main street. Suddenly, he and Michael heard a siren. Jon saw flashing lights behind him in his rear view mirror. "Cops," he muttered, stepping on the brakes and turning the steering wheel. He came to a stop next to vehicles parked on his right.

Jon opened his window as an officer approached. "Sir, your speed was over our limit. Can I have your driver's license?"

Jon slid it out of his wallet and handed it to the officer. The officer took the license and returned to his car.

Jon took a deep breath. "This will take some time, but shouldn't be a problem."

When the officer returned, Jon turned and handed him a hundred dollar bill. "Will this take care of it?" he asked, looking the officer in the eye.

The officer took the bill, gave Jon his license back, and said, "*Si senòr*, it will do."

Jon laughed as he drove on. He turned at the Tesoro station and drove to the east side of the building. He quickly braked when he saw his regular spot was occupied by another vehicle. "Damn, there's someone parked in my spot, Michael," he said, staring at the black SUV.

Jon drove three spaces over and backed into the parking spot. He stared at the SUV again, but because of the sun's glare, he couldn't see the person behind the wheel.

Suddenly, he heard several loud engines. "Michael, the trucks are arriving. We need to wait until they stop and the new drivers are in before you give the drivers in truck eight this message."

Chapter 30

PAM GOT INTO HER MAROON FORD. She waited for Nick and Marcos to leave. When they did, she followed them out of the lot. I feel a lot of tension, she thought. There's no way of knowing who's behind the theft, but I know for sure this cargo will arrive at the Tesoro station.

I see the big Tesoro sign ahead of us, she said to herself as she drove slowly, following the caravan. It's going to take those trucks quite some time to get through the stoplight.

Wow, this takes a lot of patience, she thought as the minutes dragged by. Finally, the last truck crossed the street and turned into the truck stop. She watched the black van park behind the trucks. I'll park right behind them.

Pam got out of her car. There's Hastings's silver van, she said to herself, watching it park in front of the main building. The eight drivers from the warehouse have all left their trucks and boarded the black van. The sixteen drivers who came with Hastings are heading in pairs to the trucks. So far, there's nothing shady going on, and in minutes they will all take off for Bloomington.

Pam walked toward the trucks and wandered around them. Everything appears normal she thought. I better keep wandering around so Nick will know that I'm doing my job.

JON CORLONE TAPPED HIS SON ON THE SHOULDER. "It's time to deliver this message."

Jon handed him a small cardboard slip. Again, Jon promised each driver a thousand dollars if they stopped for service at the same place north of Harlingen.

Michael walked to the far column of trucks. He stopped next to the driver's side door of truck number eight. Michael swung up onto the rung and knocked on the window. It opened, and he said, "*Amigos*, I have for you a note. You are to do what you did the last trip. You will get paid when you get there."

The driver took the note. He looked at it and smiled. Then he nodded and gave Michael a small wave while looking him in the eyes.

Michael shook the driver's hand. "See you at the service building."

The window closed. Michael stepped down and walked back to his father.

"Did you give the drivers the message?" Jon asked as Michael got back in.

"Yes, father, job all done."

Jon patted his son's shoulder.

PAM CAME AROUND THE CORNER OF ONE OF THE TRUCKS. "Master Buddy," she murmured. "Someone is up on the step talking to Joseph and Diago!"

She stared in amazement for a few moments, and then she saw the man step down and walk away. I've got to take care of this, she said to herself. Palm walked over to the truck, got up on the step, and knocked on the window. After it opened, Pam said, "Joseph and Diago, I am with Sardoza Oil. What did that man say to you?"

"We-we are to s-stop for some s-service at a certain place north of Harlingen," Joseph replied, tripping over his words.

Pam pointed her finger at Joseph. "You are to ignore what the man said."

"*Si*, but the man will pay us lot of money. We need that cash," Joseph said.

Pam raised her voice, "If you do not obey the oil company, you will be removed from your truck and get paid nothing. Do you understand?"

Joseph nodded. He looked at his partner, Diago, and nodded. "We best obey."

"I will be driving behind you when you leave. Keep that in mind."

Joseph nodded and said, "*Si*."

Chapter 31

SAMANTHA FOCUSED ON THE FUELING AREA. Uh-oh, her come the trucks, she said to herself. They are being followed a black van and a maroon car. What the heck is that all about? Who's in the maroon car?

Her view was temporarily blocked by a pickup truck that passed by. She watched it take a left and back into a parking space three stalls away. I wonder who the heck that is, she thought. Why would anyone park way over here...for what reason?

She kept an eye on the area to her left. Well, so far no one has gotten out of the black pickup truck, she thought.

Uh-oh, Nick has gotten out of the black van over on the other side of the parking lot, and eight drivers have left the trucks and are walking toward him, she said to herself.

Samantha continued to watch the black van as the drivers boarded it. She saw a woman get out of the maroon car. Who the heck is that? Well, I'm shocked, but it looks like Pam Colliton. Samantha glanced to her right. Uh-oh, here comes the silver van. Tom has arrived.

She watched Tom park in front of the food store. The sixteen drivers from Texas Palms disembarked and Nick walked over to greet them.

Sammy saw Nick lead the drivers to the trucks. That means Tom can head back to Valley Transit soon, she thought.

Samantha heard a door slam shut. She turned and saw someone get out of the black pickup truck. The guy is headed for the trucks, she thought.

She watched him disappear behind the last column of trucks.

Uh-oh, there goes Pamela, she thought. She's walking very fast, also headed for the last column. Tom is leaving with the van. The guy who was in the pickup truck has returned. The first oil truck is leaving.

Sammy watched as the oil trucks left the Tesoro one at a time. Uh-oh, the pickup truck next to me is leaving, too, she thought.

The pickup got behind truck number seven.

There goes the last truck, she thought. Pam's maroon car is following that. I better get going.

JON CORLONE TOOK OFF FROM THE STATION and followed truck number seven. He looked in his rear view mirror at truck eight. The truck is coming, he thought. I'll have six more bales of pot before long. When the Mick gets aware of that, he'll be furious, but...but he will not call the cops.

Jon looked at his son and laughed.

There goes one of the trucks onto the Expressway, he said to himself. Not sure which one it is, but soon I will do the same, and truck number eight will follow me. That damn Pam woman is still following the truck.

Jon drove onto the overpass and could see trucks ahead of him as he headed north. Pam's car has disappeared, he thought. She probably left the trucks and is heading back to Donna. There's Wilson Road...I get off at the next exit. Minutes later, he muttered, "There it is, Primera Road!" He exited the highway and drove onto the Frontage Road. The truck is still on 77, but should follow me in moments.

Jon slowed his pickup and turned onto the short gravel road leading to the warehouse.

Jon parked in front of the warehouse door and got out. "I can't believe this!" he exclaimed as he watched the truck roar up the highway. "Damn!" he exclaimed. "The maroon car is back. It's following the truck. It's that Pam woman! She has ruined my plan. By damn, she will pay."

SAMANTHA HASTINGS PASSED BY SOME OF THE OIL TRUCKS as she drove east toward Harlingen. Tom hasn't called yet, she thought. He should be at Valley Transit any minute.

She stayed in the right lane and minutes later she exited after seeing the *Valley Transit* sign. She made a U-turn under the overpass and got on the frontage road. A minute later she drove into the parking lot. There's the van, she thought. Tom is already there.

Samantha parked in front of the main building. She got out and saw Tom coming out. He walked over and opened the passenger door. "You're doing the driving, Sammy. I'll take a seat."

"How did the delivery go in Progreso?" Samantha asked.

"Real good," Tom said. "This is my fourth run. It sounds like there will be more."

"Glad to hear that. How about us stopping for lunch on the way home?"

"Sure, where would you like to stop?" Tom asked.

"Chili's in Weslaco."

"Sounds good," Tom said and closed his eyes.

SAMANTHA AND TOM ENTERED CHILI'S. "There's a booth open in the bar area, Tom. Let's grab it."

"Hey, good to see you again B.G.," Tom said to the waiter.

The smiling young man shook his hand and said, "What can I get you to drink?"

She ordered her usual Gin and tonic and Tom his Chardonnay. The waiter left. Tom said, "This guy really takes care of us. I've talked to him for close to a whole year and found out his name."

"Yes, I remember you calling him B.G. So your delivery went well, you said earlier," Sammy said.

Tom nodded. "Very smooth."

Samantha took a sip of her drink and set it down. "Tom, there is something I have to share with you."

His lips tightened. "You look very serious. What is it Sammy?"

"Today, after you picked up the van in Harlingen, I didn't go shopping. I followed you."

"You what! You followed me? Why?"

"I can't shake a gut feeling I have about what is going on with this oil company. I know you are doing your job and helping Nick out. But, something really worries me."

Tom set his glass down. "Okay, spit it out."

"This Pamela whom we met in our park is involved. She was there today. And get this: she was moving around the trucks, talking to some of the drivers. Now why! Why in the heck is she doing this? Any clue Mr. Tom?"

Tom shook his head. "The ins and outs of this oil operation really don't involve me. Why should I be concerned? It's really none of my business."

"Well, you may think it's none of your business, but if the trucks are doing something illegal, you could get involved."

Tom cleared his throat. “What could the trucks be possibly doing that’s illegal? They are simply hauling oil from Mexico to Minnesota. That is totally legal.”

Samantha leaned forward. “Why is there all this mysterious activity going on at the Tesoro station in Progreso? The black pickup truck I saw today, for example. Who is in it? And why is it there?”

Tom laughed. “You are sounding like a detective, Sammy. I’ll have another wine.”

Chapter 32

MICK AND NORM SAT IN THEIR WAREHOUSE'S OFFICE. Mick put his phone down. "The trucks are almost here. Let's open up."

Mick felt tense. Even though Pam said on the phone that all eight trucks left Progreso full of pot bales, I feel suspicious, he said to himself. If bales are missing on this trip, I'll be shocked, and right now I do not know how to handle the problem.

Mick slid his fingers through his hair. By damn, the bales better all be here today, he thought. If not, there is going to be war. We need to find out who is behind this pot stealing. I've never even thought of bumping someone off in the past...but this is different. It's me, Norm, Nick, and Pam against the enemy, and we have no choice but to win.

"Here they come!" Norm exclaimed.

"Okay, let's get 'em parked," Mick said.

Mick continued to feel tension in his stomach as he directed the trucks into their regular columns. When the last truck stopped Mick saw that Norm had the bus parked outside, ready to board drivers.

Mick anxiously opened up truck number eight. He held his breath as the tanks rotated upward. By damn, all six bales are here, he said to himself. He then pressed the button for truck number seven's tanks. "Hey, it's okay, too," he said with a sigh of relief. "We've won the battle today."

Mick got into a loader and began unloading the trucks.

JON CORLONE SAT ON A DECK CHAIR OUTSIDE HIS PARK MODEL RENTAL. Michael is coming over today, he thought. We are going out for dinner at Milano's. I need to plan a new strategy. I know the trucks will be there the morning after Hastings parks the van in front of his suite. I need to talk over the possibilities with my son. His mind is very mature and he usually has an outstanding grasp of what's going on. His mother would be real proud of him. Jon took another sip and sighed. I lost my Nora four years ago. Still hurts like hell.

Jon lifted his glass to his lips. That Pamela dame won the last battle, but she will not win the next one, he said to himself. Michael and I will see to that. He closed his eyes and stretched out, taking a deep breath. We could temporarily disable the dame, or we could force her away from the trucks. Then, maybe we could disable her car. She wouldn't be able to follow the trucks.

No matter what Michael and I do, we know she won't call the cops, he thought, laughing. The last thing that she and that Nick guy need are the cops. I heard a car door slam. Michael is here.

Jon opened the door and opened his arms. "Welcome, my son." They hugged lightly and entered Jon's rental.

"How's my grandson, Sonny?" Jon asked.

"Doing good, staying out of trouble."

"Ah, sometimes trouble is not bad. Have a seat. We need to talk," Jon said.

Michael smiled and nodded. "That's one of the reasons I'm here." He sat on the couch.

Jon sat in the armchair and leaned forward. "Michael, I'm thinking that soon, or in the near future, we could challenge the leaders of this pot smuggling ring to give us a share, or we will turn them in to the FBI."

Michael puckered his lips. "Yes, we could do that, but if the whole thing gets exposed, we could be part of the investigation. If the FBI gets the drivers to talk, the two drivers we have been using could give us away."

"You have a good point, however those two drivers do not know our names or where we live," Jon said, lifting the glass to his lips.

"Tell you what, father, let's keep that possibility in mind, but this coming Monday, I have a new plan on how to deal with this Pam woman."

Jon chuckled and raised his glass to his son. "I will look forward to that. By the way, I have given you my truck. It's now in your name. I keep all my cash in a zipped bank container in the cubby hole." Jon reached into his pocket. "Here's the extra set of keys—they are yours."

Michael beamed. "Thank you, father."

TOM PARKED THE VAN IN FRONT OF THE SUITE late Sunday afternoon. There's no way that Sammy is going to totally approve of what I'm doing, he thought. She does not trust the whole setup. Strange, but a couple of years ago, when she invested a hundred thousand dollars in a scam, she didn't have a clue. I knew that it was a fraud right from the get-go. But, the money that Nick is paying me is totally acceptable, as is the work. And having something to do...a challenge, like transporting all the drivers to Progreso on time...makes me feel good.

Tomorrow morning, I'll be off to Progreso again. The Mexicans' chatter in the back annoyed me the first trip, but now, I've gotten used to it, he said to himself. I think I best ask Sammy out for dinner.

He walked over to where Samantha was working on her computer. "Hey, Sammy, how about dinner at Milano's tonight? My treat."

Samantha gave him a wide smile. "Yes, I would like that."

"It's a deal. I'm making a lot of extra cash right now. Part of the benefits is that I can spend more on you."

Tom walked over to Sammy and hugged her.

"As long as the extra cash is obtained in an honest and legal way, I'm all for it," Sammy said as she sat down on the couch.

"I just don't see how driving truck drivers to their site would be illegal. We go through both American and Mexican customs and have no problem with either."

"Alright Tom, that's certainly good. I'll try not mention my suspicions anymore, and we will see what happens."

Chapter 33

TOM KISSED SAMANTHA AND HELD HER HAND before he headed out. Maybe this is my last trip, he thought. He took a right at Kingston Way and pulled up in front of the rooms. There's Menzo. All the rest of them are coming out.

Tom got out and opened the panel doors on both sides. He waved at all the passengers as they approached and then got back into the driver's seat.

"Okay, *amigo*, you can go," Menzo said

I'll be danged, Tom thought. There's the black pickup truck...it's following me again...but I don't see the maroon Ford. That doesn't change the chatter any though. I think everyone is talking at the same time back there. Maybe all this chatter is good for my mind.

He chuckled.

Tom waited in line at the border and finally reached the gate. Ah-ha, Tom thought, the chatter has stopped. He handed the guard his passport and told him the sixteen passengers were the same as in the past. The agent waved him on.

There it is again, the black pickup's still following me, he said to himself. Maybe Sammy is right. It seems strange that this pickup truck and sometimes the maroon Ford follow me. I'm pretty sure the Ford belongs to Pam, our neighbor. Oh well, I'm almost done with my delivery.

Tom pulled the van into its usual spot at Tesoro. Hmm, the trucks aren't here yet, he said to himself. Looking back, he said, "Everyone stay in place until the trucks come." He looked at Menzo. The man nodded.

Tom pressed some buttons, opening the windows in the rear of the van. "It gets real stuffy in here, Menzo," he said, pointing at the window next to him.

There's that black pickup truck, Tom said to himself as he watched it pass by and head toward the other side of the building.

Uh-oh, I hear the trucks, he thought. Looking to his left, Tom could see the first truck approaching from the west. It looks like a parade…all eight trucks following each other at about the same distance apart. The noise got louder as the first truck entered. Tom continued to watch. The ratcheting sound reminds me of a freight train passing.

There comes the eighth truck with the black van following close behind. Uh-huh, Tom thought. There's Pam's maroon Ford again.

Tom saw Nick step out of the van and walk towards him. "Alright, Menzo, everybody gets out now," Tom said.

As the drivers exited Tom's van, Nick walked over to the driver's door. "Good job, Tom, you got 'em all here on time."

"Thanks, Nick, I'll see you again here in a couple of weeks."

Nick walked over to the drivers and led them toward the trucks.

PAM COLLITON HAD LEFT HER SUITE SHORTLY AFTER 6:00 A.M. I don't think going this early is necessary, she thought. But Mick wants to make sure all trucks get loaded. The empty truck in Bloomington two trips ago was definitely caused by that man I saw at the Tesoro.

She shook her head. Well, I put a stop to his plot last trip and I fully intend to make sure it doesn't happen this trip either, she thought. I think the masterminds behind the theft drive a black pickup truck. I will have to keep an eye out for it on this trip.

Pam took a right on Veracruz Street and headed for the warehouse. There's Nick's car, she thought. It has the black van parked next to it, and the other vehicle must belong to Marcos.

None of the drivers are here yet. Pam looked at her watch. Nick said to be here by seven o'clock. I'm five minutes early.

Pam parked next to Nick's vehicle. She exited her car and stood next to it. Look at those streaky clouds, she said to herself. It's a beautiful morning.

Pam walked inside and looked at Nick and Marcos. They were sitting next to a table, waiting for her.

"Good morning, Pam," Nick said. "You're right on time." He glanced at his watch. "Okay, let's get the trucks loaded. The drivers will be here soon."

Pam watched the bales as they got pushed into the tanks. She placed a mark on her notepad each time a truck received its final bale. There's only one truck left, she thought. I hear some traffic outside. Pamela walked back toward the office. The drivers are likely here.

Nick and Marcus parked the loaders next to the side wall and headed for the office. Pam joined them, and when they entered, all eight drivers were seated in chairs along the wall.

"Hello, *amigos*, the trucks are ready," Nick said.

The drivers followed Nick to the trucks. Pam walked outside and got into her car. The big overhead door is opening, she said to herself. Moments later, the first truck backed out of the building. She watched the amazing parade, waiting to get behind the black van.

NICK SAT QUIETLY NEXT TO MARCOS as they headed onto Veracruz Street. I know now for certain that the loss of those pot bales didn't happen at our loading point, he said to himself. It had to take place after leaving Progreso. He looked out the rear window. Pam is right behind us. She does a great job of monitoring the drivers. On the last trip, she caught someone trying to talk the drivers into leaving the highway. This last trip the thieves failed. We are going to win this trip for sure.

He looked across a farm field. Looks scant, he thought. Minnesota gets way more rain, and the fields are real green. Here, it's dry...dry...dry. Looking ahead, he could see the Tesoro station in the distance. I wouldn't be doing this if it wasn't for the cash. Close to fifty thou a trip...wow. He frowned. Unless somebody somehow steals the pot again and I get another freaking pay cut. Well, let's make sure that stunt doesn't happen again.

The van slowed as the trucks entered Progreso. I know this truck business isn't going to go on much longer, Nick thought. We are being threatened by unknown insiders, and it's just a matter of time until the legal authorities catch onto this pot scam. Meanwhile I'll take all the bucks that I can make.

Marcos braked. We're there, Nick thought. I assume Hastings will be here with all the drivers. The trucks pulled up to the diesel pumps and stopped. Marcos stopped the black van in a space a short distance away from the pumps.

Nick looked to his left. There's Hastings, he thought. I'll be there in a couple of minutes. He looked at Marcos. "Okay, the local drivers will be back here shortly. I'll get out and get the northern drivers started."

Nick got out of the van and began walking toward Hastings.

JON WATCHED NICK LEAD THE DRIVERS AWAY FROM THE SILVER VAN. "Michael, when that Pam broad gets out of her car, I want you to execute your new plan. Take this small tool and remove the air valves from the two tires on the passenger side." He handed his son the small object. "All you have to do is unscrew the cap and stick this inside the tube. Turn it clockwise and the valve will turn itself out."

Michael took the tool and smiled at his father. "I'm so glad that you went along with my idea. When should I give the message to number eight's drivers?"

"Not until the trucks are ready to leave. We can tell when that is going to happen by watching truck number one real close. Go ahead, Michael, the broad just left her vehicle. When you go over there, make sure that she isn't watching you. Oh yes, and when the air is out of the tire, screw the valve back in and put on the cap."

Michael got out and quickly started walking toward the maroon Ford, keeping himself as close to the trucks as he could. He kept glancing to his left. I hope she stays with the trucks for a while, he thought, as he approached her maroon Ford. He dashed behind the car and got down on his knees next to the front tire. Quickly unscrewing the cap, he stuck the tool inside the short tube and turned it to the left. Hey, the air is coming out big time.

Michael walked over to the other tire and did the same.

He screwed the valves back in and did the same with the cap. Then he headed back toward the pickup truck. I don't see the broad anywhere, he thought. He quickly opened the passenger door and stepped inside. Michael chuckled and said, "I flattened the two tires. The other side of the Ford looks horrible. This side looks fine."

Jon laughed. "Good work, my son. We are not going to mess with truck number eight until the first truck starts moving. The Pam broad will be out of the way by then. And when she gets into her car, she's going to have a fit."

Jon reached across Michael's legs and unlocked the glove compartment. "See that zipped container, Michael?"

Michael nodded.

"Hand it to me, please," Jon said.

Michael did.

Jon unzipped the container and pulled out two bills. He handed them to his son. “See these two one-hundred thousand dollar bills? Have you ever seen a bill like this before, my son?” Jon chuckled. “I keep my cash in there because I have a lady come over to clean my place every week. Irma appears to be very honest, but then you never know.”

“Wow!” Michael exclaimed as he ran his fingers over the two bills.

“I want you to show them to Joseph and Diago, just before they leave. You need to tell them that they will get the money when they leave the highway and follow our pickup to our building. If they don’t show up, no money.”

Michael clasped his hands. “Father, I am ready.”

Chapter 34

PAM COLLITON PARKED HER FORD BEHIND THE BLACK VAN and got out. There goes Hastings, she thought. He's done his job and now he's headed home to that Samantha of his.

She walked to the fourth column of trucks and watched truck eight's drivers climb into the cab. I feel great that no one has come around to accost those drivers right now, Pam thought. She walked over to the next truck column. Nothing's going on there either.

There's Nick, she said to herself. Pam walked over to him. "Looks like everything is under control."

Nick smiled. "Yes it is.

"See you at Texas Palms," Pam said, smiling.

Nick nodded and walked toward the van.

Pam walked around the trucks. I really like how it's going today, she thought.

The trucks began to start their engines.

I'll follow truck eight again, she thought.

She went to her car. Something is wrong, she thought after sitting down. The dash is leaning to the right.

"Master buddy," she muttered as she got outside, "what's going on?" Pam walked to the other side of her car. "Damn, the tires are flat." I need air, she thought, and right now. Where do I get it? Someone inside will know. She dashed toward the food service building. Two of the trucks are already gone. She went inside. "Hey, ma'am, could you tell me where I can get some air for my tires?"

"Yes," the woman behind the counter replied, pointing. "At the very far end of the parking lot."

"Thanks,"

Pam dashed back out. The third truck is leaving, she said to herself.

Pam got back into her car and started it up, trying to slow her heartbeat. I have to get to the air spot, she thought. Pam remained tense as she shifted into drive. She released the clutch. Damn, it's hardly moving. This isn't going to work!

She stopped her car, got out, and headed for the food service building again. By now another truck was departing.

"I need help, someone to fill two of my tires with air," she told the woman behind the counter."

The woman nodded. "I'll call someone."

Pam took a deep breath and looked out the window. The trucks are all gone, she said to herself. She looked at the woman behind the counter again. She had just put the phone away. "Did you find someone to help me?"

"Yes, they'll be here in a few minutes."

"Good, I'll be outside at my car. It's parked at the edge of the lot," Pam said, pointing.

"I will send them over there," the woman said.

"Thanks," Pam said and headed out the door.

JON PUSHED HIS SON'S SHOULDER. "Go! You've got the cash, and the Pam dame just went inside." She's probably asking for help, he said to himself. Michael got out and looked for Pam. I don't see her.

He strode toward the remaining trucks, angling so he would arrive at truck eight. Michael hurried along, feeling his heart rate increase. There's the maroon Ford...still parked...great.

Michael stepped up to the driver's door. He knocked on the window. It opened. "What can I do for you, *amigo*?" Joseph asked.

"You need to stop for service north of Harlingen as you have done before. The woman who talked to you last time will not be following today. If you follow the black pickup, you will each get two of these."

Michael flashed his fistful of thousand dollar bills.

Joseph nodded. "We will do so."

Michael smiled. "The pickup will blink its hazard lights when you near the Primera exit north of Harlingen. Follow the pickup to the warehouse and stop in front of the overhead door. Both of you will get out and head to the office. You will get paid there."

He stepped down and walked hurriedly back to the pickup. There goes the seventh truck, he thought. Michael began to run. He got to where Jon was parked and got in. "All set, father, let's go!"

Michael held his chest as the pickup lurched forward and headed for truck seven. He glanced behind. Joseph is following, he thought. Then he glanced at Pam's maroon car. It's still parked.

Michael laughed loudly.

JON FOLLOWED THE LANE ON EXPRESSWAY-83 that led to Highway-77. He turned on his emergency lights. "They're right behind us, son."

Michael looked out the back window. "Joseph is right on our tail. It's amazing what a few bucks do," he said, chuckling.

"You're right, son. Just about anyone can be bought off."

There's the Wilson exit, Michael thought as he looked out the windshield. "Father, don't forget to put your right turn signal on," he said.

"Yes, my son, and it will be soon."

Michael watched a flock of geese hovering over a field. They are hungry for food and we are hungry for money, he said to himself. We are both going to win. Food for them and money for father and me.

He anxiously looked behind them as his father turned onto the ramp.

Thank God, he thought. Joseph is following us.

Minutes later, they reached the warehouse. Michael walked to the large overhead door. He raised an arm and waved, directing Joseph where to park.

Michael walked to the driver's door. He waved and both drivers got out.

"Follow me gentlemen," Michael said and walked toward the office door. He entered and the two drivers followed. "Have a seat," he said.

Both men sat.

Michael reached into his pocket and handed them each a one thousand dollar bill. Joseph and Diago smiled widely as they brought out their wallets and placed a bill inside.

"You both wait right here. We'll have the truck ready for you soon," Michael said.

Michael stepped outside and got behind the wheel of the truck. This is real exciting, he thought. I am so lucky to have such a successful father. He could easily be America's president. The door slowly opened. Michael pressed the accelerator and slowly moved ahead.

Michael parked and got out of the truck. His father joined him as he opened the tanks. "Holy Hell!" he exclaimed. "The compartments are empty. Empty!"

He looked at his father. Jon stood with his mouth open.

Jon sighed. "Close the tanks, son. We've lost this one." He walked to the overhead door. "Back it out, Michael. I'll get the drivers."

Michael got into the truck cab. He started the engine and backed the tanker outside. He left the engine running and stepped down onto the gravel. He had his head down as he walked into the office. "Joseph, it's ready to go."

JOSEPH WATCHED DIAGO CLIMB INTO THE CAB. He followed and got behind the wheel. He backed the truck up and headed toward the frontage road. "Diago, I didn't mention this to you before, but we're heading back to Progreso."

"Why? What the heck is going on?"

"Nick passed this information on to me at the Tesoro. They didn't fill this truck on purpose. He said that their enemies are going to try stealing it again. They can't steal anything if the truck is empty."

Diago shook his head. "Me no understand."

Joseph smiled. "You are a thousand dollars richer and don't have to do anything except help me drive this truck to Bloomington after we get it reloaded."

Chapter 35

MICK AND NORM WAITED PATIENTLY for the eighth truck to arrive. Mick looked at Norm. "It should be here pretty soon. Nick estimated that it would be about four hours behind," Mick said.

Norm shook his head and smiled. "Nick did a great job. If he wasn't on top of things, we would have lost another six bales."

"You're right Norm. I feel kind of bad that Pam wasn't part of it. When she called all flustered over her two tires getting flattened, I wanted to laugh, but couldn't. She suffered."

Norm chuckled. "Yeah, but she can handle it, even though she may feel that she was used during the last trip."

Mick laughed. "Yes, she was used, but we had to fool the tormentors, and we did." Mick put his hand over his mouth. "Sorry, but I couldn't help it."

"So now that we are sitting here, relaxing and celebrating with a beer, what's our next strategy? This enemy crew will probably come up with a plan."

"I'm going to call Nick tomorrow. The enemy's residing very close to where he is staying. I've heard so much about this black pickup truck. But then, no one is sure if they will try another hijack again. They've succeeded only once, and lost twice. What do you think Norm?"

"I think the biggest danger to us is if they spill it to the FBI," Norm said.

Mick chuckled. "Yes, they could, but! But, they would then lose any possible financial gain. So, partner Norm, I don't think they will do that."

Norm nodded. "I think you're right, Mick. So what do we do now, hire armed guards to service each truck at the Tesoro?"

"I'm mulling that possibility. We sure don't want to complicate it, and for sure we can't call the cops."

Norm laughed. "The hijackers are likely in the same position we are. But we have the upper hand. We control where the trucks go and what they carry."

"You're right, so let's go home and get some sleep and talk tomorrow," Mick said.

JON CORLONE SAT IN AN EASY CHAIR IN HIS PARK MODEL at Texas Palms. Michael has gone home, he said to himself. He lifted a glass to his lips and drank. Good whiskey, he thought. The Nick slug totally outfoxed me yesterday. What he did was very clever. This means Michael and I will have to change our strategy.

We will no longer use truck eight as our target, he thought. And the Pam broad will be on the lookout for her tires. Nothing will be the same. This is something I have to sleep on.

I wonder what Nora would have thought of all this? He said to himself. She died four years ago, much to my sorrow.

The next time I talk to Michael, I'm going to ask him to bring his cousin Frankie into the picture, Jon thought. Our enemies are going to prevent us from disabling that Pam broad's vehicle. We need extra help at the Tesoro. We can't plan ahead because our enemy uses a new strategy for each time the trucks load. But Frankie will help us.

I need to get outside and have a ride in the golf cart, Jon thought. It will do me good to drive around and see people. Michael and I can also use it to connect with the drivers at their rooms.

Jon left the house and got behind the wheel of his golf cart. He headed toward the central park buildings and parked in the lot in front of the main activity area. There are golf carts all over the place, he thought.

Jon pulled the golf cart key out of the ignition. He reached into his pocket and brought out a second key. This is for my rental unit, he said to himself. I'm going to attach it to my golf cart's key ring.

MICK STOOD NEXT TO THE DOOR IN THE OFFICE. Norm should be here pretty soon, he thought. I have a new plan for the next truck trip and I'm quite sure it will work. I feel excited because we've won all the battles but one. And I don't intend to lose another one.

He watched a vehicle turn off the street and into their parking lot.

Ah-ha, here he comes, Mick said to himself.

Mick opened the office door and stepped outside. He waited until Norm got out of his vehicle. "Hello, partner."

Norm saluted and walked over to the door. They shook hands and went inside. "Have a seat, partner, I have a new plan."

"I'm excited to hear what it is," Norm said, pumping a fist in the air.

"Our whole problem has been in what happens at the Tesoro. Eight trucks lead to a lot of openings for the enemy. This next Monday, we will move only four of the trucks to the station. The other four will remain in storage. Using only four, we can control access to them a lot better. Both Nick and Pamela will be there during the changeover. Our enemy won't have a chance."

Norm whistled. "Heavens to Betsy, that's going to work. When do we move the last four?"

"The next morning, and again both Nick and Pam will be there. What do you think of the plan?"

Norm raised a thumb and nodded his head. "It's going to shock the enemy. They won't have a chance."

Mick opened the lid of his cell phone case and plucked out his phone. He opened it and pressed three numbers. "Hopefully, Nick is available."

"Hi, Nick, have you got a minute or two?"

Mick nodded and spent the next five minutes explaining their new plan. He slammed the phone shut. "Nick's all for the idea, Norm. He'll probably have to pay his connection in Texas Palms a few more bucks, but that will not be a problem."

"Yup, that means that Hastings guy will make an extra trip just once. I assume on the return trip, he can pick up all the drivers," Norm said.

Mick nodded. "We will have four trucks coming on Tuesday and another four on Wednesday," he said.

TOM HASTINGS SAT ON THE COUCH WITH HIS LEGS UP ON A CHAIR. "Well, Sammy, what are we having for dinner this evening?"

"I made some chili soup earlier in the day when you were gone. Hope that's okay."

"Sounds yummy to me," Tom said.

"Someone is walking over this way," Sammy said. "I think it's that Nick guy."

Tom straightened up. He heard a knock. Sammy opened the door. "Hi Nick, come on in. Tom's inside."

"Hi Nick, what's up?" Tom asked.

"First of all, Tom, I appreciate all the work you've done for me. I hope you can continue to do so."

Tom smiled. "What you said makes me feel good, Nick."

"There is a change in plan for the next run. You will transport only eight drivers to Progreso. We are going to do the other eight on Tuesday morning. That means an extra trip. You will be paid for it."

Tom nodded. "I can handle that."

"Fine. The time of the run remains the same. Thanks, Tom, I need to go."

Tom stood and walked to the door. "Okay, Nick, I will handle the change."

Nick shook Tom's hand and left.

Samantha walked over to Tom and gave him a hug." Hey, Tom boy, I have talked to Tim again. He said that there are a lot of places for sale. What about having a look at some of them?"

Tom smiled. "Sure, you take control of that. I will go along with anything you want to do."

Chapter 36

TOM HASTINGS PARKED THE VAN AT THE TEXAS PALMS INN AREA early on Monday morning. Only eight drivers today, he thought. He watched eight men come out of the first four units. Heck, the other eight guys get to sleep in.

Tom got out and waved at Menzo. He waved back and opened one of the side-panel doors. Menzo stood and waited as the other seven drivers entered the van. "Okay, we're all set to go," he said.

Minutes later, Tom looked out his rear view mirror as he turned onto International Boulevard, going south. There it is again, the black pickup truck, he thought. "And," he muttered, "the maroon Ford is back!"

Half an hour later, he turned left into his usual spot at Tesoro. The black pickup's disappeared around the corner of the building, he said to himself. Pam has parked over on the south edge where the trucks come in. They aren't here yet, though.

Menzo raised a hand and his eyes widened. "They come. The trucks."

Tom looked to his left. "Yup, they are on their way, Menzo."

Tom glanced behind him. Their chatter really slows down when the trucks arrive, he thought.

He saw Nick's van stop close to where Pam was parked. Nick and another man got out to usher the four local truck drivers into the van.

Nick is on his way over here, Tom thought. "Okay, Menzo, get the boys out."

Nick helped Marcos load the four trucks. They're all done, he thought. I like this new idea. This will make the driver transfer at the Tesoro go a lot easier. Heck, Pam doesn't have to come out here to the monitor the pot loading. But, she will be at the Tesoro to watch the driver exchange.

This is sure a different ballgame, using four trucks at a time, he thought as the trucks left. We should have thought of this long time ago.

Nick opened the black van's passenger door. He got inside. "Have you heard of anything from Emile?"

"No, I have not. That is good," Marcos said.

Nick glanced at Marcos as he drove down the gravel road toward the highway. I hope he gave the Emile his hundred bucks, he thought. It wouldn't surprise me if he kept it for himself.

Minutes later, they caught up to the fourth truck.

I see Pam's vehicle is there, he thought as Marcos drove into the parking lot. She's got a perfect view of the driver's side of each truck. The enemy is going to get defeated today.

He got out and waited for the drivers to return to the van. Here they come, he thought. I better get over to Hastings's van.

He quickly headed toward the silver van. "Good morning, Tom. I see you made it on time as usual."

Tom nodded. "This is half a load today. I'm ready for tomorrow when we do the other half."

Nick smiled. "Hastings, you're right on top of it. Thanks for being here."

The two men shook hands. "So, I'm headed back to Texas Palms, and I will see you tomorrow morning," Tom said.

Nick saluted. "See you tomorrow."

Jon Corlone suddenly shifted in the driver's seat. "Holy damn! Michael. There are only four trucks!" he exclaimed.

"I see that," Michael said. "What the hell is going on?"

"The enemy is pulling a fast one. Using only four trucks, it makes it quite impossible for us to do a hijack. That Pam broad is hanging around her car. She can likely see what's going on with the drivers without leaving her vehicle. Michael, I think we are going to lose this one, but, the other four trucks will come. We just don't know when."

"I would bet on tomorrow morning," Michael said.

Jon watched as each of the trucks parked next to a pump. The four drivers have all gotten out and are headed to the black van, he thought. There comes Nick. This time he's working with only eight drivers instead of sixteen.

Jon continued to watch as Nick and the drivers walked toward the trucks. That Pam broad is hanging around her car. I bet she can see all the trucks from there.

Jon started the truck. "We are headed home. Nothing we can do here." He backed away from the building and headed toward the main street. "I'm going to call Frankie later today. We're going to need to keep an eye out on the Texas Palms motel on Sunday afternoons and beyond that. Things have changed."

Jon remained silent as the passed through Progreso. His deep frown increased as they got closer to Texas Palms. "Michael, we're going to stop at the motel. The other drivers are likely there. We can make a deal with some of them right now for their trip tomorrow, or whenever it happens."

Michael nodded. "I can do that."

Jon looked at this son. "I have a new plan. I'll explain it when we get there."

Michael lips curled into a wide smile. "Got yah."

Chapter 37

Jon Corlone felt bitterness in his heart. I need to win the next battle, he thought, as he drove into Texas Palms.

Michael jolted forward in his seat. He had fallen asleep. "Why are you parking here, father?" he asked, rubbing his eyes.

"The other four drivers are staying here. Hastings will deliver them to the Tesoro tomorrow morning. I have a plan, Michael. I want you to wake up and go talk to the drivers in rooms 4005 and 4006. The guys in 4005 are Jamie and Santos. In 4006, they are Eliogio and Javier. Jon handed Michael his keys. "Open the cubbyhole."

Michael turned the key and the small door flipped open.

"Hand me the money container," Jon said.

Jon unzipped it, reached in, and brought out two one-thousand dollar bills. "Okay, put this back and lock it up."

Michael handed the keys back to his father. Jon held up two one thousand dollar bills. "These are for Jamie and Santos. They are to follow us out of Progreso. I will have emergency lights and a turn signal on just before the Primera exit. If they get Eliogio and Jamie to follow, they will each get another thousand. Eliogio and Javier will each be paid a thousand dollars if they cooperate."

Michael grasped the bills. "Father, your plan sounds fantastic. I will take care of this end right now." He hesitated. "How the heck did you know the names of those other drivers?"

Jon smiled. "I have my way, son. Someday, you shall, too."

Michael headed for room 4005. Minutes later, he emerged and headed over to 4006.

If we win tomorrow, this battle is going to tighten up, he said to himself. If it does, I will call my nephew Frankie, who will help us win. He's a cool sharp guy and doesn't have a problem speaking up for himself or coming up with an immediate strategy to win.

Ah-ha here comes Michael, and he has a wide smile on his face, Jon thought.

"I won father," Michael said. "All four drivers are very receptive to our plan."

MICK STOOD AND CLAPPED HIS HANDS. "Norm, the first four trucks are here. I'm not expecting any problems. I think we have the enemy in hand. They are totally defeated."

"I hope you're right, Mick. We'll know in a few minutes," Norm Blaine said.

Mick and Norm walked into the storage area. Mick pressed the button to open the first overhead door. He looked back at Norm. "This is really different, Norm. We only need one door open for four trucks.

After the trucks got parked, the drivers all got into Norm's bus and headed for the motel.

Mick walked back into the office. He opened the only drawer in a desk next to the far wall. He reached in and brought out a large key ring. All eight lockbox keys are in here, he said to himself. We've never used them before, but the time has come to control access to the buttons. If I had done this sooner, the enemy wouldn't have gotten into the truck a couple of weeks ago.

Mick walked over to the first truck. He unlocked the box and pressed all three buttons inside.

Cripes, all the bales are here! He thought.

He walked to truck number two and did the same. Six more bales, he thought.

He walked around the back of truck four and opened it up. No problem. One more to go, he thought.

Mick smiled widely after opening the compartments of truck three. All six bales in here, too, he said to himself

Tomorrow, the other four trucks get here and I expect to have the same result, he thought. Then I'm going to contact Nick and have him create a large key ring like I have. No longer will each truck have a key for the lockbox. If someone hijacks the truck, they won't be able to get in.

TOM HASTINGS SAT ON THE COUCH AND SIPPED COFFEE. "Sammy, it's Tuesday today and I'm getting an extra hundred bucks for this trip. How about dinner tonight?"

Samantha smiled. "Yes, how about the Longhorn? I really like that place."

Tom nodded. "It's a deal, and it's all on me."

"I can't wait. I'll be looking forward to it all day," Samantha said.

Tom stood and looked at his watch. "It's almost time for me to go How about a big hug?"

They hugged for almost a minute. "Woo," Sammy muttered. "I need to gather my breath."

Tom laughed. "Okay, see you in a couple of hours."

He grabbed his keys and wallet and left.

Tom knocked on 4005's door. It opened and a man said, "*Si senòr,* we are coming out."

He walked back to the van and got in. Here they come, he thought. Only eight of them. It makes a much smaller load, and it's a heck of a lot quieter during the drive.

When he got on the Expressway, Tom looked into his rear view mirror. There they are again, he thought. The black pickup and maroon Ford. Well I know why Pam goes to Progreso, but I don't have an idea in hell why that black pickup tags along. But then, it's none of my business.

Twenty minutes later, he parked the van in front of the food service building at the Tesoro station. It looks like a routine trip, he thought. The trucks are almost here and Pam is parked across the way.

Tom's thoughts drifted to Samantha. She really enjoys Texas, he thought. But, she thinks this truck driver delivery has a legality problem. Well, she could be right, but I'm only doing my job and in minutes I will be heading back to deposit the van and get back to Texas Palms by noon.

Uh-oh, here comes Nick. Tom turned his head. "Okay guys, you need to get out. Your boss is on his way here."

I'm all alone again, Tom thought. I might as well get the heck out of here. He started the engine and backed away from the building.

He left the Tesoro station and headed north to get rid of the van.

Chapter 38

JON BACKED HIS PICKUP TRUCK into its usual position. "The trucks are arriving," he said, poking his son on the shoulder.

Michael sat up straight. "Hey, father, look. Jamie and Santos are headed for the first truck and Eliogio and Javier are walking to the second truck. We are right on the money."

Jon nodded. "There's that Pam broad. She's walking around all four trucks. Little does she know what's going to happen?" He laughed. "She can follow the fourth truck all day and it won't do her any good."

They watched the parking lot with anxious eyes, waiting for the first truck to move. Five minutes later, Michael said, "There it goes, father!"

Jon backed out of his parking spot and followed the first truck. "Eliogio and Javier are right behind us, Michael."

Minutes later, Jon swung into the left lane. He sped up and passed the first truck. Turning on his right turn signal, he passed the truck and adjusted his speed to keep a short distance ahead of it.

As they approached Harlingen, Jon turned on his left turn signal. He looked into his rear view mirror and smiled when the first truck signaled a left, too.

"There's the Wilson exit! Primera is next," Michael said, turning his head to look behind them. "The truck is still behind us."

Jon activated his emergency lights. When he saw the exit sign for Primera, he flicked on his right turn signal.

He anxiously glanced at his rear view mirror. "Hey, Michael, the truck has turned on its turn signal. We are going to win."

"What do you see, Michael?" Jon asked a few minutes later, as he drove toward the warehouse.

"The first truck has turned off and it looks as if the second one is slowing down."

Michael held his breath. "Yeah, father, they have both gotten off the highway and are headed this way.

Jon stopped the pickup in front of the warehouse office. "Get the overhead door open, quick," he said to his son.

Michael dashed out, unlocked the office door, and entered. Moments later the overhead door rumbled open. He stood outside and held his hand up high. The first truck came to a stop a few feet short of the door. The second truck parked behind the first one.

"I'll take care of the drivers, Michael. You take care of the trucks," Jon said.

"Okay father," Michael said.

Jon led the four drivers into the office. Michael got into the first truck and drove it inside, leaving enough space in back to park the second truck. He got out and used one of the keys to open the lockbox. He pushed all three buttons and all the tanks slowly flipped open. Then he dashed outside, drove the second truck in, and opened its tanks. "Wow!" he muttered. Six bales each. We have won this one.

A short time later, Michael had unloaded the trucks and backed them out. He hastened into the office. "All ready to go, father."

Jon and Michael watched the two trucks drive back onto the frontage road. Jon grasped his son's shoulder He raised his arm and swung it around Michael's back, grasping his shoulders. "Well done, son. You will get rewarded."

SAMANTHA HASTINGS SNAPPED HER PHONE SHUT. "Tom, Tim is coming over today to show us a couple of mobile homes that we might be interested in."

Tom looked up at her. "Great, I'm anxious to look at them. What time do you expect the guy?"

"He should be here anytime—within the hour he told me."

Tom nodded. "I suppose I better get dressed."

Minutes later, Sammy heard a quick knock on the door. She opened it and smiled. "You must be Tim."

The neatly dressed man smiled and said, "That I am. Are you guys ready?"

Samantha looked toward the bedroom. "Tom is getting ready. He'll be here shortly."

Tim nodded. "Nice suite you have here."

"Yes, it is nice and comfortable. How long have you been in real estate here at Texas Palms?"

"I moved here from St. Joseph, Missouri, two years ago and started this business. It's been doing great."

"We came through St. Joseph on our way down here. That's where the Pony Express originated, isn't it?" Sammy asked.

"Yes, it is indeed. Hello Mr. Hastings," Tim said as Tom walked into the room.

They shook hands. "I'm ready to go," Tom said.

Sammy and Tom followed Tim outside to Tim's golf cart.

Tim drove them to a mobile home "Let's go have a look," he said.

Half an hour later, Sammy said, "Let's look at the other place."

Tim drove them to another mobile home located on the same side of the street. "You're really going to like this place. It is for sale because the husband of the couple who own it had serious allergy attacks here and they had to move back to Kansas."

Tim walked up three steps and opened the door. Sammy entered and stood next to a kitchen counter. "Tom, this looks fantastic."

Half an hour later, Sammy looked at Tim and said, "We're going to go home and talk about this. You said they are asking thirty-two thousand?"

Tim nodded. "Yes, and the sellers have already turned down a twenty-five thousand dollar offer."

Sammy grabbed Tom's arm. "I love this place. We need to make an offer."

Tom laughed. "Remember now, we're going home to talk it over."

Tim dropped the couple off at their suite. "Hopefully, I'll hear from you soon," he said.

Sammy sat on the couch. "I think we should offer thirty-two thousand. What do you think, Tom?"

"How about twenty-eight instead?" he asked with a wide smile.

She nodded. "Okay, you've got Tim's number."

Tom punched in numbers on his cell phone and put it up to his ear. "Hi Tim, we're going to officially offer twenty-eight thousand for the mobile home, you just showed us." He listened for a few moments and placed his cell phone back in its case.

Half an hour later, his phone vibrated. He answered the call. "Hi."

His face broke into a wide smile. "Sammy, we just bought ourselves a new home."

MICK AND NORM STOOD OUTSIDE AND WATCHED AS THE TRUCKS approached. "This should be routine, Norm" Mick said. "Our new strategy is working."

Norm went back inside and opened the second overhead door. Looks like Mick has his two orange markers in good positions, he thought as his eyes swept across the back of the large room.

He watched as Mick directed the first truck toward the first marker. A minute later, he saw the second truck park. Norm watched Mick walk over to the second marker. Truck number three stopped when Mick raised his hand. He's got the job done. The fourth truck will park behind the first one.

Norm got in the small school bus and drove it outside. He waited until all the drivers got seated and then he drove them to the motel.

MICK WALKED OVER TO THE FIRST TRUCK and opened the compartments.

"Cripes God Almighty!" he shouted, "The bales are missing!"

He set the key fob down and walked over to the next truck. Mick hastened up into the cab and came down with the lockbox key. One minute later, he watched the tank panels opened, revealing empty compartments. "Cripes, wait until Norm sees this," he muttered. "He's going to pass out."

Mick continued to the other two trucks and opened their compartments. Santa Claus must have come, he thought. Both these two trucks are okay.

He heard the sound of a vehicle outside. Norm is here, he thought.

Mick watched the office door. He put his head down for a minute when he saw his partner enter.

"What's the problem Mick? You don't look very good," Norm said.

Mick pointed toward trucks one and two. "Take a look for yourself and let me know what you think."

Norm gasped when he saw the empty tanks. "What the hell happened?"

Mick shook his head. "Look like our enemies hijacked the two trucks after they left Mexico."

"Damn, how much is this going to cost us? Or cost Nick?"

"This time it's going to cost all three of us. We can't blame this on Nick. We are all at fault. I should have foreseen this and removed the lockbox key from all eight trucks. That's certainly what we are going to do for the next trip, I'll call Nick today."

Chapter 39

TOM AND SAMANTHA SPENT THREE DAYS MOVING INTO THEIR NEW HOME. "I can't believe the people we bought this place from left all this grand furniture," Samantha said, sitting down on the couch with a cup of coffee in hand.

"This area is so much quieter than where our suite was," Tom said.

"I love this place and will miss it when we return to Minnesota in April. This is probably the smartest move we've made since I met you Tom," Sammy said, taking another sip.

"Hey Sammy, how about if I take you out for dinner this evening? Maybe we can just walk over to the Texas Palms restaurant?"

"Yup, I'll go for that.

Two hours later, Tom and Samantha headed for the restaurant. Tom carried a cooler. They entered and Tom placed the cooler on the floor and took a seat across from Sammy at one of the tables. He reached down. "I've got your Gin and tonic all ready to go," he said.

NICK SNAPPED HIS PHONE SHUT. Pam is going to join me, he thought. We need to talk about the disaster that happened last week.

He stepped outside his suite and walked along the sidewalk.

There's Pam, he said to himself, as he arrived at Kingston Drive. He waved and walked toward her. "Hi Pam," he said, giving her a light hug.

"Nick, thanks for your phone call. I was shocked when I heard we'd been cheated again. How could that have happened? I followed truck number four all the way to Raymondville," Pam said.

Nick took a deep breath. "Let's get inside and order. Regardless of how the culprits pulled off this latest theft, we have a new strategy which will prevent it from happening in the future."

They entered the Texas Palms restaurant. Pam picked out a table in the southeast corner. "How's this, Nick?"

He nodded and sat down.

Nick and Pam studied the menu. A waitress soon came by and took their orders. "So, Nick, what's the new strategy?"

"Pam, it doesn't look like we can prevent them from hijacking the trucks. Mick's new idea is for us is to remove the keys, which open the lockbox in each truck. Without the keys, the hijackers can't open the tanks."

"Wow!" Pam exclaimed. "That's a great idea."

"Yes it is, but I'm wondering why we didn't do that in the first place," Nick said, bringing his glass to his lips.

Pam shook her head. "The whole thing is too complicated for me to understand. When do you plan on doing the key change?"

"Tomorrow morning, and I would like you to come with me. The trucks are at the warehouse and the keys should be in the ignitions. I'm going to pick up a big key ring at the hardware store before we go."

TOM AND SAMANTHA SAT AT THEIR TABLE IN THE TEXAS PALMS RESTAURANT. "Look who just came in, Tom," Samantha said, raising an arm.

"That looks like my former neighbor and my part-time boss, and the Pamela lady," Tom said.

"It sure is. I bet we'll have a chance to talk to them," Sammy said.

Tom and Sammy watched as Nick and Pamela sat down in the far corner. "They both look like they are under some kind of strain," Sammy said.

"How can you tell that?" Tom asked with a laugh.

Sammy looked Tom in the eye. "I have that universal feeling that something is wrong. That's just me."

He chuckled. "Remember when you invested a hundred thousand dollars in cash with a con guy from Italy?"

"What would that crazy thing have to do with this?"

"Well, nothing really Sammy, but you had a closed mind on that deal, and now you have a real open one regarding the oil company."

"I'm all done with dinner and ready to go home," Sammy said. "How about you?"

"Yup, me, too."

"I would like to stop and say hello to Nick and Pamela on the way out," Sammy said.

"Sure, we can do that."

They both walked to the other corner of the room. "Hi Nick," Tom said, shaking his hand. "Hello Pam."

Samantha also shook Nick's hand. She walked around to the other side of the table and placed a hand on Pamela's shoulder. "Hope all is okay with you, Pam."

Pam smiled "Just fine. I heard that you two have bought a place here in Texas Palms."

"Yes we have, a mobile on Kingston. We just moved in recently," Sammy said.

"Good for you two," Pam said.

"I guess we better head home," Tom said. "We have a ton of things to do."

Nick said to Tom, "When you pick up the drivers on Monday morning, there will be sixteen of them again."

"That's okay with me. That means I can take the van back to Harlingen that same day," Tom said.

Nick nodded.

"Alright, Sammy, let's go home," Tom said, taking his wife's hand.

Chapter 40

NICK GOT INTO HIS WHITE MUSTANG THE NEXT DAY and drove into the next concourse, parking next to Pam's maroon Ford. He tapped the horn. Within a minute, she exited her suite. There she is, Nick thought. I'm glad she is coming along. This key job will be tedious. She's also quite a chick.

"Good morning Nick," Pam said when she opened the door.

"The same to you, Pamela," Nick said.

"So, we're going to do something about the keys in the trucks, huh?" Pam asked.

"Yup, we take each lockbox key off the fob ring. We have to be sure each one of them is marked, so we all know which truck they belong to."

"How are you going to mark them?" Pam asked.

"I've got a small battery powered drill with a unique bit in it. I plan on putting a single mark on truck one's key, a double mark on truck two's, and so on." He smiled and looked at Pam. "How does that sound to you?"

She shrugged. "Anything that works is fine with me. Mick is paying me a lot of money to help with the trucks. I've got to continue to do my job."

Nick spent a minute talking to the Mexican border agent. He got waved through and he headed across the Rio Grande. "There shouldn't be anybody around our building today," he said as he drove up to the warehouse. "And I see no vehicles there."

He parked his Mustang in front of the office door. "Okay, Pam, let's go in and get the job done." Nick opened the back door of his car, reached in, and brought out a small drill with a bit in it, along with a large key ring.

He used a key from his Mustang's fob to open the office door. Nick held it open. "In you go, Pam."

Nick led the way into the main part of the building where the trucks were parked. "Okay, Pam, we are going to start with truck number one. It's in the first column and against the far wall. I want you to go up into the cab of each truck and get the keys for me. Stay on the rungs until I take the key off the fob ring, then put the ignition key back where it belongs. Okay?"

"Got it," Pam replied. She walked toward the first truck. She climbed the rungs, opened the driver's door, reached in, and pulled out the key. She stepped down and handed it to Nick.

Nick set the key down on the lockbox and held the end of it with a finger while he made a mark on the back with his drill.

An hour and a half later, Pam replaced the keys in truck eight. It's all done, she thought as she stepped down and followed Nick into the office.

Nick held up the ring of keys. "See these, Pam? Eight keys, all marked, all placed in the order of one through eight." He opened up the single drawer in the office desk and placed the keys inside. Then he used a key from his Mustang fob to lock the drawer. "Okay, Pam, let's head for home."

JON CORLONE SAT ON THE SMALL COUCH in his Texas Palms rental unit and sipped a glass of whiskey. Now that I've had a huge victory over the Minnesota pot peddlers, I have to prepare for their next move, he thought.

Michael is coming over on Sunday afternoon, Jon said to himself. He's going to visit the drivers of trucks five and six like he did two weeks ago. I think that after my win on the last trip, they will change their strategy. Jon laughed. Sooner or later they are going to remove the lockbox keys from the key fob in each truck. I'm surprised they haven't already done that. When they do, I'll need to get hold of my nephew Frankie. He's the lock expert in the family.

It amazes me how easy it is to find buyers for the marijuana bales, he thought. Sales to people across the country must be going at a high level. It's legal in three states and that's going to increase dramatically. Then there are a bunch of states which have approved it for medical purposes.

Jon got off the couch and opened a drawer. He grabbed a small ring with two keys. Jon walked outside, sat down in his golf cart, and pushed the key into the ignition. I really like this machine, he thought.

He smiled while driving down York and turning onto the street which lead to the post office. Jon then turned left on Texas Palms Boulevard. He followed it as far as it would go and stopped. Looks like that's where people poop their dogs, he thought.

He turned right and drove slowly down Kingston Drive. About three blocks later, he saw a man standing by the open door of a vehicle. Hey, that's the Hastings guy, he thought. He must have moved from the suites area.

Jon slowed and watched the man retrieve something from the vehicle. He's locking it and heading for the mobile home, Jon thought. He watched Hastings enter his unit. This man is not involved in our hijacking, so it doesn't matter where he lives.

Jon slowly did a U-turn and headed for his home.

TOM HASTINGS DROVE THE VAN DOWN KINGSLEY. It's a beautiful Sunday afternoon, he thought. It is really exciting to have a new home for Sammy and me. He slowed as he approached their mobile home.

There's our neighbor sitting on his front porch. I'm going to have to walk over there and meet him soon. He uses that porch many times in a single day.

He parked the van in the driveway and headed for the door. "Hi Sammy," he said opening his arms. He wound his arms around her waist and squeezed.

"Hey, take it easy, Tom. You could break a rib."

"Yeah, I know. I've already done that," he said with a laugh

"So, how many times have you delivered drivers to Progreso by now?" she asked.

Tom opened the refrigerator and plucked out a bottle of beer. He said, "This is going to be my sixth trip. I wonder if it's going to go on forever. It certainly isn't very hard on me. I can go on indefinitely. Actually, it's good for me—gives me something to do."

But Sammy is suspicious of this entire operation, he thought. As time goes by, we'll likely learn more, but for right now, it's a go for me. The most suspicious part of the trips is the black pickup truck that follows me every time. It could be somebody working for Nick. But then I'm only involved with delivering and picking up drivers.

Chapter 41

JON HEARD A VEHICLE OUTSIDE. He looked out the window and saw Michael pulling up in his convertible. Jon walked into his bedroom. He opened the top drawer of his dresser and brought out a ring of keys attached to a fob. Jon hastened outside and waved to his son.

"Hello father, are you ready to visit Jamie and Santos?"

Jon smiled and gave his son a light hug. "I'm ready, how about you?"

Michael fisted both hands and banged them together in front of his chest. "This should be easy for me because I've done it before. What about the next two drivers? You mentioned only Jaimie and Santos."

"This time we'll talk only to the two I mentioned. They will take care of the other two, Eulogia and Javier."

Michael got into his father's truck. Jon got behind the wheel and drove to the Inn, parking in front of room 4005.

Jon handed his son the key ring. "You know where the money is. You need two bills."

Michael got the money and walked to room 4005. He knocked. Jon watched as the door opened and Michael went inside. My son is a great salesman, he will succeed, Jon thought.

Minutes later, the door opened and Michael emerged with a smile on his face. "Father, both Jamie and Santos happily took the money," he said as he got in. "They both were delighted to know that tomorrow they will each get another thousand dollar bill."

Jon drove back to his unit. He got out and hugged his son again. "I'll see you early tomorrow morning."

Jon watched as Michael drove away in his convertible.

TOM HASTINGS OPENED UP HIS ARMS AS HE STOOD BY THEIR DOOR. "I'll be home before you know it, Sammy." He grasped her around her waist and held her tight.

"Have a good trip, Tom. I know that you always do."

Tom got into the van. This is the sixth trip by myself, he thought. I feel good that all sixteen drivers are coming this time. Even though I got paid extra last time, I'd rather have it go this way, one trip with all sixteen.

Now that Sammy and I own a home at Texas Palms, I will reconsider working for Nick, he thought. I have a lot of landscaping to do and a ton of other things inside the home. The clusters of ugly trees in our backyard have to go. I need to totally reorganize the surface behind the shop and along the side of it.

Tom made his usual stop in front of the eight Inn rooms. Today, I sure don't have my mind on the drivers, he thought as he watched them head for his van.

"Are they all in?" he asked, looking at Menzo.

Menzo nodded. "All here."

Tom drove onto the Expressway and looked in his rear view mirror. The pickup truck is behind me again, but Pam is not, he said to himself.

Half an hour later, he was parked in front of Tesoro's food shop. Tom yawned as he watched the trucks arrive from the west. Hmm, still no Pam this trip, he thought. I wonder what's going on. Here comes Nick. "Alright Menzo, it's time to get everybody out."

Tom turned his head and saw the last driver exit the van and close the door behind him. It's time to head back to Sammy, he thought, backing the van away from the building

-----

JON GLANCED AT HIS SON AS HE DROVE THE PICKUP TRUCK away from Texas Palms. "I don't see that Pam broad anywhere. She is probably already there."

"Yes father, she has been going real early recently, but it's likely we will see her there when the trucks arrive."

Jon laughed. "It really doesn't matter though, huh? We've bought four of the drivers. We own them. They will come through for us."

That Hastings guy is moving that van along at a swifter pace, Jon thought. I've got the feeling that there's something really different about this trip. As long as we get trucks five and six to make a stop at my building, it doesn't matter.

Jon turned left into the Tesoro and parked in his usual spot. Some of the trucks are already parked, he thought. After the eighth truck parked, he saw the black van come to a stop. The maroon Ford isn't here today. That's probably good, but then again, probably not.

"Michael, why wouldn't Nick have the broad monitor the drivers at the station today? Got any ideas?"

"Father, today is a crucial day regarding, what the trucks do—and we will do a successful hijack."

"We'll soon know," Jon said as he watched the first truck leave the station. He started his pickup. "Watch close, Michael. We need to be sure when truck four leaves. I need to follow it."

Michael straightened his back and stretched his neck while watching the trucks leave. "There goes number three. One more and we follow, right?"

Jon nodded. "You have it, and look, truck four is starting to move."

Jon slowly drove away from the building and got behind the truck. "Truck five is right behind me," he said. I can feel their eyes on me, Jon thought.

He drove very slow as they left the border station. Truck five has gotten through, he thought. We are on our way to my warehouse.

Jon flicked on his emergency flashers when they passed the Wilson exit. He kept his speed steady to keep pace with the truck following him. A-hah, there's Primera, he said to himself. He shut off the emergency flashers and flicked his right turn lever upward.

"Hey Michael! It's following us!"

"I see it, and—and truck five is turning, too. Looks like another win, father."

Jon parked the pickup in front of the office door. "You take care of the drivers. I'll get the overhead door open."

He unlocked the office door and walked inside. He hurried to the large section of the building and pressed the button to open the overhead door. It rumbled up and within a minute the door was open. Jon walked over to where Michael was standing with the four drivers. "Come with me, gentlemen."

Jon led the drivers into the office. "Please have a seat," he told them and then reached into his front shirt pocket. He pulled out four bills and gave one to each of the drivers.

Jon smiled and sat in the desk chair. "As before, gentlemen, it will be a few minutes."

He closed his eyes and took a deep breath.

The door opened. Jon opened his eyes and stared into his son's face. Something is wrong, he thought.

"Father, come in here for a moment," Michael said.

Jon got up and walked through the door. He closed it and said, "What? What is wrong?"

"There is no key for the lockbox!" Michael exclaimed. "There are only three keys attached to the fob. There used to be four," he added.

"Cripes almighty!" Jon said. He walked over to one of the lockboxes. "I don't think there is any way we can open that up. What do you think, Michael?"

"You are right. Even if I had a crowbar, I doubt we would get into one of those boxes."

Jon took a deep breath. "We are losing today, but I suspected all along that there was going to be a major change."

Jon smacked his fist against tank. "Back them out, Michael. I'll get the drivers."

Jon and Michael stood by the pickup and watched as the two trucks turned onto the frontage road and disappeared from view.

"Let's head for home, Michael," Jon said. I've got time to think about my new strategy on the way home, he thought. This trip just cost me six thousand dollars for nothing.

Chapter 42

MICK AND NORM OPENED THE WAREHOUSE and guided the trucks into their parking positions. Truck number eight came to a stop and the two drivers got out. They joined the other drivers boarding the bus to the motel.

Mick reached into his pocket and pulled out his ring of keys. He walked over to truck number one and opened the lockbox. Mick pressed the buttons and the panels opened. This one is okay, he thought. He did the same with the other three trucks.

Mick felt tense as he opened the lockbox of truck number five. This is the one that was hijacked recently, he said to himself. He pressed the buttons and felt his heart pound as the panels rotated upward. “Cripes almighty, the bales are all here,” he murmured with relief.

He walked over to truck six and felt the tense again. Mick pumped his fist in the air as the panels opened and he saw the six bales were all there. Minutes later, he opened the panels of trucks seven and eight. He raised his fist in the air again and then banged it against the cab of the last truck.

I’ll go into the office and wait until Norm returns, he said to himself. He sat down and brought out his cell phone. Mick opened it and pressed three numbers. “Hey, Nick, all the bales arrived. Our new strategy has worked.”

Mick smiled widely as he listened to Nick’s response. “Okay Nick, I’ll give you a call when the trucks leave.”

Mick snapped the cell phone shut and put it back into its case.

Half an hour later, Mick gave Norm a high five. “Let’s get them unloaded. Then we can take the rest of the day off. The three semi-trucks will get here tomorrow.”

Jon hugged his son after arriving back at Texas Palms. "We lost this one, but I'll get your cousin Frankie to come over and we will win the next."

He watched as Michael got into his vehicle and drove away. Jon walked inside and poured some whiskey into a small glass. He sat down on the couch and closed his eyes.

Jon punched three numbers in his cell phone and held it up to his ear. Moments later, he said, "Frankie, how the devil are you?"

Jon smiled as he listened.

"Tell you what. I need your expertise regarding locks. It will mean a lot of bucks for you. When can you come over?" Jon listened a moment. "Five o'clock sounds good," Jon said. "I need you to stay overnight, so I'll get you a room at the Inn."

"Where is the Inn?" Frankie asked.

Jon gave him directions. "Give me a call if you get lost."

"I never get lost," Frankie said.

"Good!" Jon said, laughing. "Be sure to bring all your equipment. My plan is to visit a warehouse in Mexico after midnight. So bring your passport, too."

"How do I get to your place?" Frankie asked.

"I'll come by to your room about seven. We can talk then."

Jon snapped his phone shut and picked up his whiskey glass. He took a deep sip, and then another one. Frankie is going to be here in a couple of hours, he thought. I better get over to the Inn office and get him a place to stay.

Minutes later, Jon was handed a key from the woman behind the counter at the Inn's office.

The receptionist said, "He has room number 4206."

"Ah, Thanks, but keep it until my nephew Frankie Corlone gets here," Jon said, smiling.

He turned and left the room.

FRANKIE CORLONE WORKED AS A LOCKSMITH IN EDINBURG, TEXAS. Uncle Jon sounded serious, he thought. He rarely calls me, so something big must be up. He chuckled. Whatever it is, I can handle it. I can get into anything, anywhere, anytime.

"There you are, sir. I got it opened and have made two extra keys for you," he said to a grinning customer.

"Thanks a lot, Frankie. You do a good job."

Frankie shook the man's hand and walked toward his dark brown Jeep. It's time to drive to Donna and check in at Texas Palms, he thought. Uncle Jon has rented me a room...on the house. How can I lose?

He drove to his apartment, opened a dresser drawer, and stocked his small suitcase. I'm ready to go, he thought. All my lock equipment is in my jeep. According to what my uncle said, I'll be needing it.

Frankie slipped onto Highway-281 and headed south toward Expressway-83. I really enjoy this jeep, he said to himself. The people around me hate it. He laughed. The noise is intense. I'm really getting noticed.

There it is, he thought. Texas Palms is the next exit. Minutes later, he entered the Inn's office and pulled his driver's license out of his wallet. "I'm Frankie Corlone. My uncle has gotten me a room."

"You're all set to go, Mr. Corlone. Your room is located in the first concourse, just beyond the row of rooms beyond this office," she said, pointing.

Frankie got back in his jeep and roared the engine before leaving the office area. He took two noisy lefts and parked in front of suite 4260.

He put on the television and opened a beer. Uncle Jon will be here in less than an hour, he thought.

JON LOOKED AT HIS WATCH. IT'S TIME TO GO AND SEE FRANKIE, he thought. He pulled up next to Frankie's jeep and got out. Jon knocked on the door and within a minute it opened.

"Hello, Frankie," Jon said, giving his nephew a big hug.

"Uncle Jon, you're looking great. Come on in."

Jon sat down on a two-seater.

"Can I get you a beer?" Frankie asked.

Jon laughed. "No thanks, I've already had my whiskey for the day."

Frankie opened a beer and sat down on the bed. "So you have a plan for Mexico. I did bring my passport."

"Good, you're going to need it. Tonight at about midnight, you and I are going to drive to Progreso. A few miles west of there, I need to get into a warehouse. I'm sure it will be locked."

"What are you going there for?" Frankie asked.

"To find a set of keys. I am expecting they will be somewhere in the office."

Frankie took a deep breath. "I don't suppose I should ask you what the keys are for."

"No you shouldn't. I expect to find a ring of eight keys. I need to make a duplicate of two of them. That's it."

Frankie ran a hand through the thick extension of hair behind his neck. "That will only take me a couple of minutes."

"Good, we need to get out of there as fast as we can."

Frankie laughed. "Hah, an adventure. That sounds exciting. What if we get caught?"

Jon's eyes narrowed. "I do not expect to get caught, but if we do it won't be by the cops."

"How do you know that?" Frankie asked.

"We're dealing with a company out of the Minneapolis area. It's got nothing to do with Mexico."

"Okay, I'll expect you at midnight."

Jon stood. He nodded and tightened his lips. "I'll see you at midnight, Frankie."

"I'm looking forward to the adventure," Frankie said.

Chapter 43

JON DROVE UP NEXT TO FRANKIE'S JEEP. He got out and opened one of the rear doors of his pickup. He watched as Frankie carried two large leather bags from his jeep and set them down on the back seat. Frankie closed door and opened the front passenger door to get in

"I'm ready to go, Uncle Jon."

Half an hour later, Jon and Frankie showed their passports to a Mexican border agent. Minutes later, he turned onto the gravel road that led to the warehouse.

"I'm going to park beyond the building," Jon said. "There's no way to know if someone will come around."

He drove slowly along the north side of the building. There are some trees over there, he thought. I'll park on the other side of them so if someone shows up, they won't be able to see my vehicle.

Jon stopped his vehicle and turned off the engine. He and Frankie got out. Each one of them carried a leather bag containing tools. Jon also carried a flashlight. They stopped in front of the office door. "It's quiet as a mouse," Jon said, looking around.

Frankie grabbed a ring of keys from one of the bags. Jon shined the flashlight on the door lock. Within a minute, Frankie muttered, "I've got it. We're in."

They carried the two leather bags inside. Jon slowly swept his flashlight around the room. "There's a lock in that desk drawer, Frankie. I bet that's where the keys for the trucks are."

Frankie got down on his knees and worked the lock with his tools. "This one is a little more difficult, but it shouldn't be long."

A minute later, Frankie turned a key and pulled the drawer open. Jon illuminated the drawer and exclaimed, "There it is! Looks like eight keys."

"Frankie, do you see the small marks on the back? We are looking for a key with five marks, and also one with six marks."

A few seconds later, Frankie removed two keys from the ring and set them down on the desk's top. He removed a larger tool from the bag and set it on the desk. "Just keep the light focused here and I'll make two new keys," he said, pointing.

Jon listened to the grinding sound for a few minutes. "The first one is done," Frankie said, handing the new key to his uncle.

Two more minutes went by. Frankie handed over the second key. Jon slipped both keys onto his pickup truck's key ring.

Frankie slipped the two original keys back on their ring and placed them back in the drawer. .

Jon heard a vehicle pulling up outside. He shut off his flashlight. "Cripes, someone is coming. You grab the big bag. I'll take the small one. We can hide in the warehouse if we need to."

Jon walked over to the small window. "Cripes, people are approaching. Let's get out of here." They both slipped through the door and quickly walked across the warehouse floor toward the far wall where two loaders were parked. They got behind the one of them and lowered their bodies.

EMILE SPENT HIS USUAL EVENING WATCHING TELEVISION. I always keep my drapes open so I can keep an eye out on Marcos's warehouse, he thought. Thus far, I haven't seen a sign of anyone showing up there after dark. I know that Marcos is mostly there during the day.

The evening flowed by. Emile remained on the couch, sometimes watching the screen, sometimes snoozing. Suddenly, he sat bolt upright. There's a light over at the warehouse, he thought.

He got up and walked to the window. That was a vehicle. Its headlights are off now, he thought, but there appears to be a light moving around in the office's window. Perhaps it's a flashlight.

He walked into the kitchen and picked up his phone. "Marcos, this is Emile. Something is going on at your warehouse."

MARCOS PRESSED HIS FINGERS AGAINST HIS FOREHEAD. This has never happened before, he thought. I best call Jacob. I will be safer if I take him along.

He got dressed and then he reached up to the top shelf of his front closet. He grasped a belt which had a holstered pistol attached. He strapped the belt around his waist. Jacob will have a gun, too, he thought.

Marcos looked at his watch. It's close to morning, he thought.

He walked out the door and got into his vehicle. He drove it into his neighbor's driveway and shut off the lights. He saw Jacob emerge from the side door, rubbing his eyes.

"Thank you very much for coming along," he said to Jacob as he got into the car. "This may be nothing, but did you bring your pistol?"

Jacob nodded.

"Good. I've got mine, too."

Five minutes later, they drove up the warehouse. "It doesn't look like anyone is around," Marcos said.

Jacob nodded and patted the gun holster strapped to his waist. "*Si amigo*, I may not have to use any bullets."

Marcos parked in front of the office door. "Let's check out the inside." Marcos opened the door and flicked the light switch on. "Looks okay."

He entered the warehouse, brushed all four switches, and gazed around the room. "Looks good in here too, Jacob."

Marcos turned off the switches and left the warehouse. He got his keys out and walked over to the desk. Strange, but the drawer doesn't appear to be locked, he thought as he opened the drawer.

He pulled out the drawer. The keys are all there, he said to himself, and closed the desk. "Let's go home and get some sleep," he said to Jacob.

Marcos locked the office door and walked toward his vehicle. He glanced at the houses off in a distance. Emile will make an extra fifty dollars for this, he thought.

JON HAD PLACED BOTH HANDS ON THE BACK OF THE LOADER'S REAR RUBBER TIRE. Cripes, the lights have come on, he thought. I wonder if we could crawl under the loader. He continued to squirm as he listened. "I think we're okay," he whispered to Frankie, who crouched down on his knees. "I don't hear anyone walking around. It's a good thing we didn't park out front."

Jon caught his breath when the lights in the warehouse went out. "We better wait a few minutes before we leave," he whispered

Several minutes passed. The room remained dark and quiet. Jon said, "I'll go check it out. You stay right here, Frankie."

He walked alongside the west and the north walls until he got to the small office door. He listened. I don't hear a thing, he thought. He grasped the doorknob and opened the door a crack. Cripes, it's dark in there.

Jon hustled back to Frankie and picked up the larger tool bag. "Let's go Frankie, there's nobody here."

They quickly walked to the office and stepped inside. Jon led Frankie to the outside door and opened it slightly. "It's okay out here, too. Whoever was here is gone." Jon opened the door, picked up the tool bag, and said. "Let's get the hell out of here."

Jon touched the side of his right pants pocket. I feel the keys, he thought. He led Frankie back to the truck. Before he started it up, he slipped the new keys into his key ring. "I'm driving out of here without headlights," he said as he started the motor.

Frankie said, "That should keep us safe."

JON DROVE ONTO VERACRUZ STREET AND HEADED FOR PROGRESO. I feel exhilarated, he thought. What would I do without my nephew? Frankie has saved the day. The two keys will get Michael and me into the two trucks and we'll hijack another eight bales of pot.

He smiled widely as he glanced at his nephew. "Hey Frankie, I'll have some cash for you when we get back to my place."

"No hurry. I enjoyed our adventure."

Jon chuckled. Frankie has a super-great attitude, he thought.

Minutes later, they headed up International Boulevard. A shot of whiskey is coming up in a few minutes, he thought. Frankie can have one, too. He's really earned it.

They arrived at Jon's rental unit. "Come on in Frankie, I want to treat you."

Jon put a pizza in the oven and the two men sipped whiskey for over an hour. After the last piece of pizza was gone, Frankie said, "I better head for my room now. If I have any more whiskeys, I won't be able to find it."

Jon laughed. "I could give you a ride."

Frankie stood. "Thanks for the cash, uncle. If you need any more help, just give me a call."

Jon got up from the couch and bashed knuckles with his nephew. Frankie left.

Chapter 44

TOM HASTINGS SAT DOWN ON THEIR SMALL DECK late Friday morning, sipping coffee. I feel very comfortable with my part-time job, he thought. I know Sammy has some reservations, and I respect that, but this gives me something to do, and I make extra bucks. I can take my loved one out to dinner more often, too.

He looked at his watch. According to Nick, the trucks should arrive in about an hour. I'll take off in a few minutes, he said to himself. This will be the end of my seventh trip alone. I know that I've brushed off Samantha's fears about this truck thing being something hugely illegal. I hate to admit to myself that I have the same feeling. But heck, what am I thinking? I have a totally legal job and purpose.

It's time to head out, Tom thought. He walked into their front room, where Samantha sat in her office chair, working her computer. "Hey, Sammy, I've got to go." He snuggled up to her. She raised her right hand and Tom held it tight. "I'll be back in two to three hours," he said, releasing her hand.

I really love this woman, he thought while he walked out. Without her, I would be going nowhere. He opened the door and stopped. Looking back into the room, he raised his hand. "Love you sweetie, see you in a couple of hours."

Tom felt a warm glow as he looked at Samantha and saw her wave. Half an hour later, he felt excited as he parked in front of the food service building. The trucks will be here shortly, he thought. They always show up. What would I do if they didn't show up?

Minutes later, he heard the usual sounds. The trucks have arrived, Tom thought. He got out of his van and stood by the door, his heart beating with quiet excitement as the trucks pulled into the station and parked. He opened the panel doors on each side. The drivers all waved as they approached him.

Half an hour later, Tom dropped off the drivers at the Inn. Off to Harlingen I go to get my SUV, he thought. I should be back to Sammy in about an hour. I'm taking my sweetie out for dinner at the Longhorn in Weslaco.

TOM FELT EXCITED AS HE TURNED ONTO TEXAS ROAD. He smiled and waved at the gatekeeper as he drove up Texas Boulevard. He entered his home. Samantha was practicing her piano. She stopped and dashed into the next room. "You're home, Tom! Safe and sound."

They hugged each other tight for close to a minute. "Hey, Sammy, I'm opening a beer and going to shower right away. The Longhorn restaurant awaits us. We need to go soon," Tom said as they drew apart.

"I'll get dressed," Sammy said.

"Hey, you look very sexy," Tom said when Sammy came out of the bedroom.

"Do you think I'll need a sweater or jacket?" Sammy asked.

"Hell no, it's perfect out."

Tom opened the door and followed Samantha down the steps. He hurried ahead of her and opened the passenger door. "In you go, beautiful lady," he said, smiling widely.

SAMANTHA HASTINGS WALKED THROUGH THE DOOR AT THE LONGHORN RESTAURANT. "We would like a booth for two," she said to the hostess.

"Right this way."

Samantha and Tom followed. "How's this one?" the hostess said.

Tom smiled and looked at Samantha. "This suit you okay, Sammy?"

She frowned, sat down, and looked at the hostess. "Mr. Tom thinks that it's okay."

Samantha grabbed a menu and turned a page.

"Kimberly is going to wait on you two. Enjoy!" the hostess said and walked away.

"This is sure a neat place," Tom said, gazing around the room. "Look at the size of those horns. I bet they are real."

Samantha continued to study the menu. She looked up when the waitress arrived.

"I'm Kimberly and I will be your waitress," the woman said. "Anything to drink?"

"Yes, I'll have a Gin and tonic. Bar Gin is okay. Tall glass is okay," Samantha replied.

"How about you, sir?"

"A glass of Chardonnay for me. A bar version is fine."

The waitress left.

"Kimberly is super-nice," Tom said.

"Tom, it looks like we're going to have to make a lot of improvements to our new home," Sammy said.

"What kind of improvements?" Tom asked.

"The windows and doors need replacing. The water heater and furnace are very old, and we need to update them."

"Holy cow!" Tom exclaimed. "How come I didn't know this when we bought the place?"

"Well, we got it real cheap. Doesn't that mean anything?"

Kimberly arrived and set their drinks down. “There you are. Are you ready to order?”

Samantha nodded. “I’m having the salmon and salad.”

“Any potato?” Kimberly asked.

Sammy shook her head. “I want blue cheese salad dressing on the side.”

“And you, sir?” Kimberly asked.

“I’ll have the pork chops and a baked potato. Salad dressing same as Sammy’s.”

Kimberly nodded. “Thanks folks. Shouldn’t take too long.” She walked away.

Samantha took a sip of her drink. “Tom, we are so fortunate to have found a home here.”

Tom nodded. “I agree. I love this part of the country. It’s conservative, just like you and I are.”

Chapter 45

NICK GLANCED AT HIS WATCH. It's Sunday morning and the beginning of our ninth trip, he thought. This one should be very routine since we have now secured all the lockbox keys. We should have done that with them from the beginning, but with so much going on, and we being so new at this, I can't complain.

Looks like Marcos is already here, he thought when he arrived at the warehouse at nine-thirty. Nick walked to the office door and entered. He shook his partner's hand. "Let's get 'em loaded, Marcos."

"*Si amigo*. Here are the keys."

Nick grasped the key ring and walked into the huge main room. He walked to driver's side of truck number one and opened the lockbox. He pressed all three buttons and did the same with trucks two, three, and four.

He got to the lockbox of truck five and grasped the fifth key. Hey, what the heck? He thought. The next key is for truck seven! What's going on here? Nick thumbed through the keys. Keys seven and eight are where keys five and six are supposed to be.

He walked back to truck two, where Marcos sat in a loader, guiding a bale into the storage space. Nick raised his hand to get his partner's attention. "Hey Marcos, did you make any changes to the key arrangement on this?"

Marcos shook his head. "No a*migo,* I did not."

"Okay, keep loading. I'll get the other loader going," Nick said, his mind continuing to focus on the keys. It could all be a fluke, but then on the other hand, it could be the bad guys.

Half an hour later, after all the trucks were loaded, Nick returned to the office. "Hey, good job, Marcos."

"*Si, amigo*," Marcus said.

"I'm heading out. See you tomorrow morning."

SAMANTHA HASTINGS DROVE HER NEW RED GOLF CART UP KINGSTON DRIVE and stopped in front of the post office. That was so nice of Tom to go along with me and share in the purchase of this golf cart, she thought. Now, I can get around more easily at the park when he's gone to pick up the van. This will work for both of us.

There's no mail today, but the place is open and I can get yesterday's mail. Sammy stepped inside, selected the smallest key from her neck band, and placed it into the slot of Box 79. Not much in there, she thought. No mail is actually sometimes a good thing.

She left the post office and headed for a narrow fence opening located past the main activity center. It's great to have access to the streets in the Inn area, she thought. Golf carts and bicycles can access Kingston Drive north of the gates without opening them. I wonder if the truck drivers have arrived yet.

She turned and drove onto the street. She took a left and slowed down at Kingston Way, looking up the street at the Inn's rooms.

That's where the drivers stay, she said to herself.

She drove past the Way turn and stopped the cart. Straining her neck, she looked at the parking lot just north of the Inn's buildings. Wow, there are a bunch of vehicles there, she said thought. The drivers must be here. I wonder what they do while waiting for Tom to pick them up early in the morning. An afternoon and evening off must be nice.

Sammy did a U-turn on Kingston and headed back toward the opening in the fence. Driving slowly, she turned her head. Hey, there's another golf cart parked in the Way, she thought, and it's gray. Sammy stopped her golf cart. It looks like two people are in that cart in the Way's parking lot. I've never seen it before. I wonder who it is and what they are doing there.

Hey, there's a guy getting out, she thought. Sammy watched a man leave the golf cart and head toward the rooms.

I wish Tom was here. This is likely no big deal, but somehow I have the feeling that there's something going on that is part of the truck operation.

Sammy drove her golf cart into the activity building's parking lot and parked next to a car. She had a good view of Kingston Way. She continued to watch the gray golf cart.

Soon, the man who had entered one of the rooms returned. The gray golf cart then sped away and opened the gate going west.

Uh-oh, there's Pam's brown golf cart, Sammy thought. She's heading my way. Samantha watched as Pam stopped next to her.

"Hi Samantha," Pamela said.

"Hey, great weather today, huh?" Sammy said.

"Sure is—lots of action around here. Say, I found this little gadget in the parking lot and I was wondering if it was yours—could've dropped out of your golf cart."

"Let me see it," Sammy said.

Pam handed her the gadget. Sammy grasped the device, brought it up in front of her eyes, and gave it a good look. "Nope, this isn't mine." She handed the device back. It looks like a controller of some kind, she thought.

"Okay, thanks," Pamela said and drove away.

Pam's been watching the gray golf cart just like I have been doing. I'm heading for home.

On the way, she turned into one of the suite concourses and drove slowly. There's Pam's car. 4705 must be her room number, Sammy thought. She sure uses her golf cart a lot.

Sammy did a U-turn at the end of the concourse and drove slowly toward Kingston Drive.

She took another left into the most southern concourse. There's Nick's white Mustang, she thought. And across is where Tom and I used to live. I love our new home and really appreciate all the space.

Minutes later, she drove through the gate and headed for home. Tom should be back with the van in an hour or so.

PAM COLLITON SAT DOWN ON HER COUCH. Today's Sunday, and this is the day the Minnesota drivers arrive. Mick has removed me from keeping an eye on truck loading at Progreso. That's never been a problem from day one, so he's right on track. Someone has hijacked a couple of trucks during their trip from Progreso to Minnesota. Two groups fighting to make money on pot.

Mick has ordered me to keep an eye out on the drivers, who arrive at the Inn sometime on Sunday, she thought. This is where it all starts, keeping an eye on the drivers and anyone who is messing with them. This Tony guy, who appeared to be a major problem, got toasted for his troubles. Nick is such a swell guy. He stays so cool.

I better get out there, she thought. The drivers have probably already arrived.

Pam walked out of her suite and got into her brown golf cart. Tony's been removed, so I probably won't see much going on, she thought.

Pam drove her golf cart onto Kingston and headed toward the Inn area. She took a left into the Activities Building parking lot and parked next to a couple of vehicles in the middle part of the lot. I can see the entire area next to the Way from here, she thought. I can also see every door of the eight rooms in that concourse and the beyond them I see a bunch of cars...those must belong to the truck drivers.

She yawned deeply. I feel like having a nap, but I need to hang in here for a bit longer, she thought.

"Uh-oh," Pam muttered. A gray golf cart with two men inside has just come through the west gate and parked across from the rooms.

Hey, there's another golf cart entering the parking lot where I am. It looks like Samantha Hastings. She has parked, too, and is obviously watching the gray golf cart as well.

Now a guy has left the gray golf cart and is walking toward the rooms, she said to herself.

Pam watched anxiously as a door opened and the man entered. There's no way I could physically challenge what's going on, she thought. Those guys are probably armed.

Minutes later the man came out of the room and got back into the golf cart. It left the parking lot and headed west. The cart stopped and the gate began to slide open. Pam watched the golf cart disappear around a bend in the street. I'm heading for home, she thought and took off.

Chapter 46

TOM HASTINGS STARTED THE SILVER VAN and left Valley Transit, heading for Texas Palms. It's such a great feeling to have Sammy waiting for me when I get there, he thought.

Each time I make this trip, I wonder if it's my last one, he said to himself. There's obviously something strange about those eight trucks. Sammy is likely correct in thinking that something illegal is going on. The man who was murdered at Texas Palms could've been mixed up with the trucks transportation.

Yes, Nick and Pamela appear to be so honest whenever I talk to them, Tom thought. Now that Sammy has her hands on a golf cart, she's going to do a lot of investigating. I know that girl. She's likely out there right now checking what's going on at where the drivers are staying. Pam has been doing a lot of that, too, but she works with Nick, and she needs to keep an eye on the drivers.

There's my exit, Tom said to himself. I'll be home in a few minutes. He turned the van into Texas Palms at the Inn's entrance. The drivers are all here as usual, he thought as he drove next to the parking lot. He passed by the first row of rooms where the eight drivers all stayed. Then he took a left and then a right to reach the gate. He pressed the button and watched it slide open. In minutes, Tom parked the van in the driveway of mobile home 79.

He locked the van and headed for his front door. "Hi sweetie, I'm home," Tom said loudly.

Sammy came out of their bedroom and opened up her arms. Wow, Tom thought as they hugged. One of these days, my ribs are going to get broken.

"How did the trips go?" Sammy asked.

"Perfect!" Tom replied. He headed for the refrigerator and grabbed a beer. "Would you like some of this?" he asked Sammy.

She nodded, opened a cabinet door, and brought out a small glass. Tom poured a small amount of his beer into it. "Let's go outside and sit down."

"You did such a good job building this deck," Sammy said.

"Thank you, sweetie. This is a natural spot for us to watch the birds and sit and relax. How's the golf cart working out for you?"

Samantha placed a hand over her mouth. "I'm not sure if I should share this, but I drove it over to the Inn about an hour ago. The drivers were all obviously in their rooms, but a gray golf cart pulled up into the parking lot. A guy got out and visited one of the rooms. And then, I noticed that Pamela was hanging around the same parking lot I was in."

"So there were two guys in the gray golf cart, huh?"

Samantha nodded. "Yes there were, and when the guy came back out of the room, the cart went through the western gate. So whoever it was must be staying here."

"Thanks for sharing that Sammy. But, it still doesn't change what I have to do tomorrow."

MONDAY MORNING, TOM GOT OUT OF BED AT 6:00 A.M. He made some coffee, got dressed, and returned to the bedroom. He walked over to where Samantha lay under a spread of blankets, reached down, and gently held her shoulders. "Love you, see you in about three hours," he whispered.

She uttered some words that Tom didn't understand. "Thank you sweetie, see you later."

"Good morning, Menzo," Tom said a few minutes later.

"*Si amigos*, another trip," Menzo replied.

Tom nodded and slowly drove the van out of the parking lot. The chatter back there is at an all-time high, he thought. There must be something good that's going to happen. This could be one of my last trips. I have a feeling that this is all going to end...and not very long from now. I see no problem, but that sure isn't true of Samantha. She is seriously skeptical of what's going on.

He looked into his side view mirror. Wow, there's no black pickup truck following us today, he said to himself. First time. I wonder what that could mean. The chatter hasn't slowed down any, except when I stop at the border. They all get very quiet when we stop there.

Tom turned the van into the Tesoro parking lot. As he approached his usual parking spot, he glanced to his right. The black pickup is already here, he thought. It beat me today.

NICK HAD A HARD TIME SLEEPING SUNDAY NIGHT. I keep thinking about those keys, he said to himself. Hopefully, I am totally wrong and it's no big deal. But, I was there when Marcos and I attached the keys to the ring. They were all in proper alignment. Right now, five and six are where seven and eight are supposed to be.

Is it possible that Marcos messed with the alignment, he thought. I know he does some strange things sometimes, but why in the heck would he do that?

Marcos is here, he thought as he stopped his car in front of the warehouse. Nick entered and saw Marcos sitting in a chair, eating an apple. "Good morning, Marcos, have you talked to any of the drivers?"

"*Si amigo*, they are on their way and should be here any minute."

Nick nodded. "We might as well open the overhead doors and be ready. Oh, by the way, Marcos, did you do anything to the key ring lately?"

"*No amigo*, I no do—no touch. Is something wrong?"

Nick turned his head. "Not sure Marcos. A couple of the keys appeared to be out of alignment."

Marcos took a deep breath. "I have something to tell you, Nick."

Nick looked at Marcos. "What Marcos? What?"

"Our watchdog, Emile, called me one night. He saw some lights on here after midnight. I came over with my neighbor to check it out. We didn't see anybody. No one was in the office and no one was in the warehouse. We left."

"Okay, thanks Marcos." Cripes, Nick thought. That makes it even more possible that someone messed with the keys. I'll just have to wait until the trucks get to Bloomington. If some of the pot is missing, I'm sure I'll hear about it real quick.

The two men walked into the warehouse. Marcos flicked on the lights, and Nick opened the doors.

"They are coming," Marcos said.

Two automobiles approached on the gravel road coming off Veracruz Street. They pulled up just beyond Nick's white Mustang. Four men got out and walked into the building through one of the overhead doors. Marcos said something in Spanish and each driver headed for one of the trucks.

The noise is deafening, Nick thought as he watched the trucks back into the parking area. He stood by until all the trucks were gone and Marcos had driven the black van out of the building. Nick pressed the button to close the overhead doors and headed outside. He got into his Mustang and followed the black van towards Progreso.

Chapter 47

JON CORLONE PRESSED A BUTTON TO OPEN THE WESTERN INN GATE at Texas Palms. He drove his pickup truck through and headed for the frontage road. He looked at his watch. I don't think Hastings has picked up the drivers yet, he thought. We are going to beat him to Progreso for the first time.

He glanced at his son. What would I do if I didn't have Michael to help me? He thought. Jon took a deep breath. My son will be rewarded for his help. He's going to get a chunk of those bills in the glove compartment. When I get paid for the next load, the container in the glove compartment will be pretty full.

Jon slowed as he drove down the main street of Progreso. There is no hurry, he thought. We will be there before Hastings and before the trucks. Minutes later, he parked his black pickup in its usual spot close to the southeast corner of the building. He looked at Michael. "You can have a nap. The trucks will wake us up when they rumble in."

Twenty minutes later, Jon stirred and looked out the rear window. Hastings has arrived, he said to himself. The trucks should be here soon. Moments later, he could hear them coming.

Jon heard his son stir when the fourth truck drove into the station. He's rubbing his eyes...must have had a good nap, he thought.

Jon felt amused as Nick came over to Hastings's van and directed the sixteen drivers to their trucks. They all go to the same truck every time, he thought, and chuckled. The drivers are just like the trucks. They all have a number.

Minutes later, Jon said, "We're leaving Michael. The fourth truck just left." He pulled out of his parking spot and took a right. As usual, Hastings is gone with the van, he thought.

Jon turned onto the street and drove slowly, awaiting truck five's departure.

A short time later, he led the truck through customs and then onto the Expressway. I feel very pleased that truck five is following close behind, he said to himself. After I win this one, I'm not sure what my enemies in the pot business are going to do. I'm going to have to stay on guard and have Michael do so as well. It may not be pretty.

After crossing the long overpass, he pulled into the right lane. The truck did the same, he thought. I assume truck six did, too. He passed by the Wilson exit and put on his emergency lights for a few minutes. Then he slowed, flicking on his right turn signal. He exited Highway-77 and drove onto the frontage road. "Cripes Almighty, Michael, both trucks are following us," he said.

Minutes later he pulled up in front of his green warehouse. He handed his keys to his son. "Think of your cousin Frankie when you use those keys to unlock the boxes. I'll go open the overhead door."

Michael got out and put the keys into his pocket. He walked over to the first truck, talked to the drivers, and waved them toward the office door. He did the same with the drivers of the second truck. Then he climbed into the first truck and drove it into the warehouse. He quickly did the same with the second.

Michael reached into his pocket and pulled out his father's key fob. He pushed one of the smaller keys into the lockbox's slot and turned it.

The box opened. "Wow-wee," he muttered. We win. He pressed all three buttons and felt exuberant as the tank panels opened, revealing six bales of pot. Michael did the same to the second truck and then hustled over to the loader. Within minutes, he had all twelve bales set down on the floor by the far wall.

He closed the tanks, locked the boxes, and slowly backed both trucks into the parking lot. He entered the office and heard all four drivers laughing as they held up their thousand dollar bills. "Your trucks are ready!" Michael said.

Michael looked into his father's eyes. They have a bright gleam, which I have never seen before, he said to himself. "Huge win for us," he said to his father.

TOM HASTINGS MADE BETTER TIME TO HARLINGEN THIS TRIP than he ever had before. He parked the van, locked it, and delivered the keys to the office. Then he got into his black SUV and headed for home.

I wonder why those Mexican drivers were in such a good mood, he thought. This trip was definitely different than all the others.

His thoughts turned to his new home. Our new place in Texas Palms is awesome. My spirits found me a great woman and a great home. So what the hell am I doing driving this van and delivering all those drivers to Mexico? The spirits will take care of this...someday the whole thing will dissipate...and Samantha and I can continue our lives in peace.

Tom picked up his speed to close to seventy miles per hour. I'm anxious to get home, he thought. Traffic in this stretch of Highway-83 isn't too bad. Most of it is smooth. Every once in a while, we get a radical driver who wants to control the whole road. Lots of luck, buddy. Just get the hell out of here.

Tom felt his insides tightening. Airport Road is just ahead, he thought. I'm not very far from home.

Tom turned on his right turn signal and moved over to the right lane. Minutes later he drove into the Texas Palms exit and got onto the frontage road. I'm almost home, he thought. Tom stopped at the main gate. Jesse, the agent inside, waved him on. That man is very special to this park. He has fantastic public relations skills, Tom thought.

He drove down Texas Palms Boulevard all the way to the far edge of the fenced-in park. He turned right and saw that he was on

Kingston Drive. There it is, he thought with pride. Our new home...Samantha and I are partners and we bought it together.

MICK LOOKED AT HIS WATCH. The trucks should be here within ten minutes, he thought. I feel real excited, and I think Norm does, too. I should've used this truck key strategy when we first started. Thus far, we have lost eighteen bales in our eight trips. That's eighteen out of three hundred and eighty four. Not too bad when you think about it seriously.

"Hi Norm," Mick said he entered the office. "Do you hear the trucks yet?"

"Good morning to you, too. No, I don't, but they should be here any minute."

"We're still a couple of months away from icy roads. When winter comes, it will be a new ball game," Mick said.

Norm put a hand up to his ear. "Ah-hah, I think I hear them."

"Okay," Mick said. "Let's open the doors."

They both walked inside the warehouse. The doors rumbled open.

"I see a truck!" Norm said.

Minutes later, all eight trucks had parked. The drivers headed for the bus, which Norm had parked outside. He waved as the sixteen drivers approached, then he got behind the wheel and patiently waited until all the drivers were seated.

Mick closed the overhead doors after Norm left for the motel. He came back into where the trucks were parked and walked over to the driver's side of truck one. He turned the key in the lockbox and pressed the three buttons. Mick stood with a grin on his face when he saw six bales in their proper places. He gleefully watched the second truck tank open and expose six more bales.

He repeated the process for trucks three and four. "That's twenty-four bales," he muttered. "Now for twenty-four more."

Mick pressed truck five's buttons. The tanks opened up. Mick stopped breathing. "Damn! Cripes!" He banged a fist against the cab. "I cannot believe this!"

Mick stomped his feet and stormed over to truck six. A gut feeling tells me that this truck will be empty, too, he thought. After pressing the three buttons, he placed a hand over his eyes. When the opening sound ceased, he spread his fingers to look. "Damn—cripes—same thing here." This is critical and it means we need to have a serious meeting and come up with an unbeatable strategy, he said to himself.

NORM DROVE THE BUS back to their warehouse after dropping off the drivers at the Super 8 Motel located along Interstate-494 in Bloomington. The drivers sure deserve some free time after two days and one night of heavy driving, he thought. I bet they have a great time at the motel. There's a bar and grill only half a block away.

Norm returned to the warehouse and entered the office. Something is wrong...very wrong, he thought. Mick is sitting at the desk with his head in his hands.

Norm stood silently for a few moments, and then he said lightly, "They got some more bales, huh?"

Mick lifted his head. He turned slightly to face Norm and nodded.

"What the hell are we going to do now?" Norm asked.

"I've already talked to Nick. He's going to call us back in about half an hour." Mick looked at his watch. "I'll put the call on speaker. Cripes, we need a new plan real bad—a final plan."

Chapter 48

JON CORLONE SAT IN A CHAIR AT THE KITCHEN TABLE in his Texas Palms park model. It's Sunday morning and Michael will come over today. He hasn't been here for almost two weeks.

He got up, walked outside, and opened the passenger door of his pickup truck. Jon unlocked the glove compartment and brought out an envelope. He shut the door and pressed the Lock button on his fob. The horn honked lightly as the doors locked.

He went back inside and set the envelope on the table. Then he walked into the bedroom and opened the top dresser drawer. His fingers dropped inside and he picked up one of the sets of keys. This one is for Michael, he thought. My son is going to be surprised when I tell him the news.

Jon sat on the couch, tilted his head back, and yawned deeply. He sat up straight. I hear a sound, he said to himself. Michael should be here. He got up and looked out the window. Yes, there's his convertible coming down the street.

Jon walked to the front door and opened it. "Hello, my son."

The two men hugged. "I have something to show you, Michael. Come on in for a few minutes."

Michael sat down next to the table. Jon stood next to it and picked up the envelope. He opened it and pulled out a sheet. "See this, Michael? This is the title for my pickup truck, and it now belongs to you."

Jon smiled widely.

Michael's eyes widened. He cleared his throat. "I thank you, father, but you didn't really have to do that."

"It is my wish for you to inherit my belongings, and this is one of them." Jon reached across the table and picked up a set of keys. "This is my second set of keys for the pickup, and I want you to have them right now."

Michael smiled again and extended his hand. He accepted the keys and held them up for a moment. Then he placed them into his pocket and rubbed a hand across his eyes to dry his tears.

The two men stepped outside. Jon walked over to the golf cart and sat down behind the wheel.

"I'll be with you in a moment," Michael said. He took the pickup keys and title to his car. He then locked his convertible, walked over to the golf cart, and took a seat.

Jon drove down York Drive. He waved to the driver of another golf cart that they met while on the way to the gate. Jon stopped the golf cart in front of the gate and pressed the button on the gate opener fob. The gate slid open. He passed through, took a left, and backed into a parking spot just across from the driver's rooms.

He tapped his son on the shoulder. "Knowing our enemies, this hijack may not work this time, but I'm all for giving it a shot anyhow."

Jon handed his son two one thousand dollar bills.

Michael stuffed them into his shirt pocket and said, "Okay, father, I'll get the job done."

MICHAEL STEPPED OUT OF THE GOLF CART and stood a moment. He looked around for a short time and then began his walk toward room 4005. He knocked on the door and looked back at his father. I wonder why my father is passing on all these things to me right now, he asked himself. As far as I know, he is a healthy man. Is there something I don't know regarding his health?

The door opened. "Hello Jaimie and Santos," Michael said, holding up the two thousand dollar bills.

The two Mexican drivers stood and smiled. "*Si amigo,*" Jaime said. "You wish for us to stop for service again tomorrow morning."

Michael smiled and nodded. "Yes, I do."

Jaime stepped forward and shook Michael's hand. "We shall do, right Santos?" he asked, turning his head to look at him.

Santos nodded and chuckled. "Our truck needs the service."

A loud explosion shook the room.

Michael's expression turned from genial to horrify. He dashed to the door and flung it open. "My God! Father's cart has exploded!" he shouted.

MICHAEL RAN TO THE CART. He put a hand over his face to shield it from the flames. He touched his father's shoulder. My God, he's been killed. Michael pulled the key out of the ignition and placed it in his pocket. Pain seared his palm. "My hand is burned," he muttered. Michael said to himself, this is going to hurt, but I have to do it. He pushed his father's body over slightly, reached into his back pocket, and slid out the wallet. He removed most of the cash and some paperwork. Then he pushed the wallet back into the pocket and pulled slightly on his father's shoulder, returning him to his sitting position.

Michael ran to the office and dashed through the door. "Call 911! My father's golf cart has exploded!"

He dashed back outside. He looked around and saw the drivers standing in two clusters outside their rooms, keeping back from the fire. He looked across at the Park Activities parking lot and saw a red golf cart with a blonde woman sitting inside.

Moments later, he heard a siren. Great! Help is on its way, he thought. He turned his head as the siren got louder and louder. A fire truck turned off the frontage road and drove inside the park, stopping close to the smoke and flames. Two firemen jumped out, manned two large hoses, and sprayed water on the flames. Within a minute the flames were put out.

Michael heard a second siren. Moments later an ambulance sped in close to the fire truck. Two men in white uniforms jumped out and rushed to the cart. They returned to the ambulance, pulled out a stretcher, and returned to the cart.

Michael placed a hand over his eyes as the two men carefully removed his father's remains and placed it into a body bag. They lay the bag on the stretcher and carried it to the ambulance. He approached the ambulance driver and said, "That is my father you have in there. Here is a card with my number."

The man took the card and got into the driver's seat.

The ambulance did a U-turn in the parking lot and left the scene. Suddenly two Donna City police cars pulled in and parked by the fire truck. Two officers quickly got out and talked to the two firemen. Minutes later, the fire truck also made a U-turn and left the scene.

Several people had gathered and stood around in clusters. Michael had left the golf cart and stood next to some of the onlookers. Suddenly he headed for the parking lot just beyond Kingston. Walking fast, he got around the gate and headed for his father's park model.

SAMANTHA HASTINGS HAD WAVED TO HER HUSBAND as he backed out of the driveway in their black SUV. She kissed her fingers and waved. He'll be back in an hour or so, she thought. She went back inside and sat down with her book.

Last Sunday I got to witness activity in the Inn area, which must be important because Pam was there, too, Sammy thought. I know for sure that she knows what's going on. I'm sure it has something to do with all those trucks and the drivers.

Samantha closed her eyes and dozed for a few minutes. Then she got up off her lounger. I've got to go out there and see what's going on, she thought. She got the golf cart key and headed outside. Sammy backed the cart out and waved to her neighbor Doug as she headed north. Two minutes later, she was in the parking lot of the Activities Center

Sammy looked for a vehicle to park next to. That big white SUV is perfect, she thought. It's sure a beautiful day. Tom will be back before too long. Samantha enjoyed a full yawn and coughed twice.

Oh my God, the gray golf cart with two guys in it is back, she said to herself. Just like two weeks ago, one of them has gotten out and is going across the street to the rooms. He's knocking on a door. He's going inside. He must be doing something with some of the drivers.

She heard an explosion and the gray golf cart burst into flames.

Samantha's eyes widened. Her jaw dropped as she gripped the steering wheel tightly. A golf cart has been imploded again, she said to herself. This has happened before, but Tom and I were in the restaurant then.

The man who left the golf cart and crossed the street has dashed back out to the cart. He's doing something in the fire and smoke. The man must be desperate.

Geez, the guy just took off on foot and is running toward the office, she said to herself. He must be calling for help. We need a fire truck and an ambulance, and likely the cops.

"Woah," Samantha muttered when a golf cart drove by going wide open. Hey, that could've been Pam, but I'm not sure. It looked like a woman with long dark hair. But the cart went by so fast, I'm not sure if it was her, she thought.

The sound of a siren penetrated the air. It's getting louder by the moment, she thought, anxiously watching the flames and smoke engulfing the golf cart.

The man is now running away from the cart and he's heading toward the west gate. Clusters of people are forming in the area, too.

The fire truck has arrived, she said to herself. It's come to an abrupt halt near the cart and two uniformed guys are out and they are spraying heavy water over the cart. The flames are all out...that didn't take long. I'm not positive, but it looks like there is a body in the cart. That would be the guy who stayed in the cart while the other one went into one of the rooms.

Uh-oh, here comes the ambulance, she thought. It's parking next to the fire truck. Two guys dressed in white have dashed to the golf cart. Oh my God, they're working on the guy who blew up.

Sammy cupped her hands around her face, her mouth still wide open. Moments later, she dropped her hands and regained her breathing. She continued to stare at the site of the explosion.

Here comes the stretcher, Sammy said to herself. The two guys are carrying it to the ambulance. The fire truck is leaving. A police car is here.

Chapter 49

MICHAEL CORLONE'S MIND SCREAMED AS HE WALKED FAST and at times trotted to arrive at his father's park model as fast as possible. Just before he got there, he reached into his pocket and pulled out the golf cart keys. He used one of them to enter his father's home. I really don't know what I'm doing, he said to himself. My father's gone…how can I deal with this? He stood in the living room and pushed a fist to his forehead. What do I need from here?

He opened the top drawer of a bedroom cabinet. A-hah, the main pickup keys, he said to himself. He slid the keys and fob into his front pocket. I better check all the drawers in father's unit. Minutes later, Michael walked out of the bedroom. Nothing more in there. His eyes fell upon two top drawers in the kitchen cabinet. He opened the first one. Nothing here either. Then he opened the second one. He reached inside and grabbed the handle of a small black leather satchel.

Michael looked around the room for a few moments more. This satchel could have something important in it…it's time to get the hell out of here, he thought. The cops will show up before long. Michael reached into this pocket. He brought out four sets of keys. One set belonged to his convertible. Two sets belonged to the black pickup truck. The other set was a small ring which belonged to the golf cart. He dropped it into one of the kitchen cabinet's drawers.

Michael opened the front door and turned the lock switch. He stepped out and closed the door. What the hell do I do now? He thought. I'll leave my convertible here for now and get the pickup the heck out of here, but first I need to put this satchel in my car.

After stashing the satchel in his car's trunk, he unlocked the truck and got inside. Michael worked his way to the main gate and exited onto Texas Road. I'll have to get a cab when I get home so I can return to pick up my car, he thought. And I need to do it fast. The cops are going to search father's unit for sure.

THE EMERGENCY LIGHT AND BEEPER CAME ON in the Donna Police Department on Sunday afternoon. The receptionist took the call. "Holy cats," she muttered. "There's been another golf cart blown up at Texas Palms." I hate to do this, she said to herself, but I have to call Captain Trevino.

She rang his home phone and waited. A-hah, there he is, she said to herself. "Jesse, how's your day going?"

"Fine so far, but you likely have some bad news."

She cleared her throat. "Captain, do you remember the golf cart explosion at Texas Palms a couple of months ago?"

"Sure do. I hate to think of what you are going to say next."

She chuckled, and then turned serious. "It's happened again! Same spot—a few minutes ago."

Captain Trevino licked his lips. "Not good, but tell you what, get hold of Sergeants Marie and Jesse—also at least two technicians. I'll be there in about ten minutes."

Trevino got dressed in his uniform, strapped on his gun belt and put on his hat. The captain headed out the door. He got into his police car and in minutes, he arrived at the police station. Trevino went inside and looked out the window. Maria is here, he said to himself. We can head over there right away.

Trevino walked out into the lobby and stood in front of the reception desk. "Maria and I are heading to Texas Palms right now. Have Sergeant Herarra get out there as soon as he can. Also, we're going to need some technicians. If you can connect with at least two, I would appreciate that."

"Okay, captain, I'll do the best I can."

He hustled outside and got into Maria's squad car. "Hi, Maria, thanks for showing up so quick."

Sergeant Maria Salinas reached up and activated the flashing lights and then the siren. "We're off," she said as the lights flashed and the siren blared. "Jesse will be right behind us."

Maria drove the police car with authority, moving through the traffic quickly. She sped alongside several vehicles who had stopped and then turned onto Texas Road. Minutes later, they arrived at the Suite's & Inn parking lot where the bombing had occurred.

Sergeant Salinas parked the car. "The ambulance guys are carrying a stretcher with someone on it," she said.

"I'll be damned," Captain Trevino said. "It's exactly the same place where the other bombing happened."

The two officers got out and hurried over to the ambulance. "Hello, gentlemen, looks like you have found a victim," Trevino said.

"Yes, the explosion killed a man. We're going to take him over to Forensics at the hospital. There isn't much left of him."

Captain Trevino nodded. "Okay boys, thanks for getting the body out of there. You did a great job."

One of the attendants closed the rear door and then faced Trevino. "We're heading out, but I better give you this. It's the victim's wallet."

As the ambulance left the parking lot, another police car arrived. It parked next to Salinas's. Two officers got out.

"What the heck happened—another golf cart bombing?" Sergeant Jesse Herrara asked.

"Ditto," Trevino replied. "Jesse, we need to get the markers out and secure the area. The technicians will be here in minutes."

Herrara opened the trunk. He and his partner, Officer Jenkins, removed several orange posts and two thick bands of orange. Sergeant Maria grabbed some of the posts and carried them to the site of the explosion. Minutes later, they had the area marked off.

Another police car arrived and three men got out.

"Hey, Maria, the technicians are here," Captain Trevino said.

Sergeant Maria stood next to her captain as she watched him open the wallet. "The victim's name is Jon Corlone. Other than the driver's license, there isn't much here—a small stack of bills, but that's it."

Maria said, "I think we need to contact the main office and find out where he stays—assuming he is staying in this park."

"Yup," Trevino said. "The golf cart pretty much tells us that he is living here."

Trevino stared at Sergeant Jesse as he came over. The officer held up a pipe. "Looks like the same type of bomb as last time," Jesse said.

Trevino stared at the bomb. "We still have the last one, so we can compare the two. Hey, Jesse, would you check out the office over there? See if they have an opener for the gate. Maria and I need to get through there on our way back to the station."

Herrara raised his hand. "Okay, I'll do it right away."

Sergeant Maria walked over to the dilapidated golf cart. "Hey guys, look at this."

"What?" the captain asked.

"The ignition key is missing."

Captain Trevino walked over to the golf cart. He stared at the ignition. "I'll be darned. That is very weird. There has to be a reason. What do you think, Maria?"

She shook her head. "There's no way to know until we get more evidence. We need to find witnesses who may have seen the bombing. Right now, we don't have any."

Captain Trevino said, "Ever since we got here, I have noticed a golf cart parked over there in the big parking lot. I can see there is someone in it, too." He pointed.

SAMANTHA HASTINGS CONTINUED TO STARE AT THE CRIME SCENE. This is like watching a horrific movie, she said to herself. It looks like some of them are cleaning Kingston Way with a couple of brooms. There are three police cars and about seven officers. The way it's going, they should have the street open when Tom arrives.

I remember the earlier bombing, she thought. Tom and I had been at the restaurant. We actually didn't see the bombing, but we did watch this part, the fire truck, ambulance, and the cops. Of course, from way over here, I have no idea what is going on. To me there are two things that I saw, which are very significant. The first one is the man I saw visiting that Inn room. Then the guy came out after the explosion. He ran to the cart, messed around there for about a minute, and then he ran to the office. Moments later, he dashed away, disappearing behind the western fence. The other important thing I saw was the golf cart speeding by me right after the explosion. I immediately thought it was Pam. But then, after thinking it over, I didn't really see the driver, but I did notice the person had long dark hair.

Uh-oh, here come a couple of police officers, Sammy said to herself. She awaited their arrival and tried to stay cool.

"Hello ma'am, I'm Sergeant Herrara and this is Sergeant Salinas. We need to know if you were a witness to the explosion."

Samantha nodded. "Yes, I was parked right here when it happened."

Maria got out her notepad. “We need to know your name, phone number, and address.”

Samantha cleared her throat. She reached into her purse and pulled out a card. “The information you request is on this card.”

She handed the card to Sergeant Maria. The sergeant said, “We will be getting hold of you soon, likely today or tomorrow, and we would like to come over to your home and ask you a few questions.”

Sammy nodded. “I’ll help all I can.”

The two officers left. Sammy anxiously watched the street beyond the police cars, expecting Tom to arrive at any minute.

Chapter 50

TOM HASTINGS HAD SUCCESSFULLY PICKED UP THE SILVER VAN in Harlingen and he headed for home. He was astonished by all the activity he came upon when he arrived. What the heck is going on, he thought. There are three police cars parked ahead of me.

He stopped the van when a police officer put up his hand. Tom opened the window. "What's going on, officer?"

"There's been a bombing. Do you live here?"

Tom nodded. "Yes I do. Can I get through?"

"Okay, but stay to your left as much as you can."

Tom drove slowly and saw the remains of a golf cart. Oh my God, he thought. It's happened again. I wonder if Sammy is aware of it. We both were involved in the last one, which happened about in the same spot.

Speaking of Sammy, there she is…in the red golf cart, watching this whole deal. I'm anxious to hear what she has to say, he thought.

Tom stopped the van.

OH MY GOD, TOM'S JUST ARRIVED, SAMMY THOUGHT. I don't know if he can get through there. She anxiously watched as he was stopped by one of the officers. She held her breath and patted her hands together.

Yes, they are letting Tom through, she said to herself.

Sammy watched Tom's van follow Kingston Drive and stop next to the Activity parking lot. She started her golf cart and headed toward Tom. She got out of the cart and rushed to where he stood. They hugged each other tight. "What's happened, Sammy?" Tom asked.

"I witnessed another golf cart getting blown up. Someone was killed again, too." Sammy's body shook as she lowered her head and kept holding onto Tom.

"Alright, Sammy, you better sit down. You are shaking all over."

Tom helped her slide into the golf cart's passenger seat. "Let's head for home. I'll get you a drink. You need one real bad."

Minutes later, Tom poured some Gin into a glass and grabbed some ice cubes out of the freezer. Then he added some tonic water. He carried the glass to where Sammy sat and handed the Gin and tonic to her.

Tom placed his hand on top of her head and said, "All things come to an end, Sammy. This one will, too."

Sammy stuttered. "I saw the explosion. Last time we only heard it—this time I actually saw it—so terribly frightening. I'm so glad you're home. On my own, I wouldn't be able to handle this."

Tom stood next to her lounge chair and wrapped his arms around her shoulders. "I am here for you."

"Remember the last time, Tom? The cops considered us witnesses and we were interviewed. I talked to two of the officers just before you came. They are going to call me either later today or tomorrow and come over. This time it will only be me that will be interviewed."

"Maybe so, Sammy, but they might like to hear what you told me when I got here—like what you and I are talking about right now."

"Thanks Tom, I'm sure the cops will come, and I have no problem telling them what I saw."

CAPTAIN TREVINO PLACED BOTH HANDS ON TOP OF HIS HEAD. "It's been a long, damn day. Now that we have a gate opener, on the way out, Maria and I will stop at the main office and find out if the Corlone guy was living here. If the man did live here, I'll need you all back when we find out where the place is—could be today, could be tomorrow morning. Meanwhile, for now, you can all leave."

Maria nodded. "I've seen enough here, too, so let's do it. Then Jesse and I will interview the Hastings lady later."

The four officers returned to their vehicles. Sergeant Maria drove ahead and pressed the clicker to open the gate. She took a left and stopped at Texas Boulevard. Then she took a right. Soon, she parked in the in the RV office parking lot.

Sergeant Maria and Captain Trevino got out and walked toward the main door. The other two police cars headed out of the park. Maria and Trevino entered the reception room. Maria strode forward and sat down in a chair, facing a woman. "Ma'am. We are investigating the explosion of a golf cart in your park which happened this afternoon. The victim was a man by the name of Jon Corlone. Do you have a record of this man? He was apparently staying here."

The woman stared at the officer. Then she got on her computer. "Jon Corlone, you said?"

"Yes, Jon Corlone."

The receptionist opened a file drawer, shuffled through a pack of folders, and pulled one out. "This is a document which shows that Park Model 3435 is currently being rented by a Jon Corlone."

Maria said, "Can you get out a park map and show me were 3435 is?"

"Yes." She reached down and opened a small door. "Here's a map."

Maria spread the map on the desk's top. The receptionist pointed with her pen. "It's right there."

Sergeant Salinas smiled widely. "Thank you ma'am. You've been a big help. We will do everything we can to solve this crime."

Chapter 51

MICHAEL CORLONE STRETCHED OUT ON HIS BED IN his apartment at 1450 Morland Drive in Mercedes. He had just gotten home from Texas Palms. There's no way I can handle the trucks tomorrow, he thought. Losing my father changes everything. I should feel good about all the cash I found in the pickup truck, but I don't. Money is not everything. Yet, it sure feels good to have it. I haven't even counted the money yet. The packet is stuffed with bills...this is all new to me.

The drivers of truck five will be somewhat confused tomorrow morning when the black pickup will not be there to lead them to the warehouse, he thought. Likely, they were part of the big crowd that gathered after the explosion. At least they have each already gotten a thousand bucks. That should keep them happy.

Who killed my father? Michael asked himself. Is it the same person who killed that Tony guy...a golf cart in about the same spot...I'm a lucky guy. I could have been in the cart when it blew up.

I have some deep thinking to do, he said to himself. I need to find out who the bomber is...likely it's someone who is running the pot smuggling. There's no way I'll get the cops involved. Now that my father is gone, the war is between the truck guys and me.

Michael got up off the bed. He walked into his kitchen and got a bottle of water out of the refrigerator. He sat down on the couch. That Nick guy could be the bomber, he said to himself, but I doubt it. He doesn't seem like that type of guy.

There were two golf carts in the big parking lot down from where father was killed, he thought. His brow furrowed as he tried to remember what he saw when he left his father and ran to his unit. I think that each cart had a person in it. Michael's lips tightened. One of them could have done it...could have triggered the bomb.

He heard a vehicle drive up outside. Michael looked out the window. “Angie is back from visiting her mother,” he muttered.

Michael dashed to the door and opened it. “Hi Lovie, so good to see you back home.”

He opened his arms and hugged his wife tightly. “How was your mother today?” Michael asked.

“Just fine, she suffers some from arthritis, but is in good spirits. How did your day go today?”

Michael released his wife and stepped back. “Let’s go in and sit down. I have some news which is not good.”

“Oh no,” Angie said. “What happened?”

Michael grasped her hand and led her to the couch. He sat down beside her. “I lost my father today.” He put his head down.

Tears flooded Angie’s eyes as she snuggled closer to her husband. “Can you tell me what happened, Michael?”

“Where he is staying right now—a golf cart blew up—and he was in it.”

“Oh my heavens, how the heck did that ever happen?” Angie asked, kissing him on the forehead.

Michael cleared his throat. “One of his enemies put a bomb in the cart and—and triggered it. Right now, I do not know who did it, but I plan on finding out.”

“How about the police?”

“They came in big numbers. Not sure if you remember that I told you about a golf cart bombing which happened over a month ago. The guy who got blown up worked for my father. The bombing happened in almost the exact same spot.”

TOM SET DOWN HIS CUP OF COFFEE. "Sammy, sweetie, it's time for me to go."

She sat in a chair next to the kitchen table. "I hope you get back before the cops come," she said.

Tom looked at his watch. It's almost seven, he thought. It should go smoothly today. "Hopefully, I will be back in an hour and a half."

Samantha headed for the door. She opened up her arms and they hugged each other tightly. "I sort of expect them pretty early, but maybe not by eight-thirty. You will get home about then."

Tom kissed her on the lips. He gently pushed her away and said, "See you soon, sweetie—I better get rolling."

He walked out the door and pulled the keys out of his pocket. In four minutes, he parked in front of the driver's rooms at the Inn. Hey, they are coming out, he thought as he opened the van's side doors.

"Good morning Menzo," Tom said, shaking his hand.

"Alright, Mr. Tom, men are all in," Menzo said and closed all the doors.

As Tom drove the van away from the resort, he turned his head to listen. This is really strange, he thought. There is no chatter...none...has it got something to do with the bombing? I bet the heck that it does. He glanced at Menzo, who sat in the front passenger seat. He's not talking to anyone. Maybe it's best if I didn't bring up the bombing.

Tom looked behind him as he drove onto the International Boulevard exit. No black pickup today, he thought. Half an hour later he arrived at the Tesoro. He glanced toward the far corner. No black pickup there either. Something has really changed today.

The trucks haven't changed though. Here they come.

Minutes later they had all parked and Nick walked over from his white Mustang. Tom looked at Menzo. "See you on Friday."

The drivers exited and gathered around Nick.

I'm outta' here, Tom thought. His thoughts turned to Sammy. I'll see her in about an hour or so.

THREE POLICE CARS PARKED NEAR YORK PARK MODEL 3435 early Monday morning. Seven officers got out and two of them headed to the front door and obtained fingerprints from the front doorknob. After one of them waved, Sergeant Salinas walked up to the door and used a key to open it. She pushed the door open. "Okay guys, it's all yours. We'll be checking out the units near here. Let us know when you're done."

The three officers entered.

Captain Trevino said, "I want you two to visit as many neighbors as needed to find out as much information as possible.

Maria said, "Hey Jesse, let's start with the park model next door."

Sergeant Herarra said, "Okay, let's get started."

Maria walked up to the small porch of the park model next door. She knocked and a man answered. "Hello, I'm Sergeant Salinas of the Donna Police Department. This is Sergeant Herarra. Can I ask you some questions?"

"Sure. Come on in," the man replied.

Maria entered. "Have a seat," the guy said, pulling out two chairs from the kitchen table. A woman was already seated there. "I'm Paul, and this is my wife, Nancy. What can we do for you?"

Maria and Jesse sat down. Maria said, "Your neighbor next door was killed yesterday. In an explosion here in the park. Did either of you know him?"

Paul and Nancy both shook their heads. Paul said, “The person who lived there pretty much kept to himself. He was either inside his unit all the time or traveled about in his black pickup truck.”

“Did you even notice any visitors?” Jesse asked.

“Ah yeah,” the woman said. “There was a guy who came around once in a while. He drove a fancy convertible.”

“Could either one of you give us a description of either of the individuals? Either the guy who lived here, or the visitor?” Maria asked.

Paul said, “The guy who lived here was older, I would say around seventy. His hair was brown with some gray mixed in—it was thin at the top. I think he had dark eyes and was about six feet tall.”

“Thanks. How about the visitor?”

Paul cleared his throat. “He had dark hair, was fairly slim.”

Nancy smiled and said, “He was very handsome, too.”

“Anything else?” Maria asked.

Paul said, “No, that’s about it. So our neighbor is dead.”

Maria nodded. “Yes, it happened yesterday afternoon. Oh, by the way, did you ever notice the man, who lived next to you, driving a golf cart?”

Nancy’s eyes opened wider. “Yeah, I saw the guy driving it one day recently. He didn’t have it here very long.”

Maria looked at Paul. “And you, sir, did you see it, too?”

Paul shook his head. “No, I didn’t, and the man probably parked it on the other side of his unit.”

“Thank you so much, Paul and Nancy. Hopefully, we’ll get to the bottom of this case soon,” Maria said.

Paul opened the door. Jesse and Maria stepped out onto the porch. They walked down the steps and over to Captain Trevino. Maria explained to him what they had learned.

"I checked out the unit across the street and heard about the same thing," Trevino said.

"I see the technicians are gone," Maria said.

"Yeah, they got some fingerprints and not much else. But there was one thing. They found two keys. One of them was for the front door and the other could be for the golf cart. Remember that the golf cart's key was missing?"

"Let's go check that out, and then we need to visit Hastings."

Chapter 52

SAMANTHA PACED AROUND THEIR MOBILE HOME. Geez, I hope that Tom gets here before the police do, she thought. She stepped out onto the small deck. I wonder if we should talk out here or inside. She looked up at the blue sky. We better do it inside. Our neighbors might hear us. This has got to be private.

Sammy went back inside. She turned on the TV and sat down to watch. Oh heck, she thought, I can't focus. She heard a vehicle come to a stop outside. She dashed to the window. "It's Tom. He's back." Then she saw another vehicle pull up. "It's a police car," she muttered. "Wow!"

She opened the door. "You made it!"

"Yup, just in time, too. I see the cops are here."

Tom and Samantha remained standing on the stoop as they watched two police officers get out of the car and walk toward them.

"Good morning folks," the female officer said. "I'm Sergeant Salinas and this is Sergeant Herarra. As you both know, we are investigating the golf cart bombing, and we did talk to you yesterday in the parking lot, Mrs. Hastings."

Sergeant Herarra said, "I remember you, Mr. Hastings, from the original bombing. You were in one of the suites then."

Tom shook the sergeant's hand. "I remember that. It never got solved, did it—the first bombing, I mean."

"You are correct, Mr. Hastings, that crime has not been solved yet. But we are determined to solve this one, and we strongly suspect that the two bombings are related," Sergeant Herarra said.

Sergeant Salinas raised an arm. "Today, we need to know exactly what Samantha witnessed regarding the new bombing. I hope you understand that, Mr. Hastings."

Tom nodded. "I'll back off and let you continue."

Sergeant Maria said, "Thank you, Mr. Hastings." She turned to Samantha. "We want you to relax and tell us what you saw."

Sammy inhaled deeply and then let the air out. "The reason I was in the parking lot of the Activities area is because I was waiting for Tom's return from Progreso. As you both know from our last visit, he assists a guy who works for Sardoza Oil in Mexico."

Sammy brought an arm up to her chin.

"Please continue, Samantha," Maria said.

Samantha tightened her lips. "As I was killing time, sitting in our golf cart, another golf cart showed up. It had two men in it and it parked in the Way's parking lot across from the eight Inn rooms.

"I saw the passenger get out. He walked to one of the rooms and knocked on the door. It opened and he entered."

Samantha placed a hand on her forehead. "Then—then, the golf cart exploded. Fire and smoke and debris." She took a deep breath. "I couldn't believe what I saw—a terrible experience."

"Samantha, we really appreciate you sharing all this. Please do the best you can, and continue," Sergeant Maria said.

"A short time later, the guy who went in one of the rooms came out. He dashed to the golf cart—it looked like he got his hands in there—and then he took off.

"Actually, he ran towards me, and then turned towards the west gate. He ran by it and disappeared."

"Samantha, thanks, and please try to relax. What did the guy that ran toward the gate look like?" Sergeant Maria asked.

Sammy's expression remained stoic. She lifted her chin. "The guy looked like a movie star. He was extremely handsome. Dark hair, a tanned face, dark eyebrows, dark eyes. Extremely unusual. I don't think he was a park resident."

"I assume that you have never seen him before," Maria said.

Sammy shook her head. "No, never."

The two officers stood. "Thank you very much, Samantha. If we come up with a picture, can we come over and have you look at it?"

Sammy nodded. "There is one more thing that happened on that day which you may be interested in."

"What's that?" Sergeant Herarra asked.

Samantha looked at Tom and then faced the two officers. "Moments after the explosion, a golf cart sped by me, heading toward the suites. I think it was a woman, but cannot be sure."

Maria said, "By speeding, you mean what?"

"Very fast—as fast as I've ever seen a golf cart go."

Sergeant Herarra said, "Do you remember the color of the golf cart—the one which sped by you?"

Samantha placed her right thumb on her lips. "Again, I'm not totally certain, but a dark color sticks in my mind. The cart was either brown or black."

"Thank you very much, Mrs. Hastings. If any memories return regarding your view of what happened, please give us a call," Sergeant Maria said.

Samantha nodded. "I sure will."

The two officers left.

CAPTAIN TREVINO SAT BEHIND HIS DESK. His two sergeants entered and sat in chairs, one in front and one to the side.

"We have only one witness. What do you think, sergeants?" he asked.

Sergeant Herarra said, “This case is the most unusual I’ve ever worked on. We’ve had two murders, and not a single suspect. There appears to be a secret criminal society or something here in Donna—I’m totally stumped.”

The captain placed both hands on top of his head. He looked at Sergeant Maria. “What’s your view, Maria?”

She tightened her lips. “I agree with Jesse that this case is very unusual. I think the reason why is because two powers are fighting to win a smuggling battle. I understand that the FBI has investigated the possibility, but I don’t think they have even come close to what’s really going on.”

“I appreciate your comments, both of you. We have two big mysteries going on. One is: *who was the person who walked away from the golf cart just before it exploded?* The second mystery is: *who was driving the golf cart which sped by Samantha Hastings right after the explosion?*”

Maria said, “The fingerprints we got from the park model likely belong to your first mystery person.”

Sergeant Jesse said, “Also, I think that guy, the first mystery person, removed the keys from the destroyed golf cart and used the second key to get into the park model.”

“Why do you think the first mystery person needed to get back into the victim’s rental place?”

Maria said, “I think because he needed the keys for the truck the victim drove.”

“That makes sense, Maria. It’s also possible that there were other valuables in the park model that suspect number one may have needed,” Captain Trevino said. “Okay, and now, what do you two think about the golf cart seen speeding away by the Hastings woman?”

Maria said, “It is likely that cart was driven by the bomber.”

Sergeant Jesse added, "We have a third mystery. Was the person speeding away in the golf cart from the second bombing the same as the person in the first bombing? If so, we know who the bomber is. It's Pam Colliton."

Maria nodded. "I think we should get a court order to search the suite the Colliton woman is staying in."

Captain Trevino said, "Great idea, Maria. I'll get Selina on it immediately."

Maria looked at Sergeant Jesse and said, "Great. Soon as we get the court order, I want you to join me in questioning Pam Colliton and searching her suite. I assume we are looking for a detonator which could trigger a pipe bomb, probably a small one."

PAMELA COLLITON WALKED BACK TO SUITE 4705 after eating breakfast at the Texas Palms Restaurant. That was a great breakfast, she thought. I would be very surprised if the cops didn't come over today. I'm totally ready for them, just as I was the last time they came.

It's Tuesday, and the drivers won't be back until Friday, she said to herself. I've got a bunch of days off now, because the next truck run north won't happen until a week from Monday. Mick has called me only once since the Corlone guy got blown up. I kind of feel that he doesn't need me any longer.

I hear a vehicle outside. I bet it's the cops, she thought. Pam sat on the couch and put her hands on both sides of her head. In moments, she heard a knock. Well, here goes, she said to herself and headed for the door.

Pamela opened it. "Yes, what can I do for you?"

"Hello, I'm Sergeant Salinas and this is Sergeant Herarra of the Donna Police Department. We have a search warrant for your suite, your car, and your golf cart." He handed Pam the document.

"Why! What the heck is that for?"

Sergeant Herrara said, "We have evidence that you may have been involved in the recent bombing that happened here in this park."

"Go to hell! Where's your evidence?" Pam loudly demanded.

"Someone here in the park said that you left the bombing scene right after it happened—seen leaving in a golf cart. It doesn't matter whether you agree or not right now. We have legal authority to do a search, and will do it whether you like it or not," Sergeant Maria said.

"We will need a key to your car," Sergeant Maria said. She looked at her partner. "Call in the technicians, Jesse."

Pamela threw her car keys at Maria and stormed into her bathroom.

Chapter 53

Sergeant Maria sat down on the couch next to Sergeant Jesse. "We'll have to wait until she comes out of the bathroom. Meanwhile it shouldn't take the guys long to make the search," she said.

She watched one of the technicians go through all the kitchen drawers. He was done in minutes. The technician met with one of his partners who had searched the bedroom. "Nothing I could find in here," he said.

When Pamela returned, Maria stood. "I want you to sit down because we need to ask you some questions."

Pam flipped up her hands. "Where do you want me to sit?"

"Anywhere you want," Maria said.

Pam sat in a chair next to the kitchen table.

One of the technicians walked over to Maria. "We're all finished in here, so thanks for your help. I assume the guys outside are also done. See you again."

"Hey, good job," Maria said. "But don't leave until we are finished with Miss Colliton. It shouldn't take along."

The two technicians left.

Maria looked at Pam. "I assume that you are aware that a golf cart was blown up near here this past Sunday afternoon."

"Yes, I have. It's terrible what happened—a person getting killed."

Sergeant Herarra said, "From this moment on, our conversation will be recorded. I want you to be aware of that, Pamela Colliton."

Pam smirked and nodded.

Maria opened up her notepad. "Pamela, we would like to know where you were this past Sunday afternoon at about three o'clock."

Pam rubbed her nose with a finger. "I was home, right here.

Sergeant Maria said, "We have information from a person who witnessed the explosion. Her testimony included saying she saw you drive by in a golf cart, going top speed, and heading toward your suite.

Pam looked up at the ceiling. "Whoever this person is—is wrong. I was right here in my suite, not anywhere near the bombing area."

Maria looked down at her notepad. "I am recording your answer, even though in my view it is questionable. If you are telling the truth, there will be no problem.

"I'm sure you remember that we interviewed you after the previous bombing. To update you, that one happened in the same spot, close to two months ago. After that bombing you were seen speeding away in your golf cart, and you agreed that you did exactly that."

Pamela flipped up her hands. "Yeah, I told you guys that the explosion scared the hell out of me."

Jesse nodded. "And now you claim that it wasn't you speeding away in the golf cart that left the scene after the second explosion."

There was a knock at the door. Everyone turned to look.

One of the technicians entered. "We're all done, Maria—and we found this." He held up a clear plastic bag. "It looks like some sort of electronic instrument—could be a detonator."

"Where did you find it?" Maria asked.

"In a narrow slot in the golf cart where golf balls are normally stored."

The two sergeants got up off the couch. Sergeant Maria looked at the technician and said, "Would you get a set of fingerprints from Miss Colliton?"

Pamela said, "Let me see that."

The technician held the plastic bag in front of her eyes.

"That's not mine! I've never seen it before."

Maria said, "Miss Colliton, if your fingerprints do not match the ones on the detonator, than you have nothing to worry about."

The technician sat down next to Pam and took her fingerprints. "All done, sergeant. We'll compare them to the detonator prints. Should be finished within a half an hour. I'll give you a call." He walked out the door.

Maria placed a hand on Pam's shoulder. "Thank you, Miss Colliton. Sergeant Herarra and I are going to wait here for the results. It shouldn't take long."

"I have total confidence that I will be cleared," Pam said.

They sat in silence for close to half an hour. Minutes later, Sergeant Maria's phone finally rang. She flipped it open and said, "Hello."

Maria nodded twice and then put the phone away. "Pamela, you are cleared for now. Your prints did not match the ones on the detonator."

Pam clapped her hands together. "I told you so."

SERGEANT MARIA STEPPED OUTSIDE AND SAT IN THE POLICE CAR. She looked at her partner and said, "If Pam did the bombing, why the heck would she leave the detonator in her golf cart? This totally confuses me."

Jesse scratched his left ear. "Maybe she had someone else handle the detonator and wanted it to be found by us so she could get off the hook."

“If it was me, I would’ve gotten rid of it—the detonator,” Maria said.

“Pamela needs us to find a second suspect, and she may get one,” Jesse said.

Maria fastened her seatbelt and said, “Right now, we don’t have enough evidence to arrest anyone. It’s a lot like the first bombing.”

Jesse said, “It’s a total mystery, especially when you think about the person who was originally in the golf cart with the victim and then disappeared.”

“Pamela has won this session, but she is far from being cleared. The next thing we need is fingerprints from the others who were involved in the first bombing.”

CAPTAIN TREVINO SAT BEHIND HIS DESK. ”Searching Pamela Colliton’s suite and golf cart was a great thing to do. There’s no way to know for certain if the detonator we have in our possession initiated the explosion. But—but, we have to assume it did.”

Sergeant Maria nodded. “What puzzles the heck out of me is the fact that somebody else’s fingerprints are on it. I totally expected them to be hers.”

Sergeant Herarra smiled and said, “I would have bet money on it.”

The captain chewed on his upper lip. He took a deep breath. “This is a long shot, but since you suggested Pamela, we need to get fingerprints from the other people we interviewed after the first bombing—namely Nick Giggs, and Tom and Samantha Hastings.”

Chapter 54

TOM SIPPED COFFEE AND SCANNED HIS INTERNET NEWS. He clicked the Obituaries icon. Moments later, he stopped. My God, he thought. Our farming neighbor has just passed away. Steve Bruhn is gone.

Our neighbor managed the farmland adjoining my property in Minnesota for many years, Tom said to himself. I'll have to share this with Sammy, although she never met the man.

My fondest memory of him is waving to him when I drove by his tractor cab as he sat inside it working his field. I read his full obituary and it had so many good things to say about him. Steve was very active in the community, Tom said to himself. He farmed land and raised turkeys. The community of Vergas, Minnesota, will certainly miss him.

His mother-in-law Marjorie Schwandt was my neighbor for the past forty years or longer, he thought. Her husband had passed away a few years ago. I remember Sammy visiting Margie many times. They would sit in the kitchen and share coffee and experiences.

Tom stood and walked to the window. Sammy should be home pretty soon, he thought. She is enjoying her daily early morning walk. She has her mind replaying the bombing incident right now, and perhaps passing on the bad news might not be wise.

Sammy has gone through so much since we met, Tom said to himself. Back in Minnesota, she saved my life with her Glock pistol. Bone Erlock was determined to get revenge and eliminate me, mainly because my grandfather had shot and killed his grandfather after that Erlock had escaped from jail in the late eighteen-hundreds.

Recently Bone Erlock stole a UPS truck and drove it into my yard, hoping that I would not be suspicious, Tom said to himself. It worked. I walked out to get my package, and Bone Erlock took advantage and pulled a gun on me with the full intention to kill me and get his revenge.

Earlier, Sammy had spent a lot of time learning how to shoot with the Glock. During my desperate moment with Erlock, she snuck up on him, fired her gun, and killed him, he said to himself.

"Uh-oh, here comes Sammy," Tom muttered while watching his wife walking toward their house.

Tom stood in the kitchen and waited for the door to open. Moments later, Sammy entered. "How was your walk?" he asked.

"Uh," she replied. "There was this guy. He wanted to walk with me."

"What happened?" Tom asked.

"I told him that I would rather walk alone."

Tom chuckled. Then he turned sober. "Sammy, I have some bad news. Our farming neighbor Steve Bruhn passed away." Tom reached out his hand.

"Oh, I'm so sorry," Sammy said, sitting on the couch.

"I really liked and respected that man," Tom said as he sat next to her.

NORM BLAINE DROVE THE BUS OUT OF THEIR WAREHOUSE and parked it outside. There goes the eighth truck into the building, he said to himself. The drivers will all be coming out soon. They've done this ten times so the parking is pretty routine to them. He chuckled. Mick does watch over them like a hawk. Since the first hijacking, I always saw tension building up in Mick whenever the trucks approached, he said to himself. But he's calm today. He must be a hundred percent sure the trucks are all full of bales...six in each one.

Here they come, the drivers, he thought. Sixteen smiling men are headed for my bus. I can see this is the favorite part of their trip. Their rooms at the motel are all paid for. Then they get to go out, have some drinks, and who knows what the heck they do. I would guess they do some partying.

Norm chuckled again.

"Okay Menzo, do you have them all inside?" Norm asked.

"*Si amigo*, they are all set."

Norm headed for the motel. A half an hour later, he dropped off his passengers and headed back. When he arrived, he drove through one of the big overhead doors and parked along the south wall. Norm laughed. Mick looks like he's won the World Series. All the bales were intact, I bet. I better get rolling and help him unload the trucks.

Norm stepped up into the second loader. He roared off to the trucks, plucked out a bale, and deposited it near where his mini-bus was parked. Norm did several more and thought, this is my last one, as he watched Mick and his loader leaving a truck. Norm picked up the bale and dumped it off with all the others. He parked the loader.

"Looks like forty-eight bales, Mick," he said when they were finished.

Mick turned and smiled. "The last battle has ended. Our adversities are all finished, Norm. We have defeated them."

Norm smiled and headed for the two overhead doors. He pressed the buttons and the big doors rumbled down. He walked into the office and saw Mick sitting at the desk, writing in a large sketchbook which Norm had seen so many times in the past. "It's time for me to head out, Mick. I'll be back tomorrow when the three semis arrive."

Mick looked at Norm and nodded. "Yeah, Norm, we got all forty-eight bales this time. I think this will always happen in the future, too."

"Okay, see you tomorrow."

NICK RETURNED FROM PROGRESO Monday afternoon. He spent the next two days relaxing, anxiously waiting for a call from Mick. I don't think that any of the trucks got hijacked on this trip, he thought. The guy getting bombed and killed in the golf cart is probably the reason why. I think about all this a lot, but actually the less I know of what's going on, the better off I am.

He heard a knock on his door. Nick opened it and saw two police officers, a man and a woman.

"Mr. Nick Giggs, I assume?" the male officer said.

"Yes, I am Nick Giggs, and you have been here before."

The officer nodded and chuckled. "Yup, I'm Sergeant Jesse Herarra and my partner is Sergeant Maria Salinas. As you likely know, there's been another bombing. We have been instructed to obtain fingerprints from all the people we talked to during the first bombing—and you are one of them."

Nick laughed. "Well, first of all, I was in Mexico when the second bombing occurred, but I'll go along with the fingerprints."

Sergeant Maria waved to the police car parked next to theirs. She looked back at Nick. "Okay, Mr. Giggs, our technician will do it for us. He's on his way in. Would you have a seat at the table?"

Nick followed her request. Maria placed a chair next to him. "Right over here, Santos," she said.

Samantha Hastings sat in her lounge chair, watching her recorded soap on television.

She heard a knock on the door.

"I'll get it," Tom said. He got up from his computer chair in the office and headed for the door.

"Thanks," Sammy said.

He opened the door and said, "I've seen you two before."

Sergeant Maria laughed. "You have a good memory, Mr. Hastings. As you both likely know, there's been another bombing and we have been instructed to get fingerprints from all the people we questioned after the first bombing."

"Sure," Tom said. He looked at Samantha. "Okay with you, sweetie?"

"Yes, where do you want me to sit?"

The sergeant pointed. "Next to the countertop would be fine. A technician will be in momentarily to print both of you."

Minutes later, after all the officers had left, Sammy said, "You and I have nothing to worry about, but I bet Pamela Colliton is in deep trouble."

Chapter 55

CAPTAIN TREVINO SAT BEHIND HIS DESK. He had both his knuckles planted on the desk's top. His two sergeants had just come in the door and got seated. "Good afternoon, Maria and Jesse. The results are in."

Maria scratched the tip of her nose. "You have that look, captain. "Did somebody's fingerprints match those on the detonator?"

The captain nodded. "Samantha Hasting's prints did it. They match the ones on the detonator." He held up a sheet that had fingerprints displayed.

Maria shook her head. "This is unbelievable. Something is wrong here."

Sergeant Herarra said, "It looks like we were leaning in the wrong direction when we suspected Pamela Colliton."

Sergeant Maria said, "I'm definitely not going to conclude that, Jesse. I want to hear from Samantha first."

The captain said, "You will soon, Maria. I am issuing an order to arrest Samantha Hastings on suspicion of murder."

TOM HASTINGS HEARD THE KNOCK ON THE DOOR. "Who the heck could that be?" he said and walked over to answer. He opened the door and felt a stab of fear in his stomach. "Hello officers. Why did you guys come back so soon?" he asked.

Sergeant Herarra said, "We are here to see Samantha."

Tom turned. "Sammy, the cops are here to see you."

She came out of the bedroom and stopped. What the heck, she thought. Why do they want to see me?

Samantha looked at Tom, who had turned toward her. He backed off a couple of steps. "Come on over here, please," he said.

She slowly walked toward the police officers. "Why do you want to see me? I've already told you all I know."

"Samantha Hastings, we are arresting you on the suspicion of murdering Jon Corlone this past Sunday," Sergeant Herarra said. "You have the right to remain silent," he said and continued reading Samantha her rights. After he finished, he grabbed both of Samantha's hands and brought them around to her back. Then he snapped a cuff on each wrist. "You have the right to seek legal consul."

"You guys are crazy. I didn't blow up the golf cart. Why the heck are you arresting me?" Samantha protested.

Sergeant Maria said, "It's your fingerprints, Mrs. Hastings They matched the prints on the detonator."

"The detonator!" Sammy exclaimed. "What the hell is that?"

"It's the instrument which set off the pipe bomb used in the explosion."

"I don't have a detonator. What the hell are you guys talking about?"

"We're taking you into custody and to police headquarters. If you wish your husband Tom to come along, he can follow us in your vehicle," Sergeant Herarra said.

Sammy felt the hand of one of the officers on the top of her head as he assisted her into the back seat of the squad car.

Tom said, "I'll be there with you, Sammy. We'll get this mess straightened out." He stood by the squad car while his wife was getting settled into the back seat.

Sergeant Maria removed the handcuffs from Samantha's wrists. Sammy brought her hands forward and loosened her fingers.

Tom was given permission to enter the interrogation room. He took a seat in the far corner. He clasped his hands together and nervously slid his fingers back and forth.

Sergeant Maria said, "Samantha, we want to hear your side of the story. Try to relax and express yourself in any way you wish."

Samantha took a deep breath. "The detonator—that's what you found my fingerprints on—I'll tell you why.

"Two weeks before the explosion, the day which Tom leaves for Harlingen to pick up the van—a Sunday afternoon, I drove out to the Activities parking lot, just to see what's going on. Pam Colliton came by with her golf cart. She handed me a small gadget. She told me that she found it in the parking lot and wondered if it was mine.

"I held it in my hands for a few moments and looked it over. Then I told her that it was not mine."

Samantha looked around the room. "Actually, the reason I was in the parking area near the suite rooms was because I'm suspicious of what's going on with the truck drivers Tom delivers to Progreso and back every two weeks. I know that what Tom is doing is perfectly legal, but I suspect that what the trucks are hauling is illegal."

She shook her head and placed both hands over her face.

Sergeant Maria said, "Samantha, I believe you—regarding the detonator." She walked over to Sammy and placed a hand on her shoulder. Sammy began to cry. Tom gasped and lowered his head.

Maria stood and looked at Captain Trevino. "You may not agree with me, but I think—I think that Pamela woman has set off both pipe bombs. If you remember, she was seen by creditable witnesses speedily leaving the scene of the explosion after the first bombing. Then a golf cart was seen speedily leaving the scene of the second bombing. Our witness said she thought it was a woman, because she had long, dark hair."

Captain Trevino took a deep breath. "Yeah, and our witness is now here on suspicion of murder."

Maria cleared her throat. "Yes, but only because her fingerprints were on the detonator. You are perfectly aware that she absolutely has no criminal record—not even a speeding ticket."

Captain Trevino looked at Sergeant Herarra. "What do you think, Jesse?"

The sergeant raised both hands and spread his fingers. "I have to go with Maria's view—this hasn't been mentioned, but we both agreed that Pamela Colliton lied when we questioned her about entering the first victim's suite. Pamela had said she was looking for the cleaning lady. Then she said she was a general consultant for different companies and organizations, but that all means basically nothing. We really don't know why she is here."

"Thanks Jesse," the captain said. He placed both hands on the desk. "I'm going to request the county to hold a hearing on this whole case. Meanwhile, I'm going to release Samantha Hastings. I am requesting that her husband, Tom, guarantee us that she will not leave the territory."

Tom got up from his chair. "Captain, you have my word that Samantha will not leave this area. We have a new home at Texas Palms, and will remain here until this case is solved."

"Thank you, Mr. Hastings. Your wife can now officially leave."

Chapter 56

PAMELA WALKED TO THE TEXAS PALMS RESTAURANT. She sat down and looked around the room. Not many people in here right now, she thought. I've got to be feeling good. The cops hauled Samantha Hastings away yesterday. I held my breath when I saw one of the officers push her head down as she got into the back seat of the police car.

She chuckled. That could've been me, but I'm a free woman, she thought. It's mainly because of my detonator strategy. Mick doesn't know what happened yet, but I'll clue him in when we talk again.

I've got the feeling that the next truck trip will be the last one, she thought. Mick didn't say that directly, but he hinted at it. That means that I will need to get out of here, and pronto. Meanwhile I can just relax and take it easy. I will need to drive to Progreso for the next truck trip. Mick has made that clear to me. I don't have to go to the warehouse, though. I like that. My job is to make sure no one messes with our drivers at the Tesoro.

Pam chuckled again. I can just see Samantha standing behind bars in the Donna City jail, she said to herself

-----

MICHAEL CORLONE COULDN'T SLEEP. HE PATTED HIS WIFE ON THE SHOULDER and left the bedroom. Michael opened a cabinet and brought out a bottle. My father drank this stuff, and I know I shouldn't, but right now I need it, he said to himself, pouring whiskey into a small glass. He added a little water and sat on the couch.

I've got enough money and don't need any more, he thought. Maybe down the road I will...but there's always a way. My father was a great teacher. One time he told me that people with lots of money have big weaknesses.

Right now, my mind is not on money, but avenging my father's death, he said to himself. I need to know who detonated the bomb, and I also need to know who ordered the bomber to do it. Regardless of what I learn about the culprits, I have a plan to shut down the entire truck operation. It's been on my mind for some time now, and with each passing day, my ideas grow.

Michael took another sip of whiskey. My father will be proud of me. I know that he's in heaven and directing traffic there. He was a great teacher and always knew how to get the job done and drain the swamp.

He thought about his visit to the Hawkins Funeral Home in Donna. After I paid them, they provided me with a brown leather bag. It contained my father's ashes, he said to himself. I'm lost right now...don't know what to do with them. Perhaps after I gain my revenge for his loss, it will come to me.

Michael got up and filled his glass again. He took another sip and sat down on the easy chair. I remember seeing two golf carts parked nearby right after the explosion, he thought. I gazed at both of them as I headed for father's park model. One of the carts was brown and it had a woman sitting in it with long dark hair. The other cart was red and the woman in that one had blond hair. He took another sip. One of them is likely the bomber. The newspaper isn't going to tell me who they are. Do I dare visit the police department to find out? No. I will need another way to learn who the killer is.

TOM SAT ON THE COUCH, CLOSE TO SAMANTHA. He kept an arm around her shoulder. "This shall soon pass," he said.

Samantha stuttered when she said, "I've never been arrested before—my God, what have I done? I haven't hurt a soul."

Tom released her. "Sammy, you are a victim. The two explosions are a result of criminal activity. I think you are right in that the whole thing has something to do with my part-time job involving the trucks."

Samantha turned her head and lifted her chin. "Maybe if I had stayed out of it, this wouldn't have happened."

"What do you mean by that?" Tom asked.

"Well, I have always suspected that this truck operation was involved in something shady. That's why I traveled to Progreso to check things out. That's why I spent time on my golf cart keeping an eye out on the Inn area."

Tom grabbed her hand. "I have to appreciate your concern and care. You are doing this for me—for us."

"Thank you, Tom. I don't know how I could have handled this without you. You are the best person that I have ever known."

Tom put his arm around her shoulders and gave her a gentle squeeze. "Sammy, you're so special to me. We will survive and win this—the police will eventually expose the real truth behind this complicated case."

Chapter 57

MICHAEL CORLONE GOT INTO HIS CONVERTIBLE and headed for Texas Palms, anxious to revisit the scene of the crime. I need to sit there and do some deep thinking, he thought. I'm real positive that one of the women, who were sitting parked in their golf carts in the parking lot just south of us, ignited the bomb that killed my father.

He pressed the brakes and stopped right next to the spot where his father had died. I'm still screaming inside, he said to himself. Michael looked ahead into the parking lot where he had seen the two golf carts. Long dark hair and blonde hair...which one did it?

He drove his car ahead and turned right, then drove into the parking lot where he had seen the golf carts. Michael spun his vehicle around and faced the Inn area. This is the view that the bomber in the golf cart had. She sure wasn't very far away, he thought. A detonator could easily ignite the bomb from here.

Michael left the parking lot and drove onto Kingston Drive, driving slowly away from the Inn. There's a big concourse, he thought. He drove into it and eyed all the vehicles and golf carts. Turning around, he drove back onto Kingston and drove into the second concourse. Oh my God, he thought, there's a brown golf cart and a maroon car. He stopped his vehicle and stared. That car looks just like the one I sabotaged at the Tesoro awhile back.

His eyes hardened. I think I found the bomber, he thought. It's the woman who manipulated the sixteen truck drivers in Progreso. She stays here in Suite 4705.

Michael drove to the end of the concourse and turned around. He pulled up to a suite about four units away from 4705. Sooner or later, she is going to come out, he thought. I have to make sure she is the same woman I saw at the Tesoro. Michael looked at his watch. This could take some time, he thought. Suddenly, someone came out the door and hustled over to the maroon Ford Focus.

"It's her!" he exclaimed. "That Pam woman killed my father. And now I know where she lives."

SAMANTHA SET TWO BOWLS OF OATMEAL on the kitchen table. "It's ready, Tom, add the syrup anytime you wish."

Tom reached into the refrigerator. He brought out a bottle of syrup and poured a small amount into each bowl. "That should do it," he said.

Sammy sat down, extended her hand, and grasped Tom's. She said a short prayer.

After taking a couple of bites, she said, "I couldn't sleep again last night. It's been a few days now, and I need to do something about it."

Tom put a hand on her shoulder. "It's obvious what's bothering you, sweetie. What's on your mind?"

"I need to confront Pamela. She set me up to get arrested, and it worked. I spent some time behind bars and she hasn't. There is no doubt in your mind, Tom, and mine, that she is guilty of the bombings. She should be in jail right now, as I speak."

"I totally believe you, but the problem is that the cops don't have enough evidence to arrest her. Lot of it is your word against hers—no fundamental proof."

Samantha took two deep breaths. "There is only one solution to my problem. I have to confront her—the sooner the better."

Tom gritted his teeth. "If Pamela is the bomber, and she likely is, you are talking about a very dangerous person. If I was going to take her on, I wouldn't do it without being armed."

Sammy pushed her chair back. She walked over to the two chairs that were pushed under the countertop. Her purse was stored on one of them. She took out her purse and reached inside. She pulled out her pistol. "See this Tom? It's my Glock 42. Do you remember when you helped me pick it out?"

Tom nodded. "Sure do, and you saved my life with it. How could I ever forget that guy—Bone Erlock—who tried to do me in—you and our neighbor Pete took him out for good."

"Real soon, I'm going to knock on Pam's door and confront her. She is a brutal liar. I'll have the pistol in my purse with my hand on it."

"Whoa, Sammy, I don't like the sound of this."

"You can come with me. I know that you have a pistol, too, Tom."

SAMMY GOT BEHIND THE WHEEL OF HER GOLF CART. She set her purse down next to her. Tom sat in the passenger seat. "Here I go," she said.

Sammy drove the golf cart up Kingston Drive and turned toward the Activities building where she snaked through a narrow portal to get around the gate of Kingston Drive. She turned right at the second suite concourse. There's Pamela's maroon Ford Focus, Tom thought.

Sammy pulled alongside the brown golf cart and parked at the curb. She got out and looked at Tom. "I've got to do this. My life depends on it."

Tom nodded. He patted the holster he had fastened to his belt on the right side of his waist.

He held his breath as he watched Sammy walk up to the door and bang on it four times with her fist.

The door opened.

There she is, Tom thought.

Pamela Colliton stood in the doorway. He mouth opened partially. "What can I do for you?" she asked.

Samantha replied, "You faked me into getting my fingerprints on the detonator which you used to murder the men in the golf carts!"

"You are wrong. Please go away."

"I am not wrong and you know it!" Sammy exclaimed.

Tom held his breath as he listened. Geez, Pamela just slammed the door shut, he said to himself.

Samantha banged on the door again with her two fists. Moments later, she turned and looked at Tom. She pulled her Glock out of her purse and aimed it at the door. Then she returned the gun to her purse and raised a fist. Tom anxiously waited, and felt relieved when Samantha returned to the golf cart.

Chapter 58

MICHAEL CORLONE GRASPED HIS WALLET AND PULLED IT OUT OF HIS POCKET. He brought out a wad of hundred dollar bills. "I need to pay you for the two rooms I rented. Mine is for a week, the other for two days, today and Sunday."

The woman behind the counter at the Texas Inn stood in front of the printer. She plucked out a sheet and set it down in front of Michael. "I'll get you some change."

She handed Michael some bills and also two keys. "Your rooms are 4013 and 4012. They are in the first concourse just around the corner. Have a good time," she pointed and said.

Michael said, "Thank you," and headed out the door. He got into the black pickup truck and drove into the concourse, parking in front of his room. Frankie should be here real soon, he thought. He said that he would bring a pipe bomb. I feel amazed that he could come up with one so quickly.

As he entered his room, his mind drifted back to the explosion which killed his father. I knew immediately that my father was gone, the thought. The pot smuggling devils, who are making a fortune spreading the drug marijuana, had murdered my father.

Michael entered his room, reached into his belt holster, and brought out his phone. He pressed two numbers and waited. "Frankie, I've got us a couple of rooms and yours is ready for you."

He listened and nodded. "Okay, see you in a few minutes."

Michael used his key to get into his room. This is going to be the biggest two days of my life, he thought.

Minutes later, he heard a vehicle drive up. Michael opened his door and said to himself, "It's Frankie!"

Michael stepped outside and shook his cousin's hand. "Your room is ready. Here's the key. It's 4112."

"Howdy, Michael, thanks," Frankie said as he accepted the key.

"How about a little whiskey, Frankie?"

"No thanks. I know your father used whiskey a lot to calm his stress, but I'm not at that point yet."

Michael chuckled. "That's fine, cousin. More important is the pipe bomb. Do you have it?"

"I sure do."

Michael's face lit up. "Great. Can I have a look at it?"

Frankie opened his Jeep's passenger door. "There it is, right on the seat."

Michael leaned into the Jeep and brought out the pipe bomb. He held it up in front of his eyes. "Thank you very much, Michael. I'm not sure exactly when I'm going to use this, but I will keep it in a safe place."

He picked up the bomb and carried it into his truck.

He returned to Frankie. "I got you here for a second reason. I want you to come with me early Monday morning. I need to direct one of the pot trucks to a special place near here. My plan is to put a stop to the smuggling deliveries to Minnesota. I'm doing that to get revenge for my father's death. We may need your tools to penetrate a lock. "

Frankie nodded. "I could see that coming, and now that your father has been killed, I felt that you were going to take serious action."

Michael's eyes hardened. "The truck drivers will arrive tomorrow afternoon and I need to connect with the drivers of truck five. Meanwhile, this evening, we can go out for dinner. I'll take you to Milano's."

TOM AND SAMANTHA WERE AT THE TEXAS PALMS RESTAURANT. I'm sure glad that she didn't notice that Pam Colliton is here, he thought. Fortunately, Pam is sitting in the far corner behind a bunch of people. It looks like a guy is with her, likely Nick Giggs.

"How's your breakfast, Sammy?" he asked.

"Nothing seems to taste good since I spent a few hours behind bars."

Tom took a sip of coffee. "Sammy, I know that there's nothing I can say which will remove that problem, but I still love you and will do anything I can to help."

Samantha forced a smile. "I really appreciate that. I keep thinking that: *this, too, shall pass.*"

"After we get back to our home, I'll be leaving for Harlingen to pick up the van. I have a hunch that this will be my last trip. Actually, if you wish, you could go along. Getting away from here for a time would do you good."

"Thanks Tom, but I would rather stay here. I won't do anything rash like I did when I confronted Pamela. Actually, I feel a lot better since I did it. There is something about standing up for yourself."

Tom stood. "Okay, Sammy, let's go home."

Tom stopped at the station next to the front door and dropped off some bills. He held Sammy's hand as they walked into the parking lot. They got into their SUV and he headed down Kingston Drive. Tom drove into their driveway and got out. "I'll unlock the door for you, and I will be on my way."

MICHAEL LOOKED AT HIS WATCH SUNDAY AFTERNOON. The truck drivers should be here, he thought. It's time to connect with Jamie and Santos.

Michael knocked on their door and glanced at the Activities Building's parking lot. There she is, the Pam broad. I'm not sure if she spotted me or not, but it really doesn't matter. Four thousand dollars will do the talking.

The door opened and Michael entered. He chatted with the two men and handed each one of them a thousand dollar bill. Then he shook their hands and left the room. Again, he gazed at the Activities parking lot as he walked around the end of the concourse, heading back to his room. She's watching me again, he thought. Not a hell of a lot she can do.

Michael chuckled as he got his key out.

Michael left his room and knocked on Frankie's door. He smiled when his cousin appeared. "Time to set the bomb, Frankie."

They both got into Michael's pickup truck. He drove onto Kingston Drive and slowly turned into the second suite concourse. "There it is," he said. "The gray golf cart alongside the maroon Ford Focus.

Michael parked four units away from Pam's door. A gut feeling made him pause before he got out. This may be the wrong thing to do, he thought. If I blow her up, it could interfere with the cops investigating the truck. "Hey, Frankie, I changed my mind. We're going back to my room and I want you to take the bomb back."

Frankie said, "Anything you say, cousin."

There are other ways of avenging my father, Michael thought as they drove back.

Chapter 59

TOM SET HIS CUP OF COFFEE DOWN AND HEADED FOR THE BEDROOM. "Hey, Sammy, have a good morning. I'll be home in about three hours."

He gently squeezed her shoulders. She smiled.

"Have a good trip, Tom. Be careful."

This could be the end, he thought as he watched Menzo and the other drivers head for his van. Tom chuckled. I used to get irritated listening to all that chatter, but now I feel that I will miss these guys. I have so much respect for them because they are such hard workers.

As he prepared to leave, Tom said to himself with a chuckle, the chatter in the back has returned. "Hey, Menzo, your guys have all come alive again."

"*Si, amigo* Tom. The word from my comrades is that this could be our last trip to Bloomington."

"Now, where the heck did that news come from?" Tom asked.

"The spirits, I think," Menzo replied.

"All ready to go," Menzo added.

Tom headed for the frontage road and looked in his side view mirror. I'll be darned, he thought. The black pickup is back...it's close behind.

An hour later, he arrived at the Tesoro. "The trucks are already here," Tom said to Menzo. He remained behind the wheel as Menzo guided the drivers out of the van. There comes Nick, he thought. Pam doesn't seem to be here. Looks like I'll be heading home in minutes.

PARKING HERE MAKES ME VERY SAD, MICHAEL THOUGHT. My father did the same thing so many times. He had such a cool way directing me out there to do my job. He's probably looking down on me right now.

Michael wiped a tear from his eye.

There go the Minnesota drivers, he said to himself. They don't know it, but this is the last time they will be doing this. Well, maybe Jamie and Santos know, because they are going to follow me west. Only seven trucks will arrive in Bloomington. The head guy Mick will be furious. Michael chuckled. He and his partner in Bloomington are going to pay for killing my father.

I expect both Nick and the Pamela broad will leave when the trucks do, Michael thought. I'm sure that they are totally confident that none of the trucks will be confronted.

There goes Hastings, Michael thought. The van has just left. Minutes later, the first truck moved out of the station. He started the pickup. There goes number four. He backed up and followed it out onto the main street. Jamie and Santos are right behind me, he anxiously said to himself.

"Look at that little girl standing on the corner of the sidewalk. She has a basket and it's probably full of cash," Michael said.

"There's one on every corner of Benito Juárez," Michael said. "I've always wondered if they work for rich people."

Frankie chuckled. "If your father was down there, he'd probably put a hundred dollar bill in the basket."

Michael smiled. "Thanks, Frankie. My father was a very generous man."

He got them through American customs and drove away slowly, waiting for truck five to catch up. "There it is, Frankie. They're right behind me."

Minutes later, they were cruising along International Boulevard, heading for Expressway-83.

Michael turned on the emergency lights as he approached the frontage road. “Come on, *amigo’s,* follow us,” he said.

“They did it!” Frankie exclaimed.

Michael raised a fist in the air as he headed toward Texas Palms. “I wonder if any of the other trucks saw number five head west,” he said.

Frankie laughed.

Michael remained on the frontage road until they got to Airport Road. Then he took a right and immediately got onto Pike Boulevard. He followed it for a short distance and took a left. He slowed, watching the truck behind them. “They’re still with us. They will each make two thousand dollars for doing this. And then they get to go home.”

He turned into a parking lot of a large building. The lot contained many vehicles. Michael led the truck to the side of the building and stopped. “Okay, Frankie, get your tools out, I’ll take care of the power cord.”

They walked over to the lockbox and Frankie set down his tools.

Michael said, “I’ll talk to the drivers. I know it won’t take you long to get it open.” He stepped up to the cab. Michael talked in a low tone to Jamie and Santos and then stepped back down.

“How’s it going, Frankie?”

“A-hah, I just got it!”

“Great, be sure to make a spare key,” Michael said. “When you’re finished, would you get the power cord and your tools back into the truck? I’ll go pay the people inside the three hundred bucks they charged us for parking here.”

MICHAEL AND FRANKIE LED THE BIG TRUCK BACK ONTO THE FRONTAGE ROAD and drove west, getting off at the Texas Road exit. They turned to their left, headed over the overpass, and turned left onto the frontage road to go east. Michael put on his right turn signal. He turned into the Texas Palms entrance, but then took a quick left and drove onto a grassy area, lined by a large hedge protecting the Inn's rooms from the highway. He drove to the end of the grassy area and stopped. The truck came to a halt behind him.

Both Pam and Nick should be at their homes by now, Michael thought. If they came by now and saw the truck, they would panic and get the heck out of here now.

Michael and Frankie got out. They walked to the driver's side of the truck. Michael said, "Come on down, Jamie and Santos, I wish to pay you both extra for your cooperation, and then you can both go to your vehicles and leave."

The two drivers stepped down the rungs and smiled widely as they stood on the grass. Michael handed each one a thousand dollar bill and said, "Thank you very much for your cooperation."

Jamie and Santos left, waving goodbye with happy smiles on their faces. Michael waved back as they left. He walked over to the lockbox and placed a key into the slot. He turned it and the top flipped open. He pressed a button and one of the compartments slowly opened. "It works, Frankie. Great job." He pressed the button again and the top of the tank returned to its original position. Michael close the lockbox and left the key in the slot.

Michael reached into his breast pocket and brought out a large piece of paper. I created and printed this in the computer room here at Texas Palms, he said to himself. I faked my name when I signed in. The head guy did give me a strange look. I got the job done and got the heck out.

"Frankie, we're all set. I'm going to leave this message on the driver's seat and we'll leave the ignition key in place."

Michael stepped up into the cab. He returned in moments. "Get in the truck, Frankie, and I'll drive you to your Jeep."

Michael drove the pickup down to the curb, took an illegal left, and quickly drove into the Texas Palms resort. He took a left and stopped in back of Frankie's jeep. "Thank you, cousin, here's your pay." Michael handed his cousin a small stack of bills.

Frankie smiled and saluted. He got into his Jeep and took off. Michael drove into the first Inn concourse, stopped his vehicle, and entered his room. I've had it for the day, he thought, but I have to call the Donna police.

Chapter 60

CAPTAIN TREVINO HELD HIS PHONE TO HIS EAR, LISTENING. He flipped it shut and called his secretary. "I need Sergeants Herrara and Salinas in here immediately."

A minute later, he heard a knock. "Come on in."

"What's up, captain?" Herrara asked.

"You two are not going to believe this, but one of the trucks involved in the golf cart bombing case at Texas Palms is parked on their property right next to the frontage road. Let's get over there and fast. Jesse, take at least one of the technicians with you. Maria, you come with me."

The captain drove northward and entered the frontage road. In minutes, he said, "Maria, there it is—the truck." He pulled up behind it at Texas Palms. "Okay Maria, let's check this out."

Maria climbed up to the cab. She opened the door and looked inside. "Captain, the key is in the ignition and there's a sheet of paper here. Looks like a message."

She grabbed the paper and came down to hand the message to the captain.

He read it: *This is one of eight trucks which has been smuggling marijuana from Mexico to Bloomington, Minnesota. The other Sardoza Oil trucks will arrive at their destination sometime tomorrow afternoon. Each truck has two drivers, so they travel all night long. To access the pot in this truck, go to the small lockbox just behind the cab and at the bottom of the tank. Turn the key and open the lockbox. Press a button and the tank will open. The drivers of the trucks were not aware they smuggled marijuana. They believe they were hauling oil. I prefer to remain anonymous.*

Captain Trevino walked over to the lockbox. He turned the key and the metal top flipped open. He pressed a button and the two police officers stood in awe as the top of the tank slowly opened.

"My God, what do we have here?" the captain asked.

"Looks like two bales of hay," Maria replied.

A second police car pulled up. "Great!" Captain Trevino said. "We're really going to need the tech guys. What do you think it is, Maria?"

"Pot!"

"My God, it's likely the two golf cart murders are connected," Trevino said.

"Very likely," Maria said.

Sergeant Herarra approached. "Whackers, what the heck is going on?"

"Maria, would you get on the phone and call either FBI Agent Sam Perkins or Bill Malone? I'm sure they are going to take over this case. Tell them they will need the DEA, too."

The captain pressed a second button and stood in amazement as a second tank compartment opened. Then he pressed the third button. "Holy mackerel," he said. "There are six bales in this truck."

"I'LL BE BACK BEFORE YOU KNOW IT, SAMMY," TOM SAID as he headed out to his vehicle. He got in his SUV and headed for the frontage road. As he approached, he saw flashing lights to his right. Tom stopped. I can't believe this, he thought. It's a Sardoza truck! How the deuce did that ever get here?

He slowly drove onto the frontage road and drove by the truck. Two police cars are there, he thought.

I'll have to try to remember what I am going to the grocery store for after seeing this, he thought.

Tom turned right on Westgate and in minutes walked into H.E.B. He hurried to make his purchases. I feel very nervous about what I saw. Yet, I really don't know what is going on. He paid for his groceries and headed outside, walking quickly to his SUV.

Tom didn't enter Texas Palms at the main gate. Instead he drove to the Inn gate. Holy smokes, the truck is still parked here, he thought. There are more police cars, a lot more. The Feds will probably be here soon. I better get home to Sammy.

He parked and entered his home at 79 Kingston Drive. Tom set two bags on the table and walked into the room where Samantha was playing her piano. "Hi Sammy, I'm back," he said.

"Anything happen?" she asked.

Tom cleared his throat and took a deep breath. "This is a toughie. One of the Sardoza Oil trucks is parked in the narrow green area between the Inn and the frontage road. I saw all kinds of police cars."

Sammy stopped playing. She turned to face Tom. "I told you so. I've suspected all along that the trucks were involved in some type of scandalous operation. I can't wait to read the paper tomorrow."

"I better get up early and bike to the Activities area. The newspapers are going to be sold out early," Tom said.

FBI Agents Perkins and Malone left their office in McAllen and hastily drove to the city of Donna. The slightly pudgy Malone was behind the wheel and Perkins sat in the passenger seat. "I've got four other agents to help us with the investigation. They should arrive at the scene within an hour," Sam said. "The DEA is sending people in, too."

Agent Malone licked his lips. "I remember our investigation of the trucks after the first murder at Texas Palms. Obviously, something was missing, but it looks like we're going to have some answers, and soon."

Agent Perkins blinked. "The phone call I got from Captain Trevino said one main thing. There is marijuana in the truck. I didn't get any details of what part of the truck it was in, but within minutes we shall see for ourselves."

Twenty minutes later, Malone drove onto the Texas Road exit. He worked his way around the overpass and continued on the frontage road. "I see flashing lights, just ahead."

He parked their car in a safe zone and they both got out. They walked over to the scene. "Captain Trevino, what has happened here?" Agent Perkins asked.

"We don't know how the truck got here. We do know that some anonymous person called us about it. Then when we got here, there was a typed note on the driver's seat, apparently from the anonymous tipster. Here it is," the captain said.

Agent Perkins stood close to his partner. They both read the note. Perkins said, "It looks like there are two parties involved in all of this. The party who used the trucks to smuggle the marijuana, and second, a party who was at war with them. This somewhat explains the two golf cart murders."

Captain Trevino nodded and pressed the lockbox button. He smiled while watching the expressions on the faces of the two agents. "I assume you are going to take over the truck. If so, I'll get my people out of here. Give me a call if you need us for anything," Trevino said.

The captain pressed the button again and the tank cover closed. He closed the lockbox and said, "I'll leave the key in the slot."

Chapter 61

THE TWO MCALLEN FBI AGENTS TOOK CONTROL OF THE TRUCK. Their staff busied themselves looking for clues and obtaining fingerprints. They all marveled at how the truck was designed to haul marijuana and disguise it to get past the border agents. The DEA agents who joined them were similarly impressed.

After the staff had completed their work, Agent Perkins ordered the truck to be moved to the secure area close to their McAllen office.

Perkins stood next to Malone and said, "I think it's time to take two of our suspects from the first bombing into custody. I'm talking about Pamela Colliton and Nick Giggs."

"You've got it absolutely right, Sam. We've got to collar them before they leave the area."

Agent Perkins said, "Let's take agents Colleen and Butch with us. We need a woman for sure. I've already talked to the two of them."

"Okay, let's go do it. Colleen and Butch will follow us," Agent Malone said.

Two FBI vehicles drove into the second suite concourse and parked close to suite 4705. Perkins and Malone got out of their car and walked over to the door. They knocked. The door opened, revealing Pam Colliton in the doorway. Agents Colleen and Butch stood a short distance away.

Pam said, "Yes?"

"Pamela Colliton, you are under arrest for suspicion of being involved in the smuggling of marijuana from Mexico to the United States," Agent Perkins said.

Perkins turned his head. "Agent Colleen, secure this woman with handcuffs and place her in your vehicle. You will transport her to the county jail in McAllen."

"What!" Pam exclaimed.

Agent Perkins read Pamela her Miranda rights. "You let Agent Colleen know what personal items you need. She will get them for you from your suite."

Pamela staggered as Colleen and Butch partially dragged her to one of the FBI vehicles. They secured her in the back seat.

Perkins nodded to Malone. "Okay, let's go get Giggs."

Half an hour later Nick Giggs was handcuffed and placed into the back seat of the second FBI vehicle. The agents left Texas Palms and headed for McAllen.

AGENT MALONE CALLED THE FBI OFFICE IN MINNEAPOLIS. He explained what was happening and issued an order to send a helicopter out in the morning to monitor Interstate-35 and look for the seven pot trucks heading for Bloomington.

Within two hours, Perkins and Malone boarded a Southwest Airline flight at the McAllen airport. The plane's destination was the Minneapolis/St. Paul International Airport.

After landing, they communicated with the Minneapolis FBI office. "Hey, Sam, they found the trucks," Agent Malone told his partner. "They are currently north of Ames, Iowa, The Minneapolis agents are on the way to pick us up. We've got about four hours before the trucks arrive."

At 4 P.M., Perkins and Malone joined six other agents and a van loaded with an eight member tactical squad. They parked in a secure and safe distance from the Bloomington warehouse and waited for the trucks to arrive.

They lay in wait as the trucks made their way into the building. Minutes later, they saw a small former school bus exit the building and drive away. "They're on the way to the Super 8 motel. We need to wait until the bus returns and the driver gets back inside," Agent Perkins said.

Within half an hour, the bus returned. "Let's wait five more minutes," Perkins said.

After five minutes passed, Perkins said, "Now."

The FBI vehicles headed for the building. The agents and tactical squad swiftly got out and deployed.

"Go!" Perkins ordered.

One member of the team kicked in the office door and they stormed the building. Within minutes, the two overhead doors opened. Led by Agents Perkins and Malone, all the FBI agents entered. Mick Brown and Norm Blaine were arrested, handcuffed, and were secured in the rear seat of an FBI vehicle.

Chapter 62

TOM OPENED THE DOOR. Sergeant Maria Salinas gave him a wide smile as she stood on the carpeted stoop. "Hello, Mr. Hastings, I came over to share some of the results of the trucks case. Is Samantha home?"

"She sure is. Come on in," Tom said.

He pointed to the couch. "Have a seat. I'll go get her."

He walked into their office. Sammy was practicing on the piano. "Hey, Sammy, remember Maria—one of the police officers that arrested you? She wants to talk to you."

The piano music stopped.

Sammy got up and walked through the door. "Hello, Sergeant Maria."

The sergeant sat down. "Yah know, I feel real bad that we arrested you, Samantha."

"I totally understand. You matched my fingerprints to the detonator."

"Yes, and it was very confusing. Thank you for understanding."

"I feel real good that Tom doesn't do any more runs to Progreso. I suspected all along that something strange and illegal was going on."

Sergeant Maria laughed. "Strange is a good word. The marijuana gang smuggled tons of pot to Bloomington, expertly working their way through our border agents."

"Geez," Tom said. "How was that possible?"

"They used a very high level of technology to get away with it. What cooked their goose was another gang of hoodlums. They obviously were onto the pot smugglers. That led to two of the rival gang getting murdered in those golf cart bombings. But a mysterious tipster, probably from the rival gang, decided to swipe a truck and leave it for law enforcement as a gift complete with a note about where the other trucks were going."

"Wow," Sammy said.

"Four of the pot smugglers will get tried in court for the smuggling. Two of them will also be tried for murder."

"Wow!" Sammy exclaimed. "I'm really thankful that nothing serious happened to me and Tom."

Sergeant Maria got up off the couch. "Well, I've got to go. Thanks for listening."

"Thank you so much, Maria. I really appreciate this," Sammy said.

The sergeant walked out the door and turned. She shook both their hands and walked down the steps.

Tom held Samantha's hand. "It's all over and we have a new home, sweetie.

Samantha looked up and kissed him on the lips. "Welcome home, Tom," she whispered.

END

EPILOGUE

Mick Brown, Norm Blaine, Nick Giggs, and Pamela Colliton were all found innocent of smuggling marijuana from Mexico. Their defense attorney did a miraculous job and successfully convinced the jury that the substance was legal where it was being delivered to.

Pamela Colliton was found guilty of murdering Tony Fabzonni and Jon Corlone. Her sentence was reduced because she testified against her boss, Mick Brown, who was identified as ordering her to commit the crime. Her sentence was reduced to five years with a possible parole in two years.

Mick Brown was found guilty of orchestrating the Fabzonni and Corlone murders. He was sentenced to 30 years in prison.

Michael Corlone safely returned to his home in Mercedes, Texas, to live with his wife, Angie, and his son, Sonny. Each day when he walked into their garage, he would stop, meditate, and gaze at the black pickup truck in memory of his father. He didn't need an income because of the huge amount of cash he inherited. Michael felt good that he didn't kill Pamela Colliton. The police did not connect to him in their investigations.

The sixteen truck drivers and Tom Hastings were not prosecuted for their part in the smuggling. The judge declared them to have a neutral position in the scandal.

Tom and Samantha Hastings settled into their new home in Texas Palms. Every night, he would wake up and think about the truck drivers and his visits to Progreso.

Frankie Corlone moved to Grand Forks, North Dakota, to join a business, EZ Locksmith, owned by Greg Barta.

AUTHOR'S NOTES

My fourteenth novel is well under way and it involves the wall being built between the U.S. and Mexico. Tom and Samantha Hastings visit the construction site. Samantha is obsessed with the protestors and takes action. The title of the novel will be *The Wall*.